I0824663

TO THE END OF RECKONING

TO THE END OF RECKONING

JOSEPH MOLDOVER

THE MYSTERIOUS PRESS
NEW YORK

TO THE END OF RECKONING

Mysterious Press
An Imprint of Penzler Publishers
58 Warren Street
New York, N.Y. 10007

First edition

Interior design by Maria Fernandez

Library of Congress Control Number: 2025946941

ISBN: 978-1-61316-758-8
eBook: 978-1-61316-759-5

10 9 8 7 6 5 4 3 2 1

Printed in the United States of America
Distributed by Simon & Schuster

For my father, Jonathan R. Moldover, MD
Who is always true and relevant

And for Leah
My partner in solving all mysteries

Truth is truth
To the end of reckoning

—William Shakespeare
Measure for Measure

Truth, after all, is not a matter of facts.

—Sloan Wilson

Personal communication, 1942

PROLOGUE

Lake Prout is the largest man-made body of water in the Catskill Mountains. It runs almost four miles from north to south and is just shy of two miles wide from one bank to the other at its broadest point.

It wasn't meant to be so big. The state of New York created it in 1932 by deliberately flooding a series of three connected quarries. The planners intended to leave part dry but there was a mistake and they filled too much, too fast. I have no idea what happened; maybe some junior engineer forgot to carry the one or divide by the square root of pi. I imagine him in a hard hat, standing alongside his boss, watching two hundred billion gallons of water go where it shouldn't while rechecking his calculations and starting to think about another line of work. I have a strong sense of empathy for that guy.

Due to good luck, or maybe cautious management, no one was hurt in the flood. A lot of things were lost at the bottom of the newly formed lake, though. Pieces of construction equipment and work sheds and partly excavated rock formations were submerged underwater down to seventy-five feet. All sorts of crags for something to catch on and never come up to the surface.

Jason Grant's shoes and watch were discovered at the edge of the lake in April 2013, neatly set on a stone near a spot where the water quickly became deep. His car was parked nearby. There was a long search, as the Grants were some of the area's most well-respected citizens and Jason was only thirty-one years old. Volunteers with dogs combed the banks for weeks. They went out in boats. The county sent divers. His body was never found.

One year later, on the morning of the memorial, the people of Faith, New York, had long since traded their search for a story: Dr. Grant, a promising young psychiatrist just coming into his prime, ended his own life by walking into the lake. His reasons for doing so would remain unknown and unknowable, as would the precise location of his final resting place. In this, he would join at least seventeen other residents of Ulster County who had chosen the lake as their point of departure from the world in the eighty-one years since the lake's formation, and more than forty-one thousand Americans who died by suicide in 2013. His case was tragic but unexceptional. We had moved on.

Only two people were troubled by doubt. They each had their reasons, neither particularly well-ounded. For one, the problem was memory. There was an event he could not recall, tickling the back of his damaged mind, insisting there was more to Jason's disappearance than was yet known. For the other, the problem was hope. She knew that Jason would not willingly leave her. She knew that the people of Faith could look as long and as hard as they wanted, but they weren't going to recover a body because it had never been in the lake to begin with. She knew, with all the conviction of her broken heart, that the only thing to be found with all that misdirected searching would be two hundred billion gallons of empty water.

CHAPTER ONE

The line pulled taut at three in the morning. I was exhausted, so I started with the basics. "Your name is Richard Moore," I said. "You're on the couch in our living room. You're fifty-six years old." I kicked my way out of the sleeping bag on the floor. "You're recovering from a traumatic brain injury. You're agitated. You're confused. You're home."

"I'm not confused," my father said, "and I know I'm home. I have to pee."

I stood and reached out to him. He took my arm and pulled himself up, staggering a little. "Easy," I said, "there's no rush."

"That's what you think."

We walked to the downstairs bathroom, the cord slack between us. Dad flipped on the light and I turned my back, ready for what I had come to recognize as an inevitable delay.

"Lukas, what time is the memorial?" Dad asked.

"Ten thirty."

"You're sure we'll make it?"

"I am. The doctor always runs on time."

He grunted and I finally heard the sound of liquid on porcelain. It wasn't steady. "This is something you have to look forward to," he muttered.

"I am. I really, really am."

He finished and washed his hands. "Were you sleeping?" Dad asked.

"Yeah."

"You should have ordered an air mattress."

"I don't think this situation will last much longer. Let's see what the doctor says."

Dad shrugged and patted my arm. A physician himself, he had less faith in the medical profession than I did. At age twenty-three, I thought all doctors seemed so much older than me, and impossibly competent.

We went back to the living room. He sat on the couch and I sat on my sleeping bag. I looked at him in the light from the front hall. He seemed lucid. He'd stumbled a bit going to the bathroom but he would have made it on his own. I could almost convince myself that the cord, a lightweight yellow rope, was no longer needed, that he and I could consider going to our respective bedrooms, and in the not-too-distant future I could leave altogether. The problem was nights like the one before, when I'd woken to my father pulling me out of my sleeping bag like a dog straining at a leash, agitated and confused, trying to get to the front door where, I knew from experience, he would continue into the neighborhood with little orientation to his surroundings.

Dad leaned back, tugging the line connecting our wrists so that I had to maneuver slightly closer to him. "Something is bothering me," he murmured, "but I can't say what it is."

"It's the memorial. You're getting stuck on it. You're perseverating." At the time I was a high school graduate who had skipped college in favor of the New York theater scene, but my clinical vocabulary had grown tremendously in the twelve months since Dad's brain injury.

Dad tapped his fingers on his knee. He wore red flannel pajama bottoms, an ancient Yale Medical School T-shirt, and mismatched gym socks. His black hair stuck out in all directions. Tap tap, tap tap. Long, bony fingers on flannel, deep and intrusive, like a leaky faucet. "I just don't think it was suicide," he finally said.

"I know you don't."

"He had plans."

"So you've said. People with plans die by suicide. Plans change. People give up." It was a basic fact that he, a board-certified psychiatrist, seemed to keep losing track of.

"There was no history of depression."

I shrugged. I knew the family; they were not the type to disclose that sort of thing, even to one another, even to themselves. "None that we know of."

"I'd like to know about substance use. I'd like to have toxicology, if they found a body."

"Well," I said, cracking my knuckles, "they haven't and at this point they probably won't. Can we go back to sleep?"

"Do you want the couch?" he asked.

"No, you need to rest. You can't rest on the floor."

"You said you were fine sleeping on the floor."

"You need to sleep well."

"You're not sleeping well?"

"Just lie down, Dad."

He lay on the couch and covered himself with a blanket. "We'll talk more in the morning," he said. "We need a better solution."

"We'll see the doctor in the morning. He'll have something." I lay down in the sleeping bag, careful not to yank on the line that connected my left wrist to his right.

"There was something," Dad said. He was lying on his back, staring at the ceiling, his untethered hand on his forehead. "In the research proposal he showed me just before my accident. Something was off about it. I know that I wanted to follow up." He rubbed his eyes. "I understand that plans for the future don't keep people from killing themselves, Lukas. I know that. But there was something, I know there was something."

We'd had the conversation many times. Dad had played the undesirable role of pedestrian in a "pedestrian vs. motor vehicle incident" just over a year before that night. He'd been in a coma for two weeks and woke to several pieces of distressing news. The first was that he had suffered a traumatic brain injury and was unlikely to work as a physician again. The second was that, due to the awkward circumstances of the accident, his wife was leaving him. The third was that his former colleague in the department of psychiatry at New Birmingham Medical Center, Dr. Jason Grant, was missing and presumed dead by suicide in Lake Prout.

Dad found that last item the most troubling, not because he had been close to Jason Grant—he had not—but because the public narrative that had formed in the time Dad had been unconscious did not fit with an encounter they'd had shortly before his accident and Jason's disappearance. The issue was that he could not remember anything about their conversation, other than that it involved a research proposal.

"It wasn't suicide, Lukas."

"Great. Good. Heard. Can we sleep now?"

"I'm not even convinced that he's dead."

"Then this memorial service is going to be a bit awkward."

"If I could just remember."

"I know. It's frustrating. I understand."

There was another moment of silence. I believed, as everyone else in town believed, as all of Ulster County believed, that Jason Grant was somewhere beneath the waters of Lake Prout, caught on a piece of detritus that kept him from coming up to the surface. I also knew that it was pointless to try to convince Dad of that fact. I wasn't completely unsympathetic; I knew something about what it meant to only have part of a story. I knew how that incompleteness could hound you and insist upon conclusion. I still needed to sleep.

"Good night, Lukas," Dad finally said.

"Good night, Dad." I closed my eyes.

CHAPTER TWO

In the morning I was the first to wake. I'd slept very fitfully, as was true every night since adopting this approach. I had spent five years in New York City trying to make it as an actor, sleeping on lots of couches and more than one floor, but the situation with my father was wearing on me. I got up and cut the line with scissors I kept nearby. Dad could be hard to rouse, but he got up easily that day and started right in on his morning physical therapy routine while I cooked breakfast. The PT had prescribed a series of exercises that Dad viewed as insufficiently rigorous, so he amplified it two and in some cases three times over. On that particular morning, he did dozens of push-ups while I cooked eggs, push-ups not having been something the therapist recommended in the first place.

After his routine Dad got dressed. I made bacon and toast and set two places at the table. "Shit," Dad said from the bathroom. "Shit, damn, fuck." He said it as one run-on word so that it sounded like "shitdamnfuck," an omnibus expletive appropriate for a variety of occasions and audiences. I still wasn't used to hearing him curse, something he'd never done before the accident.

"What's the matter?" I called, even though I knew.

"This tie." He came into the kitchen, dressed in a suit and white dress shirt, the collar open. He wrapped a tie around his neck and made an effort at a knot, but it all went wrong as the rabbit went around the tree and down the hole (the way I'd learned it from a costume designer for the first musical in which I had a leading role: Professor Harold Hill in *The Music Man*, in a performance that the *Ulster County Courier* called "undeniably vigorous"). He finally dropped one end and slammed his fist on the counter, knocking the bottom row of the spice rack over.

"You could wear the collar open," I offered.

"Ridiculous."

"Then let me do it."

"I don't have the bilateral coordination."

"Bilateral coordination isn't all it's cracked up to be."

"You miss it when it's gone."

I took the tie from him and knotted it around my own neck, then loosened it, took it off, and handed it back to him. It looked like a paisley noose. He looked at it critically—Dad always took great pride in the knot of his ties—but slipped it over his own head and drew it tight. "I'm thinking of phasing in a PT module emphasizing interhemispheric transfer," he said. "I think it might help with things like this. I'm going to ask Dr. Kellogg about it this morning. Are we running late?"

"No, we're right on time."

We ate quickly, him at the head of the table and me by his side. He poured hot sauce and shook pepper onto his eggs. Neither of us looked at the empty chair facing him. When we were done I took our dishes to the sink, fixed the spice rack, and went upstairs.

We were more or less boycotting the second floor of the house. Dad hadn't wanted to sleep in his own bed since Mom left and I felt that putting my things away would be a tacit admission that I had come home to stay. I went into my bedroom in search of a decent shirt, flipping on the light and pausing to look around. The walls were still covered with pictures. I stood in my doorway and looked at them: Daniel Day Lewis, Al Pacino, Leonardo DiCaprio. Marlon Brando at various stages of his career. I crossed to my dresser, opening the top drawer and glancing up at the only photo of me.

I was sixteen, onstage at Tricounty Regional High School. The camera caught me staring into Yorick's skeletal face at the start of act five of *Hamlet*. Casting a sophomore in the lead resulted in a lot of blowback for our drama teacher, Mr. Jollett; there were juniors and seniors who felt entitled to the part. Getting that role was the first time I knew that I could make it in professional theater. I let my eyes linger on the photo, then looked down into what turned out to be an empty dresser drawer.

"Lukas," Dad called from the foot of the stairs, "when did we go grocery shopping?"

"Tuesday," I replied, leaving my room and walking down the hall to the closed door of the master bedroom. "Why?"

"I thought it was Wednesday."

"It wasn't. It was Tuesday."

"Dammit, I was sure it was Wednesday. Did we get peanut butter?"

"We did. Extra chunky. It's in the cabinet."

I opened the door and went inside. My mother had left the king-sized bed in the center of the room neatly made. It would be far more comfortable than the couch, but I understood why my father refused to sleep in it. There was a stillness to the space, a vacancy. It was a place whose time had passed. Books were piled on the table by what had been Dad's side, a clip-on reading light still slanted toward the pillows. The table on my mother's side was empty save for a framed photo. I walked over and picked it up. It was of the two of them astride camels almost thirty years before, during their honeymoon in Egypt. He was looking into the camera but her gaze was slightly to one side, giving her young face a quality of uncertainty and anticipation.

"It's not in the cabinet!"

"You're looking in the wrong cabinet," I called. "Look in the one above the microwave." I put the picture down and opened one of Dad's drawers, riffling through shirts, looking for one that might fit me. I selected a polo, closed the drawer, and studied myself in the mirror. I looked tired; blond hair tousled and in need of a trim, blue eyes a bit bloodshot. Pale. A far cry from the leading man my headshots tried to portray.

I saw a bottle of my mother's perfume nestled toward the back of the dresser behind a box of tissues. I reached out and then paused, not sure that I wanted to smell it. Instead, I pulled my phone from my back pocket and tapped the screen.

"Lukas?"

"Hi, Mom."

"Is everything okay?"

I looked around the room, phone held to one ear. "Everything is fine. I, uh . . . found something you left. A bottle of your perfume. I wondered if you wanted me to send it to you?"

"Oh, Lukas, that's very sweet but I bought myself a new bottle. Really, it's not worth the expense to send it internationally."

"Ah. Well, good." I looked at the glass bottle, wondering what the hell we would do with it. The line was silent for a moment.

"How is your father?"

"Fine. We have an appointment this morning, actually. A follow-up with the doctor. I'm hoping it will be helpful."

"Yes, here's hoping. And you?"

"Yeah, good. Really. Good."

"Plans for heading back to the city? Auditions?"

"Oh yeah, there's a lot going on. My agent's been in touch, he has plenty of leads."

"You know how sorry I am you had to give up that role."

"It's no big deal, Mom. Really. I wasn't excited about it anyway, and this situation is temporary. Dad's almost all better and I'll be heading back soon. Maybe come up to visit you?"

"I'd love that. I have to go now, Lukas. I have an early meeting."

Something crashed to the floor in the kitchen below. "I have to go too. I love you, Mom."

"I love you too."

I hung up and hurried back downstairs, pulling the polo over my head and pushing my hair into some semblance of place. "Why do you need peanut butter anyway?" I asked, retrieving the jar from the exact cabinet I'd told Dad it was in.

"I'm making a sandwich for later."

I couldn't object; planning for the future had been one of the targets set by the occupational therapist at the rehab hospital and Dad doubtless would like a sandwich by midday. I put the blanket, pillow, and sleeping bag in the corner of the living room and tucked the spool of rope on the second shelf of the bookcase. "Ready?"

Dad slipped a pair of sunglasses on, even though we could see through the window that it was overcast. Photosensitivity was another word I had learned. "I am."

We went out to the car. It was April and there was a chill in the morning air. Dad walked down to the end of the short driveway. It was good to see him in a suit again. At fifty-six he was still an impressive presence: taller than most men, broad in the shoulders, with hair that was just a little gray and thick enough to mostly conceal the scar from his brain surgery. I joined him and peered at the biggest house in the neighborhood, perched at the top of the hill.

The Grant family was gathering to mourn their eldest son. Cars were parked outside their house, lining the street. Several people stood on the wide front porch, heads close together, talking. I shielded my eyes against the sunrise and scanned the group. Somewhere up there were the parents, Owen and Lucia Grant. Somewhere, I guessed, was Jason's younger brother, Garrett, who had once been my closest friend but whom I had not seen or heard from in years. And somewhere was Garrett's twin sister, Misty.

"Today's the funeral," a voice called from across the street.

Emery Quinlan was sitting on his front steps, running his fingers through his dog Rufus's fur, studying us.

"It's about time," Dad called back.

"They were waiting to find the corpse," Emery said. He didn't say it loud, but the morning air was very still and I imagined his words carrying up the hill to the mourners.

"Quiet down, Emery," I said. He shrugged and kept petting his dog. "It's a memorial service anyway," I added, hoping to take the edge off my abrupt response with a little bit of education. "Not a funeral. It's been a year. It's a memorial."

"That's because there's no corpse," Emery said matter-of-factly. If anything, he spoke a bit louder than before. "If they ever find the corpse they'll do a funeral, though if they find him now they'll have to ID him with dental records because his fingerprints will have dissolved and his face will have been eaten by fishes."

I sighed and turned to my father, who was still looking up the hill and nodding slightly, though whether at Emery's assessment of the effect of freshwater on a submerged corpse or at some thought of his own it was hard to tell. I looked down. "Careful, there's a dog turd by your left foot."

"I know," he said. "There's another two and a half meters to your right and a third a half meter beyond that. It looks like Peaches has a bit of a GI infection"

"Oh."

"Mrs. Macarthur can't bend over to pick it up, you know."

"Then she should get someone else to walk her dog."

Dad shrugged. "When you get older, Lukas, you'll find that the ordinary things are the hardest to give up."

You're not the one picking up someone else's dog shit on our front lawn, I thought. "We should go."

Dad scratched his jaw. "Emery," he said, "when was the last time you saw Jason Grant?"

Emery thought for a moment, tugging at his dog's fur with excessive vigor, though the dog seemed used to it. "Before he disappeared?" he asked.

"You've seen him since?" Dad asked.

"No."

"Then yes, the last time you saw him before he disappeared."

"Jesus, Dad," I said, "we need to get going. The police questioned everyone a year ago. Emery doesn't have any clues."

"The police never questioned me," Emery said. "They questioned my mom but they didn't talk to me."

"All right," I said, "you're being questioned. When did you last see Jason?"

"He disappeared on a Thursday," Emery said, clearly relishing his moment in our dim limelight. "I remember by the next Monday people were really worried, what with his stuff being found by the lake and all.

I wanted to go out with the people who were looking along the shore, but Mom said I had to go to school."

"I'm sure you would have been a huge asset," I said.

"I'm good at looking for things," he acknowledged. "Alice loses things a lot and I'm always the one who finds them. Also, once when he was still living here my dad lost his wedding ring and I found it in the cup holder in his car. He hadn't even known it was missing. It made Mom really upset."

Alice was Emery's younger sister. She had Down syndrome. His father had moved out more than two years before. "That's great, Emery," I said. "You're a world-class talent. We really do have to go, though, and my father won't leave until you answer his question, so please . . ." I trailed off. Dad waited patiently. Emery kneaded the dog's ears.

"I saw him the week before," he finally said. "He was walking up the street toward his parents' house late at night."

"He was out for a walk?" Dad asked.

Emery shook his head. "He drove up to the house, and then he drove right back down the street and parked at the bottom of the hill and walked back up."

"Why would he do that?"

Emery shrugged. "How should I know? It was late. After dark. I was outside, scouting locations for a rocket launch."

"How late was it?"

"Maybe ten thirty."

"Did your mother know you were out that late?" I asked.

"Nope."

"Why can't you scout launch locations during the day?"

"Because then people would see me."

"Why . . . never mind." I turned to Dad. "You got your answer. I can't see how it matters. Can we go?"

"Did you see Jason come back down the hill?" Dad asked.

Emery shook his head. "I had to go back inside. I think he was talking to someone, off to the side, there." Emery pointed up the hill, toward the woods behind the houses on our side of the street. "I could see what was maybe the tip of a cigarette," he explained. "It was orange and it would sort of light up and then fade away and then light up and then fade away, like someone was puffing on it, you know?" Emery held two fingers up like he had a cigarette in his hand and puffed hard.

Dad looked up the hill at the Grants' house, then at the woods. "Yes," he said, "interesting. Thank you, Emery. You've been very helpful. Have a good day at school."

"Sixth grade blows," the boy replied.

"It does," Dad agreed. "How is your mother?"

"Grumpy."

"Tell her I say hello."

Emery shrugged. "Sure."

Dad turned and walked to the car, getting in on the passenger side.

"Your father is cool," Emery said.

"Is he?" I asked.

Emery nodded. "He didn't used to be, but now he is."

I wanted to tell Emery that if he wanted to be cool then maybe he should get himself run over by a car, but that seemed excessive and also possibly the sort of thing he might take literally. I looked up the hill at the big house and then once more at Rufus the dog, whom I liked much more than I liked his owner. I nodded in their general direction and turned away.

We were halfway to the town line when I realized Dad left his peanut butter sandwich at home on the counter.

CHAPTER THREE

New Birmingham was a twenty-minute drive from our house in Faith. The medical center was on the east side but it was a small city and nothing was really that far. That was fortunate for Dad, who had been found lying at the intersection of Forty-Third and Vine on the west side of town but was nonetheless whisked into surgery within twenty-five minutes of the ambulance's arrival. The entire process of saving his life was fast, professional, and efficient. The questions left behind—why he'd been outside a hotel on the west side of New Birmingham at that time on a Friday night and who was the intended recipient of the bouquet of lilacs found beside his body—were considerably messier.

We sat in the waiting room of the outpatient clinic. There were a few pregnant couples and an old man with a much younger woman in scrubs who was reading a magazine. An extremely thin girl and her father sat across from us. She might have been eleven or twelve years old, about Emery's age, and she looked scared. There were dark rings under her eyes, brought out by the harsh fluorescent lights. Her father was on his phone. He seemed angry and was talking to someone about the timing of the Japanese markets.

I tried to focus on my own phone, scrolling through a list of upcoming auditions I couldn't go to and then scanning recent texts, clicking on one from Jules Pierre. It had come the afternoon before and I read it again: Bro I got intel on auditions for the Albrecht production that's coming up next year and if you're not back here rehearsing to be the king of Scotland in 3 weeks we are fucking done.

I thought about texting back with an explanation that Macbeth starts the play as a mere thane, not the king, but it seemed pedantic and needlessly provocative given that Jules Pierre was my sole remaining link to the New York theater scene and it was kind of him to think of me.

Jules was junior assistant to my agent, Michael Kasdan of Kasdan and Associates, a distant figure who, as far as I knew, had long forgotten that I existed. Jules, in contrast, saw me as something of a pet project, enough of a nobody for him to pull off the scrap heap without stepping on anyone's toes. He had a vision and it was of me (or one of his other minor clients) breaking through to stardom and catapulting him from getting coffee for Mr. Kasdan to founding his own agency. You had to admire his ambition and work ethic; most of his texts came at one or two in the morning and tried to cajole me into auditioning for parts I had no hope of getting. Everyone knew that Albrecht was planning to cast William H. Macy as Macbeth.

I started to compose a reply to Jules conveying that I appreciated his attention but that three weeks was not going to be enough time to rehabilitate my father and also that he was completely nuts to think that I had a shot at that audition. As so often happened, however, I was interrupted.

"I've been researching telepathy," Dad said, his voice louder and his speech slower than necessary. "Do you know what telepathy is, Lukas?"

I looked up. So did the little girl across from us and a few of the other people nearby. "Um . . ."

"It's mind reading. Mind . . . reading."

"Right."

"Now, I never believed in mind reading. I am a board-certified psychiatrist with a degree from the Yale University School of Medicine."

"I'm familiar with your credentials. You might want to speak a bit more—"

"There's a science to it," Dad went on, "but most of the studies are poorly done. The problem is that the stimuli are too impersonal." He had a small audience now, although the girl's father, who had earbuds in, was entirely unaware of the lecture unfolding across from him. "Do you know what I mean by impersonal stimuli, Lukas?"

"I can't say that I do." I was, at that point, a high school graduate who had spent most of his working life waiting tables in Manhattan, and I did not remember the term "impersonal stimuli" from ninth-grade bio.

"What it means," Dad continued, "is that when they do experiments to test for telepathy—mind reading—they ask the subjects to remember silly, random things. Numbers written on a slip of paper, or words picked out of a dictionary. Things that make no . . . no impression." He held his hands up, palms out, as though making an impression on the air around him. "And that is not the way these things work at all. People who are telepathic . . . who have the gift . . . can only pick up on things that are real."

"Dad," I said, "this is very interesting, but did you take all of your medication this morning?"

"Young lady," Dad said a bit more quietly. He leaned forward, his eyes on the girl across from us. "In what town or city do you think my son, Lukas, here was born?"

She looked back at him. Her father was partly turned away in his seat, furiously tapping on his phone while telling someone that the fucking bond market was too fucked for them to be fucking with. "New Birmingham?" she said. Her voice was gentle and very hoarse, like wind over sand.

Dad nodded. "Yes."

Pretty much everyone in Ulster County was born in New Birmingham but I didn't want to intrude on the moment.

"Moore?" a nurse called from the doorway. "Richard Moore."

"Now," Dad said, "tell me this: What is my son's middle name? My son, Lukas, right here." He patted my knee. "What is his . . . middle name?"

"Dad, they're calling us."

Dad didn't move. Neither did the girl. "Try it," he said. "You might surprise yourself."

"Edward." The girl said it softly, so that I barely heard.

Dad sank back in his seat. He looked at her for another moment. The father, finally catching on that something was happening, stared at us. "Edward," Dad said. He smiled and nodded. "Yes. Edward." The girl's eyes widened and after a moment she also smiled. Then Dad stood and I followed him back into the clinic.

The nurse weighed Dad and took his blood pressure and then brought us to Dr. Kellogg's office, where we were seated by the window in a pair of institutional armchairs with stain-resistant cushions. She left us there, waiting for the doctor. "I never understood," I said, "why you and Mom didn't give me a middle name."

"We couldn't agree on one. I wanted Oxford. She wanted Hortense."

"You couldn't come up with something normal?"

"Oxford is a noble name."

"What about Hortense?"

He snorted. "Family name of your mother's. Her Uncle Hortense was an alcoholic, a semiprofessional golfer, and a devout Lutheran. I wouldn't have it."

"So, I wound up with nothing?"

"So you wound up with nothing."

"Well, now that kid is going to spend years thinking she's telepathic and trying to read everyone's thoughts."

"I doubt her father has thoughts worth reading, and that little girl is about to be diagnosed with idiopathic subglottic tracheal stenosis, which, if it proves treatable at all, will require several painful surgeries and possibly use of a feeding tube, so she'll need something interesting to think about and it won't hurt for her to feel special as well as cursed."

"She has what?"

"I hope they send her down to Mount Sinai," he said. "She'll get the best surgical care on that unit. I wonder if I should . . ."

Shaken by the realization that my father had just demonstrated a level of sensitivity and consideration for a stranger unprecedented in the history of raising me, his only child, I missed the remainder of his musings. The hospital pamphlets said that personality change could be a consequence of brain injury but this kindness seemed extreme. I wondered whether it was permanent and if it would generalize to non-strangers, possibly even family.

The door opened and a doctor came in but it was not Dr. Kellogg. "Good morning," he said. "I'm Dr. Newman. Dr. Kellogg was called to give grand rounds at the last minute and I'll be covering for him."

Dr. Kellogg usually sat behind his desk, partway across the room, and held forth on the nature of traumatic brain injury. Dr. Newman took Dr. Kellogg's chair and rolled it out so that he was sitting directly across from us. He set Dad's file down on a table by the window, crossed his legs, and smiled. He was young and blond. Instead of a white coat he wore an ordinary tweed blazer with leather patches on the sleeves and he had an absolutely epic mustache. Dad looked on disapprovingly. "My appointment is with Kellogg," he said.

Newman nodded. "Yes. Dr. Kellogg was called to give grand rounds—"

"When will he be back?"

"Not until ten, but I'm covering for him. I've reviewed your file."

"I'll wait to see him."

"Dad," I said, "there's no time. The memorial for Jason is at ten thirty."

My father shifted in his chair. This was how it happened since he came home from the hospital. His brain was a station with two trains arriving at the same time—in this case, the wish for his usual doctor and the determination to be at Jason Grant's memorial—and while once there had been a conductor, now there was nothing and the two engines were likely to come in at full speed and plow right into each other. "You have oatmeal in your mustache," he said. "What medical school did you go to?"

Dr. Newman took a paper napkin from his pocket and dabbed at a spot above his mouth. "University of New England."

"My God, you're an osteopath?"

Newman did not seem rattled. "You can reschedule if you like," he said, "but I've been looking forward to speaking with you. Your test results are back."

Dad, who looked as if he was about to get up, sat back in his chair. "Already?"

"They rushed it, at our request."

My father had been through a battery of psychological tests and brain scans the week before. It was meant to measure his progress since being discharged from the hospital.

"Would you like me to review it with you?" Newman asked.

"I can review it myself." Dad held out his hand for the file.

"Your son might like to hear it explained in layman's terms."

"Let the doctor explain it," I said, "in case I have questions."

Dad shrugged, nodded, and adjusted his tie. His hand was trembling a little.

Dr. Newman opened the file and looked at me. "Your father," he said, "is utterly fascinating."

I felt flattered, though in the years since I have learned that you never want to be fascinating to a doctor. At that time in my life being ordinary still seemed like the worst possible fate, and if I had to put my Broadway dreams on hold then I could at least have interesting family in the Catskills.

Newman took a set of colorful scans out of the file. "The biggest problem with research on traumatic brain injury," he said, "is a lack of premorbid data."

"What does that mean?" I asked.

"It means that people rarely do us the courtesy of being evaluated before their injuries, so when we see them it can be hard to tell whether some of their deficits were preexisting. The population isn't entirely random, you know. People are more likely to be injured if they drink hard, drive fast, that sort of thing. Engage in reckless behavior."

"I don't get why that's a problem."

"It's a problem for science because it means that, if we find that people who have sustained brain injuries tend to show poor judgment or lack of planning or limited impulse control, there is always the strong possibility that they were that way to begin with. But your father . . ." He drew air in through his mustache, as though savoring something delicious. "Your father has a pristine set of data from five years before his accident."

I was finding this guy to be increasingly pretentious, but Dad seemed to be warming to him. "The data from the Alzheimer's study," he said.

Newman nodded.

"But you don't have Alzheimer's," I said.

"I was in the control group, Lukas. I volunteered. They were studying Alzheimer's in unusually gifted people to determine whether superior intelligence cushions the symptoms, and they needed a high-functioning control, people without the disease but with a very high level of achievement, for comparison."

A high-functioning control group sounded like exactly the sort of thing my father would sign up for. Newman rubbed his hands together, looking like a kid on Christmas morning. "So, we have the data from five years ago and we have data from a week ago, for a patient with no history of pre-injury deficits. It's perfect."

Dad, who did not seem to mind hearing his close encounter with a Toyota driven by a drunk teenager described as perfect, eagerly leaned forward. For my part, I wasn't sure that some sort of "reckless behavior" hadn't played a role in my father's injury given that my mother had never liked lilacs.

"The MRI," Dr. Newman said, "reveals considerable atrophy in the frontal lobes. In fact, if we compare the current scan with the old one, there's been a seven percent reduction in cortical volume." He held out two of the colorful sheets. Dad took them and frowned, holding them side by side.

"What does that mean for him?" I asked.

"The frontal lobes," Newman said, "are absolutely crucial as we make our way in the world. Inhibition, self-awareness, mental flexibility, multistep planning, all are dependent on the frontal lobes. They are the seat of the civilized mind."

I was coming to hate this man and his mustache but Dad was practically jumping out of his chair with excitement. "This is fascinating," he said, looking first at one scan and then at the other.

"The really fascinating thing," Newman said to me, "is that you can be highly intelligent without particularly functional frontal lobes. You can be knowledgeable, perceptive, and clever without having any insight or self-control."

That sounded troublingly familiar.

"Your father had an intelligence test five years ago, and he had one last week, and despite the injury his IQ now tests thirteen points *higher*."

Dad let out a low, soft whistle. "That's statistically significant?"

"It certainly is."

"You should write it up for publication."

"Dr. Kellogg and I are preparing a manuscript for the *Archives of Clinical Neuroscience*."

"Very nice."

"What I want to know," I said, "is when I can get some goddamn sleep."

They both stared at me. "You're having a hard time sleeping?" Newman asked.

"He's having a hard time sleeping. He falls asleep fine but then he wakes up in the middle of the night and sometimes he's confused and agitated and I think it's getting worse. There have been a few times when he's left the house and I found him wandering in the street. I've started having to . . . keep a close eye all night." I didn't want to explain about the cord because that would bring up the question of where my mother was and I didn't particularly want to get into a long discussion of our sad family dynamic. “I need to sleep,” I said. “Is there something you can give him?”

Newman frowned. Dad shifted in his chair, looking embarrassed. Neither one seemed to appreciate being interrupted by an actual medical problem. “Late insomnia is hard,” Newman said. Dad nodded his agreement. “We could, uh, make a few adjustments in his night-time regimen . . .” He looked at the chart. “Although some of these medications are already at their maximum dosage.”

“That’s it?” I asked. “You’re going to tweak his meds?”

“I told you we should order an air mattress,” Dad said.

They spoke for a few more minutes, reviewing the test findings and swapping stories about residency. I usually listened carefully at Dad’s appointments and took notes, but as they went on and on I stared out the window at the hospital parking lot and let the words wash over me. I watched people walk to and from their cars, wondering what kind of problems they were having. There were old couples leaning on each other and young couples cradling children in their arms. Some people came alone. I didn’t see any pairs like me and my father.

“Well,” Dad finally said, “I don’t want to take any more of your time. This has been a true pleasure. I hope that you’ll join Dr. Kellogg and me for my next consultation.”

“I’d be honored,” Newman said.

We all stood and shook hands and then Dad and I returned to the waiting room, where I made the next appointment. We exited the clinic to the hospital lobby. It was a newly constructed cavernous space, stone walls five stories high with interior windows looking down and a desk curving in a lazy parabola across from the front doors. A fountain on the far wall was malfunctioning, spraying a jet of water onto the marble floor in a recurrent pattern. A janitor had it marked off with cones and was engaged in the Sisyphean process of mopping up.

Dad glanced around, sunglasses on. “When I started here,” he said, “this was a fraction of the size it is now.”

“Well,” I said, “that was a long time ago. The city is growing.”

“Now they have all this but only one person working the desk.”

I saw his point. There was a long line and the woman behind the reception desk seemed frazzled.

“I’d like to go down to the morgue,” he said.

“Seriously?” I asked. “We really don’t have time. We need to—”

He spotted someone on the far side of the lobby. “Dr. Lee!” he called. “Over here!” He pulled his sunglasses off and hurried away.

Dr. Lee was a small woman in a long white coat who stared as Dad charged across the lobby. I hurried to catch up. By the time I got to him he had just stopped pumping her arm with an overly enthusiastic handshake and, visibly flustered, she was smoothing her coat and rearranging her stethoscope.

“This is my son, Lukas,” he said. “Damn, it’s good to see you. It really is. I’ve been thinking about your research, your team’s hypotheses about acetylcholine, and I keep meaning to email and ask if you have any data?”

Her face brightened at his mention of the research. “As a matter of fact,” she said, “we do have some preliminary findings.”

“I left something in the clinic,” I told Dad. “I’ll be right back. We absolutely have to go in five minutes.”

He nodded, completely focused on Dr. Lee, and I made my way back through the waiting area, into the clinic, and down the hall to the office where Dr. Newman was still writing notes in the chart.

“Dr. Newman?”

"Lukas. Is everything okay?"

"I wanted to ask you something else."

His eyes flickered to the empty hall behind me. "I really can't give you information from your father's file without his permission."

"Just generally, then, about strategies to help him."

"All right. I have a moment."

I stepped into the office. "Do you think my father's memory will come back? I mean, does a patient at this stage of recovery still have a shot at some improvement in that regard?"

"When you say 'memory,' you mean his ability to learn new things?"

"More his ability to remember old ones. Like what happened in the day or two before the accident, and what he was doing that night."

Newman nodded. "I believe he has retrograde amnesia for a period of about seventy-two hours?"

"He does." It meant that Dad remembered having lunch a few days before his accident, and then nothing else about the circumstances that brought him to Forty-Third and Vine.

"That type of recovery only happens in the movies, Lukas. The issue is that those events were never consolidated in long term memory to begin with, due to the physical trauma. People imagine that these things are like pieces of paper in a file cabinet, waiting to be found, when in fact there's nothing there."

"So, there's no way he can tell us what he was doing that night?"

"He would be inferring it, like the rest of us. Of course, he might have clues from deeper in his memory, previous times he visited that area, associations to the location, an appointment he made . . ." Newman paused. "He doesn't have any ideas about it?"

"He says he doesn't know."

"I see."

"And another thing: the perseveration. He's so stuck on an idea."

"Which is?"

"A colleague of his, here at the medical center. Dr. Jason Grant, the psychiatrist. You probably know about him?"

"Yes. Tragic."

"Well, Dad has this idea that the whole thing is a mistake. Or, I don't know, a cover-up or something. That's the thing, he doesn't really have a coherent idea, just the sense that something's wrong."

"Dr. Grant died by suicide, I believe? Last year?"

"He disappeared a year ago today. We're on our way to the memorial now. He disappeared while Dad was in the coma and when he woke up and found out about it he was convinced something was wrong. He thought he knew something, something no one else knew, from a conversation with Dr. Grant just before the accident."

"What did they talk about?"

"That's the thing, Dad has no idea. They weren't friends; I think it was probably the only time they ever spoke. Dad's a researcher, he spent all his time in the basement with his lab rats. Dr. Grant was upstairs seeing actual patients. Children. Dad hates children . . . or at least he used to. Anyway, Dr. Grant had a research proposal, an idea and an application for funding, and he wanted to run it by Dad since that's what he does. So they talked, and Dad said there was something wrong with the proposal, or odd about it, but again, he has no idea."

"Peculiar."

"It is. It also doesn't matter. Jason Grant is obviously dead. He's been gone for a year; they found his stuff next to the lake. The point is that Dad is stuck on this and I don't know how to get him unstuck."

Dr. Newman put the cap on his pen. "Lukas, something I've learned in studying the brain is how profoundly people can change and at the same time how little they change at all. Tiny changes, microscopic alterations in neurotransmitter reuptake, may profoundly change how we feel, how we think. An injury like your father's can alter the entire personality. And yet, at the same time, if you ask me to engineer a simple change in someone's functioning, make them a tad more independent, improve their judgment or their mental flexibility just a little bit . . ." He spread his hands helplessly over the chart.

"Yes," I said, "it seems like a real paradox. The thing is that I can't stay here, at home. I have to go back to the city. I have a life, I'm an actor. I gave up a major part to come back and take care of him. Stanley Kowalski in a revival of *Streetcar*."

Newman stared at me blankly.

"*A Streetcar Named Desire*. Tennessee Williams?"

He shrugged slightly.

"Well, it was off-Broadway but it was big, really exciting, and that shot's gone but I still have connections. If I stay, though, they're going to dry up. I'm going to get older. I know that sounds stupid because I'm only twenty-three, but . . . I have to be able to leave him, you know? And if he can't let go of things, if he keeps wandering at night . . ."

"Hire help."

"We've tried. They get fed up with him. He has a knack for picking up on details about people, noticing things, and then he comments . . . no one stays for long."

"Mmm." Dr. Newman stroked his mustache. "My impression has always been that progress happens most for the people who have meaning in their lives, who have direction."

"How do you help someone find meaning? Is that, like, a hobby or something?"

"It's going to be rooted in his life prior to the accident. What did he care about, what was he passionate about?"

"I have absolutely no idea."

"Well." He looked at his watch. "We're starting from scratch then, aren't we?"

A nurse appeared in the doorway. "Dr. Newman? Your next patient is ready."

The doctor shuffled through the papers in Dad's file. He clearly wanted to get back to publishing his findings about IQ and frontal lobe volume. "I'll think about the perseveration," he said. "If I come up with any strategies I'll let you know."

I thanked Dr. Newman with all the sincerity I could find, given that I wanted to punch him in his absurd mustache. In the waiting room I spotted the telepathic girl. Her father was talking to a nurse. His phone was nowhere to be seen and he looked stunned. The girl looked at me and I tapped my forehead and winked. She smiled. Then I went to free Dr. Lee from my father, with his extra thirteen IQ points and his 7 percent reduction in frontal lobe volume, pack him up in the car, and take him to Jason Grant's memorial while we were still able to get there on time.

CHAPTER FOUR

Clouds were gathering over Tricounty Regional High School, though the rain was supposed to hold off. Rows of chairs were set up on the front lawn, facing and gently curving around a wooden bench with a stone base and a metal plaque. A sapling was planted next to it. A line stretched to the parking lot and moved slowly but steadily forward. As people reached the bench they stooped to read the plaque, sometimes touched the wood, said something to the couple standing beside the sapling, and went to find a seat.

"So, we're waiting to look at a bench?" Dad asked. "I can see it from here."

"Shh," I said, as the woman in front of us turned. "You wanted to come. We're paying our respects."

Dad craned his neck. "Christ, look at Owen," he said. "He's half the man he was."

"Well, he lost his son."

Dad was right, our neighbor from up the hill had declined precipitously. He had been a larger-than-life presence in my childhood. Owen Grant was rarely home when I went over to see Garrett, who had the best collection of Matchbox cars in our elementary school, but I remembered him from the holidays. In those days their house was the largest in town and the day after every Thanksgiving a crew of workers showed up to wrap it in what must have been miles of garland and lights. For the rest of the year it glittered on top of the hill, lighting up the entire neighborhood with the Grant family's good cheer. Owen descended from his home on Christmas Eve, laden with a bag full of oversized candy canes and gingerbread for us kids and bottles of red wine and single-malt scotch for the adults, Santa Claus hat pulled down over his block of a skull. His sons, Jason and Garrett, were always right beside him, soaking up their father's reflected glow. Misty trailed behind when she was little, already looking faintly embarrassed, and then disappeared from the scene in later years. I was generally aware that Owen Grant was a rich and important man, a builder and a leader, the chairman of the board at the medical center where my father worked, whatever that meant. I just liked the candy canes.

The line moved forward. Each mourner, upon reaching the front, said a few words to Owen and to his wife, Lucia, studied the bench for a moment, and then moved on to the seating area. Watching this pattern repeat, it occurred to me that coming might have been a terrible mistake. A year out from his injury, nine months from his lonely homecoming, Dad had been in very few social situations, and the ones he had experienced tended not to end well. The home health aides were only the tip of the iceberg; there was the cashier at the supermarket he'd reduced to tears, the waiter at his favorite Italian restaurant who'd needed to be physically restrained. It wasn't just what he said, it was the number of times he said it. He was disinhibited, to be sure, but he wasn't the first person to complain about the service at L'Italiano. The waiter probably didn't even know what "limited dendritic arborization" meant (I had to look it up). The issue was the perseveration, the relentlessness, the step too far, beyond the signals that would warn other people to stop. And if there was one thing Dad had been perseverating on, as we approached this anniversary, it was what he perceived as the mystery around Jason Grant's disappearance. I had a sinking feeling that once we reached the front of the line he would have a few questions for the grieving parents.

"You know, Dad . . ." I began.

"Where are the twins?" he asked as the line again inched forward.

I looked around. "Garrett's over there. I don't see Misty."

Dad followed my gaze to where Jason's younger brother, Garrett, sat in the second row. "That kid is a damn shame," he said.

Garrett wasn't a kid anymore; he was my age. He was, however, a damn shame. As a child he looked like his twin sister, Misty. They were both gorgeous, redheads with chocolate eyes and smears of freckles across full cheeks. He was the only person, other than my father, wearing sunglasses under the overcast sky. Even from a distance he looked gaunt, the bones standing out in his face. He wore the five years since we left high school heavily; they, and whatever drugs he had filled them with, seemed to have melted his youth away.

"Do you ever talk to him?" Dad asked.

"Garrett? No. Not in years."

"Maybe you should reconnect."

"Why would I want to do that?"

Dad shrugged. "He was a nice boy. Didn't he used to come over and race cars with you?"

"Yes. You usually yelled at us for being too loud."

"Well. Times change."

"They do. He and I would have nothing to talk about. Listen, Dad, just remember this is a memorial, all right?"

"Of course this is a memorial."

"Yeah. Right. So, let's not ask Owen and Lucia any questions about Jason when we get to the front of the line, okay?"

Dad turned to look at me. "Do you think I need lessons on social skills, Lukas?"

"It's not that, it's just that when you get an idea in your head you can sometimes hyperfocus on it and forget, you know, social niceties. And I've noticed, with this getting closer, you've been pretty stuck on the whole Jason Grant and the lake . . . thing."

"We don't even know he's in the lake."

The poor woman in front of us turned to look again. I smiled in a manner that I hoped somehow conveyed my predicament. She turned away without reciprocating.

"Of course he's in the lake," I hissed back. "He's been in the lake for a year and that's where he's going to stay. Where the hell else would he be, Dad? His car, shoes, and watch were at the lake. His body is there too. Just because they haven't found it doesn't mean it isn't there. It is a big . . . fucking . . . lake."

The woman got out of line and walked away. I realized I had allowed my voice to rise. "Now who's being inappropriate at a memorial service?" Dad asked.

Nothing else was said until we reached the front of the line. Standing in front of his son's memorial bench, Owen was a man who had been hollowed out. His cheeks were sunken, his hairline receding, and his eyes had retreated into his head. He didn't seem robust enough to hoist a sack of presents and he looked like he would never have the inclination to do so again anyway. "I'm sorry," I said, not knowing what else to say. He nodded and gripped my hand, a trace of his old power still there. I moved along to Owen's wife, Lucia, mumbling a similar apology. She was a diminutive woman with dark, short-cut hair. She had always melted into her husband's outsized presence and grief had diminished her further. She looked up when I spoke but her gaze, vague and unfocused, went right through me.

Dad followed behind. I heard him offer similar sentiments, the Grants make similar non-replies, and then we were through it. I led us to seats on the far side of the field, glancing at Garrett as we passed. His head didn't move, though with the sunglasses on it was hard to tell whether he saw me. We settled into seats midway back.

"I didn't have to ask them anything," Dad said. "I went over and asked my questions last week."

"You what?"

"Last week. Tuesday, was it? Wednesday? When did you go to the dentist?"

"Thursday."

"Thursday, then. All the days blend together."

"You went to see the Grants on Thursday?"

"Indeed I did."

"Without me?"

"Obviously without you, if you weren't there."

I stared at him. Dad needed me by his side during the night, when he was prone to wake up agitated and confused. He couldn't drive and generally wasn't to be trusted in stores and restaurants. Staying home by himself during waking hours, however, was supposed to be safe. "What did you do?"

"I went for a walk," he responded, "and knocked on their door, and they invited me in for coffee."

The Grants' house was maybe seventy-five yards up the hill from ours but they had become a rather long seventy-five yards. My childhood friendship with Garrett and adolescent infatuation with Misty notwithstanding, there was a social gulf between them and the lesser houses on the street. My mother had once been our chief emissary to the community, but with her departure our little family didn't have an outward face. The thought of my father trudging over to have coffee with the Grants while I had a cavity filled was dreadful. "What did you talk about?" I asked.

"Oh, this and that," Dad said. "I hadn't been over there in years and years. You know, Lukas, I wonder whether I tended to work too much before my accident."

"It's possible."

"Well, we caught up. Misty finished Yale Drama and is in New York."

"I know."

"Do you ever see her?"

"No."

"And Garrett has had quite a few problems, as you know. I suggested some programs but they had already tried them all."

"That was nice of you."

"I'm a researcher rather than a clinician, but I am still a psychiatrist. We talked a bit about the medical center; Owen is still chairman of the board and they're expanding very aggressively."

"Did you, ah, ask them anything about Jason? Anything sensitive?"

"Let me see." He dug into the inner pocket of his blazer and withdrew a red leather notebook, flipped it open, and frowned at the contents. "Major behavioral changes in the weeks leading up to his disappearance? Negative. Suicidal ideation, vegetative symptoms, appetite reduction, loss of interest in previously enjoyed activities? Nothing there. Shifts in libido? They weren't sure about that one, but nothing to report—"

"Jesus Christ, Dad, how did they feel about all those questions?"

Dad seemed confused. "How did they feel? Fine, I suppose. Unfortunately they didn't know anything about a research proposal. It wasn't a very productive line of questioning but it seemed to spark something, in Lucia at least. She came after me when I left and we had a short follow-up in the street."

"What did she say?"

Dad closed the notebook and tapped it against his chin. "It was about Garrett. Owen told me that the last time he and Lucia saw Jason was several weeks before his disappearance. He had a condo near the medical center and had been working too much to come out and see his parents."

"But Emery said—"

"Right. That he was out on the street a few days before he went missing. It fits with what Lucia told me: that she thinks Garrett, who had been staying with them, was sneaking out to see Jason."

"Why would she think that? And why would Garrett sneak out to see his own brother?"

Dad shrugged. "She didn't know. Garrett denied it. And as for why she thought it was the case, she caught him sneaking back in and when she checked the security footage she saw that he had cut a wide path around the side of the house, avoiding the scope of the camera."

"So?"

"So, Garrett didn't know the camera had been installed. At least, he wasn't supposed to. His parents don't trust him. Jason was the only person, other than Lucia and Owen, who knew about the security system."

"How do you avoid the camera?" I asked, though I guessed that I knew the answer.

“The woods. Where Emery saw the glow of the cigarette.”

“All right,” I said, “so Jason wanted to talk to Garrett and he wanted to do it without his parents knowing. Why didn’t he just call? Why didn’t he meet Garrett at the diner?”

“Good questions,” Dad said. “And ones only Garrett can answer.”

“Is that why you want me to reconnect with him?”

“It’s why I suggested it, yes.”

I thought for a moment. “Another question might be why Lucia wanted to tell you that without Owen hearing.”

“She said that he’s been emotionally fragile. She probably thought that it would upset him.”

“I’m guessing it would have. I don’t think you should be stirring things up, Dad. Whatever was going on with Jason and his brother is history now.”

Dad shrugged, reopened the red notebook, and flipped through the pages, studying his own cramped handwriting. “Did they say anything about Misty?” I finally asked.

“Misty? Not really. Just that she’s in New York, doing well, getting auditions and such. I’m not surprised; Yale is the finest theater conservatory in the country, of course.”

“Of course.” As far as Dad was concerned, all things Yale were unquestionably the finest.

“She’s supposed to be here.”

“Is she?”

Dad nodded without looking up. “They said they were expecting her. I hope she arrives in time to find a seat.”

“There are plenty of seats.”

“There are eighty-seven chairs set up and thirty-five free ones but forty-one people are still on line, plus the Grants.”

I craned my neck and scanned our surroundings. I was, by that time, used to the idiosyncratic observations my father had been issuing since coming home from the hospital. They were generally detailed, precise, and extremely irrelevant. I took a moment to count the empty chairs. Thirty-five. A moment later a man sat down. Thirty-four. "Maybe I'll save her one," I said. "Like, go and put a sign on one in front."

"That would be nice. You could strike up a conversation with Garrett."

"I am not going to question Garrett."

"I didn't say question him, I just said—"

"I know what you said. You'll stay here? Don't wander off and accost anyone."

"I'm just reviewing my notes, Lukas. I'm not a cat. I don't wander."

I got up and walked away.

I was surprised by how many people had come. It was strange, in a way, that the school was doing this at all, considering that it had been over a decade since Jason graduated. He wasn't the only person to have something bad happen, not by a long shot. Brad Roxbury, a kid in my graduating class, drove his car off Route 31 the previous winter and would spend the rest of his life in a wheelchair. Someone in the freshman class had OD'd just a few months before.

Jason had been different, though. He'd been golden. He was a success in everything he did. He was one of those kids; the town followed his exploits long after he left, keeping track of where he was going to school and how he was doing and where he was on summer internship. When he disappeared into the lake it landed on the town of Faith with mythic force. Even he couldn't handle the stresses of modern life; even he wasn't immune to whatever had ailed him. The search for his body became a community project. People sensed that he had been the hero of a tragic story and though they didn't know the plot or the other characters they at least knew that it should have a proper ending, and they now realized that this ceremony was the closest they were going to get.

I walked away from my father, circling around the back of the seats, nodding to a few former teachers but not stopping to chat. I had been gone for five years and this was not the way I'd imagined a return. I thought that I'd come back to talk about my career as an actor and to inspire the theater students with the arc of my story, the way I'd passed through years of doubt and deprivation before arriving at great success. It wasn't the sort of journey you wanted to stop halfway through.

There were many people I only half recognized, which was a common feeling after growing up in a place like Faith. It was a small town but not an isolated one. Nearby New Birmingham was a little city that was in the process of becoming midsized and more people were coming and going every year, mixing with the ones who had always been there. When I was a kid it was exceptional that my father was a doctor and my mother a lawyer. Most of my friends had parents who were working class, periodically unemployed, and I was painfully self-conscious about being a "rich kid." The Grants were our one truly wealthy family. By the time Jason disappeared, though, Faith was turning into an upscale suburb. Doctors and lawyers were no longer rarities, and even the Grants' house was overshadowed by the massive homes being built by newcomers from New Birmingham's growing financial sector.

I spotted the father of the guy who had played Horatio to my Hamlet, the woman who ran the hair salon my mother used to go to, and my old math tutor's younger brother among a collage of strange and unremarkable faces. Some people chatted with one another as if it were any other event, a basketball game or graduation, while others stood awkwardly or wandered aimlessly. I kept moving.

I finally saw her standing alone in the shade underneath an oak tree, wrapped tight in a purple, knee-length coat. It had been years, but she looked just the same. High cheekbones, a sharp chin set below gently pursed lips, as though holding in a comment that would be hilarious or devastating or both. Her long, red hair was tied back with a white ribbon. She looked at me and she started to laugh. "Lukas," she said, "you look like hell."

I probably did. "I'm sorry about your brother," I told her.

She squinted at me. "You are?"

"Of course I am."

She nodded and looked away from me and over what were, according to my father, ninety-three people who had come to pay their respects to her and her family. "You came all the way back here for a bench?" she asked. "You can't even sit on it. I mean, you could, but it would be rude during the ceremony."

"It wasn't that far out of my way. I'm living back home now. I left the city about nine months ago."

"Why?"

"To take care of my father. Didn't you hear he'd been in an accident?"

She shook her head. "No."

"He was hit by a car."

"Huh. I saw the two of you on line. He seems to be getting around okay."

"Yeah, his body is in pretty good shape."

"So what isn't?"

"Well, his arms and legs and all that are good. He has a TBI, though. A traumatic brain injury. I've been taking care of him."

"Is that why you look the way you do?"

"Do I look that bad? I haven't been sleeping particularly well."

"It's not so much that you look bad as that you look . . . concerned."

The wind picked up and an older woman waiting on line lost her hat. A man ran to retrieve it. I stepped farther back under the oak tree, closer to Misty. "How are your parents?" I asked.

She wrinkled her nose. "Terrible."

"I suppose that's to be expected?" I didn't really know. At twenty-three I'd had very little contact with tragedy.

"I guess."

"I saw Garrett."

"He basically lives with them now. Except when he doesn't. He bounces back and forth between their house and our Uncle Frank's, in Boston. Wears out his welcome in one place and then moves on to the other."

"I didn't know you had an Uncle Frank."

"My dad's big brother."

"Oh. And what about you? Are you just here for the ceremony?"

"Yeah. I need to get back. I have auditions lined up." Misty spoke without looking at me, her eyes scanning the crowd. She stood on tiptoe, craning her neck.

"Are you waiting for someone?" I asked.

"I am."

I felt an unexpected rush of jealousy, imagining a boyfriend arriving from Manhattan in time to support her through the ordeal. "Who?"

Misty glanced at me. "I don't know her name. I just know what she looks like."

"Oh." I glanced down at Misty's hands. She wasn't holding a phone or a picture.

"How is your career going, Lukas?" she asked, eyes back on the milling attendees in front of us.

"Uh, good, actually. Great. Or, it was. I was cast as Stanley Kowalski in *Streetcar.*"

"The Myrton Styles role?"

"Before it was the Myrton Styles role it was the Lukas Moore role. He was my understudy."

"Huh. I hear they're doing a four-page write-up on him in *Playbill.* You left that behind to come back here?"

"Uh-uh."

"To take care of your father?"

"Yup." I was having a hard time managing multiple syllables in the wake of the *Playbill* news.

Misty shifted her eyes away from the crowd to look at me. We stood in silence for a long moment. I felt the disappointment that had been curdling in my gut dissolving, a little bit at a time, as she gazed at me with those chocolate eyes.

"People! Please find your way to your seats, the ceremony is going to be getting underway." Principal O'Brien hadn't aged a day since Misty and I were in school. People broke out of the groups they had been standing in and began to make their way toward the seats. I wondered whether Dad's calculation had been correct and, if so, whether more chairs had been found. "I guess we should . . ."

Misty stiffened, her face draining of color, one hand reaching out to grip my forearm.

"What is it?" I stared at her and, not receiving an answer, turned to follow her gaze.

A man was standing midway across the field, close to the dwindling receiving line. He looked like an accountant. He was wearing a dark suit, like many of the men present. He was slight and blond and wore glasses. A cowlick stood up on the back of his head. One hand was tucked in his pocket and he shifted from one foot to another, looking around until he turned to look at us, looking back at him. We stood like that for what seemed like a long moment, though in reality it was probably only a second or two, and then he turned on his heel and disappeared behind the later-arriving mourners.

"Oh," Misty hissed, "no fucking way." I started to reply but it was too late; she was off, running across the grass, pivoting around one couple, and pushing a surprised member of our graduating class out of the way. I had no choice but to follow.

Running through a memorial service, even one that had yet to get underway, was an awkward experience. I made an effort to run casually, sort of a light jog that implied I was trying to get to my seat or perhaps assist an elderly person, but Misty was in a full-out sprint. She was wearing canvas sneakers and had hitched her dress up high enough to have a full range of motion. She had always been fast; if she hadn't done theater in high school she would have been on the track team. I, on the other hand, never had any discernable athletic talents, a fact which I partially attributed to genetics and partially to my father's historic disinclination to toss a baseball, shoot hoops, teach me to ride a bike, or otherwise invest in my physical development. Misty easily outdistanced me.

I would have been all right if it hadn't been for the baby. Who brings a baby to a memorial service? Though to be fair, the baby was being well-behaved. I believe that he or she was sleeping. It was in one of those car seat carriers that snaps out of the base, set on the ground and revealed at the last moment as someone ducked out of my way. I jumped and cleared it but tripped on the other side, flying headfirst like a failed and awkward Superman, landing with the wind knocked out of me in front of the bench.

Scrambling to my knees as rapidly as I could, considering that I wasn't able to breathe, I was deeply relieved to find that Owen and Lucia Grant's backs were to me. They, along with a minister who had recently appeared and most everyone else, were watching Misty's progress across the parking lot. Rising unsteadily to my feet I craned my neck to see her actually hurdle over the hood of a parked sedan. Ahead of her a black BMW was gliding toward the street.

"She's always been a strange girl."

I turned to find Garrett standing behind me, sunglasses still on.

"Lukas."

"Hello, Garrett," I gasped, my breath returning.

He slid the glasses down his nose and studied the muddy knees of my trousers, the dirt on the polo I'd borrowed from Dad, the fresh scrape on one elbow. "You took a spill."

"Someone left a baby lying around."

"You seem to still be chasing after my little sister."

Garrett had been born six minutes before his twin and always insisted on reinforcing his seniority. I didn't have a witty response to his accurate observation. Turning, I saw that the BMW was turning onto the state highway beyond the lot and that Misty was finally slowing down, apparently recognizing the futility of the situation. "Who was she chasing?" I asked.

"I have no idea."

"Did you see him?"

"I did. Never seen him before, though."

"She said she was looking for someone but I think it was a woman."

"Is that right?" For the first time, Garrett sounded interested.

"How are you?" I asked, turning back to him.

"Fine. Wonderful, actually. Fit as a fiddle."

It was obviously not the case. "I'm sorry about Jason."

He nodded, eyes again hidden as he pushed the sunglasses up the bridge of his nose.

"I've been home," I said. "With my dad. For a while now, actually. I'm surprised we haven't run into each other."

"I spend as little time in Faith as possible. I'm usually in Boston."

"With your Uncle Frank."

He raised his eyebrows. "You've met?"

"Not formally." There was no point in being evasive except that I felt I wanted some sort of advantage in the interaction.

I felt Garrett scanning me, looking for chinks in my armor. I didn't think they would be hard to find. "Have you given up the theater, Lukas?"

"Things are on hold."

"Ah. While you get your father sorted out? I did hear about his accident."

"He's nearly back to one hundred percent."

"That's not my understanding."

"Then you've been talking to the wrong people."

"I hear he's half vegetable. I was impressed to see him so ambulatory when the two of you arrived."

"I'm impressed you know the word 'ambulatory.'"

"Cornell, my friend."

"A whole three and a half semesters, right?"

"Ladies and gentlemen, please!" Principal O'Brien was beside us, facing the crowd, clapping his hands. I almost expected a rhythmic clap back, kindergarten style. "We're running behind. Please take your seats!"

Garrett smiled, dipped his head, and pivoted to his seat. I made a half-hearted effort to brush the mud off my shirt and knees. A moment later Misty was back by my side, breathing hard and seizing my elbow. "I want to get drunk, Lukas," she hissed in my ear. "Like, really, really drunk. Will you get drunk with me tonight?"

"Um," I said, "maybe. What time were you thinking?"

"What time is good for you?"

"Well, the thing is that my father can get a little confused at night. Agitated and confused. I was hoping the doctor was going to give him something for it this morning, but . . . anyway, it usually happens after one A.M., so until then I'm free."

"Your mom can't watch him?"

"Mom left. Packed up and moved back to Quebec, near her sister. While he was still in the hospital. That's why I'm here, there's no one else to take care of him."

Misty regarded me for a moment and I felt myself peeling away under the intensity of her gaze. "All right," she finally said, "we'll get drunk before one in the morning."

"Yeah," I said, "sounds good."

I made my way back to my father before the principal could remind us again. "That," he said when I joined him, "was very interesting."

"I'm glad you enjoyed it."

"Not particularly appropriate behavior for a memorial service, though. And your pants are a mess."

I sat back and sighed. "Let's just get through this, Dad."

He steepled his fingers and shut his eyes. "That's what I'm doing, Lukas. That is what I am doing."

I gritted my teeth and sat back myself, waiting for the service to begin.

CHAPTER FIVE

After dinner Dad read for a short bit and then switched over to TV. He chose a movie he'd seen about twenty times since his accident (and which he never would have watched before) and I sat beside him until my phone buzzed with two words: Outside. Vodka.

"I'm going out," I said. "I won't be late."

"Jesus," Dad said, "Jesus Christ."

I followed his gaze to the screen where Hugh Grant was running through the rain. "He makes it," I said. "You know he gets there before she leaves."

"I know," Dad said, "but it still gets me every time."

"Did you—"

"Quiet please, Lukas!" The rain was coming down harder. Hugh was getting close to the airport.

Dad's newfound love of rom-coms would keep him occupied. I put my shoes on and joined Misty on our front steps, where she drew a sizable bottle of vodka and pair of plastic cups from a backpack. "I'm not much of a liquor guy," I said. "I may just grab a beer."

"That's fine," she said. "More for me." She poured into one cup and took a long drink. I went back inside and took a six pack from the fridge and then rejoined her. She was wearing jeans and a loose-fitting sweater and her red hair was tied back. The sun had just gone down, but it was not fully dark. I opened a beer and sat on the stoop. "Why did your mom leave?" Misty asked without preamble. "Was taking care of your father too much for her?"

I took a long drink of my beer before answering. "Yes. No. She didn't even try. It was the accident, the way it happened." I told the story then, laid out end to end in a way that I had not told it to anybody before. I had been in the city, in early rehearsals for *Streetcar*, when I got the call. At first they didn't know if he was going to make it, and I rushed home and huddled with my mother in a miserable hospital waiting room for almost twenty hours while various surgeons shuttled in and out, offering explanations about intracranial pressure and the dynamics of skull fracture, until finally an older doctor, the head of the team, came in and told us the only thing we cared about, which was that Dad was going to live.

The details emerged later: where in the city he had been hit and the circumstances of the accident. Dad was supposed to have been working late that night, but the medical center was nowhere near Forty-Third and Vine. Even if he had stepped out for a late dinner it would not have brought him there. The flowers were the clincher, though. There was no reason we should have found out about them; I don't think families are generally informed about every detail of the tableau when their loved ones are peeled off the asphalt. Mom insisted on thanking the paramedics, though. That's the way she was: bottles of wine for the garbage men at the holidays; a box of cigars for the mailman (who she knew didn't drink); a twenty for the kid who delivered the newspaper. Thoughtful gifts for my teachers every last day of school. If an ambulance crew rushed out into the rain to save her husband's life there was no way she wasn't going to show up at the station with heartfelt thanks and a plate full of homemade cookies, and that was when a paramedic with a vivid memory and a big mouth told her about the striking scene of her husband lying on the wet pavement in front of a hotel, a bouquet of lilacs spread beside him, loose petals clinging to the blood and rain on his upturned face.

My mother had been unhappy for a very long time. She was also a lawyer at a massive firm with a half dozen offices; she had grown up in Quebec and spoke fluent French. It was easy to arrange a transfer to Montreal.

Misty listened and she drank and when I finished it was much darker and I'd had almost two beers. "What's your father doing now?" she asked.

"Not much. He's not working. His medical license is suspended and his lab is shuttered. Maybe he could do some sort of consulting on grant proposals, or teach, but he keeps acting like he's just days away from everything being back to normal, so we never get to plan B. And then he sits around and reads old psychiatric journals and watches rom-coms."

"He didn't used to do that, did he?"

"Never. Definitely not the rom-coms."

"That's a weird change."

"The accident changed him in some ways, though in other ways it just made him more of who he always was."

"Has he lost his memory? That's what happens when people get hit in the head, right?"

"There's a hole in his memory. His brain wasn't able to make new memories for the time right before and after the accident. But anything outside of that gap, he remembers. That's not it, though. His biggest problem is that he notices everything."

"Like what?"

"Well, like, all the people at the service this morning. You and I just saw a crowd, right? Sort of one thing. A single chunk. 'People.' Or 'chairs.' But he sees every single one of them. He knew how many there were. He knew, I don't know, that Mrs. Macarthur's dog has a stomach problem because instead of just seeing a dog turd he noticed something about it, probably something disgusting. It's like normal people have a filter so that we don't get barraged by every single thing going on around us, and his filter is broken."

"That's sort of cool. It's almost like a superpower."

"It's exhausting. For him, I mean. He gets wiped just by being out in the world. And I have to tell you, it's fucking exhausting for me too, because it seems like that filter is supposed to work both ways. He says every damn thing he thinks of—it just comes out."

"It's not easy when parents change, is it? They're supposed to stay the same. We're the ones who are supposed to do all the changing."

"I guess that's right." I drank the rest of the second beer. We sat quietly, the faint sound of another rom-com drifting through the door behind us, and then a rocket took off across the street. It rose from a backyard and emerged from behind a house. It seemed to ascend slowly, though I knew that was only an optical illusion, and it rode a plume of red and orange fire. We watched in silence until it bent in its arc and Misty asked: "Is it coming toward us?"

"I think it is."

In retrospect we probably should have stood up and moved, but she'd had the vodka and I'd had the beers and felt tired, and in any event it is very difficult to judge the exact trajectory of a projectile as it comes in your direction so for all I knew we could have moved right into the rocket's path. We sat still and Misty took another sip and the rocket, which was not very large, crashed into the hedge about ten feet to our right.

No one had taken care of the leaves the autumn before and it had been dry, and things immediately began to burn. Smoke rose from the shrubbery along with the smell of what I could only assume was some sort of rocket fuel.

"How high did it go?" We looked across the street. Emery was running toward us. "Tell me." He gasped as he arrived on my front lawn. "Your best estimate."

"A mile," I said.

"Really?"

"No," Misty said, "a hundred feet at most."

Emery frowned. "You had a better view," he said. "It's hard to tell from right underneath." He looked at the bushes. "If I had more money I'd install an altimeter so that when I recover them I could know for sure."

"Do they usually burn up?" I asked. The fire seemed to be growing.

"No. This is the first time. It's probably your fault, you have too much flammable brush in your yard."

I tried not to hate Emery but the beer and the fire and the fatigue made it hard. "There's a big bucket in the shed in the backyard," I said, "and the spigot is on the side of the house. Can you please put it out?"

Emery trudged away. Misty squinted at the house across the street. "I remember him being much smaller."

"He's grown."

"I guess that happens. What about Alice?"

"Her too. You haven't been home much, have you?"

Misty shook her head. "Hardly at all."

Emery returned with a bucket and dumped it on the bushes. There was a loud hiss and an eruption of foul-smelling steam. "Another bucket," I called. He scowled and walked away.

"Is Garrett around?" I asked.

"He went out after the service. He'll get in late, if he gets in at all."

"How are your parents?"

"Sleeping. Dad drank most of a bottle of scotch. Mom took some of her pills." She refilled her cup with an alarming amount of vodka and watched as Emery brought another bucket of water and doused the embers from the fire. Then he dropped to his knees and crawled under the bush, reaching out.

"I wouldn't do that, Emery," I called. He yelped and snatched his hand back from the still-smoldering fuselage. "No one's going to take it," I said. "You can begin recovery operations tomorrow after school."

He stood, fingers in his mouth, ingesting who-knew-what chemicals, and then nodded and turned to us. "That's the best I ever did," he said.

"It was impressive," Misty replied.

"Would you like to buy me an altimeter?"

"Not really."

"But your family's rich."

"They're rich, but I'm not," Misty said.

"What's the difference?"

"About a hundred and fifty thousand dollars in student loan debt."

"So what's a lousy altimeter?" I asked.

Misty burped. "I'll think about it."

"Your dad was going to get me an altimeter," Emery told me.

"I doubt that."

"He was. He said so."

"Yeah, well, he's been saying all sorts of things lately. His frontal lobes aren't working very well. Good night, Emery."

"Good night," he said. He turned and crossed the street, disappearing inside his own house.

"How drunk are you, Lukas?"

"I'm not drunk," I told her. "I only had two beers. Though the vapor from that fire is doing something to my head."

"Good," she said. "You drive."

"Where?"

"I'll tell you where." She stood, bottle in one hand and cup in the other. "You have time, right?"

I still heard the rom-com. Dad would be up for another hour or so. "I have a bit of time."

"Then let's go." She put the bottle in her backpack and stood.

I followed her to the car, though my path was considerably more linear. She got in on the passenger side and I got into the driver's seat as loud voices drifted across the street. "I think Emery's in trouble," I said.

"I like Emery," Misty said, obviously drunk. "He's sweet and he's smart and he's trying to do something great."

"Burn my house down?"

"Just drive to the lake," Misty said, sitting back and closing her eyes. "And take the turns slow. I don't want to throw up."

CHAPTER SIX

I had never been fond of Lake Prout. Part of it was that I didn't like to swim. That was all of it, actually. I found water terrifying when I was a kid. At night more than during the day, lakes more than the ocean. There's something about a lake, the way it is self-contained and still. A river and the ocean move on, but a lake isn't going anywhere. It sits with its secrets. Like every other kid in Faith, I'd visited Lake Prout for field trips and birthday parties, and every time I looked out at its gray water I felt a chill and the urge to stay away. It seemed to be waiting for me.

Misty directed us to a small lot and we parked and got out. There weren't any clouds and there was plenty of moonlight. This wasn't one of the more popular spots as there was not a good beach, just rocks and gravel along the water. Misty brought the backpack down to the shore. I had put the rest of the beer in the back seat but I didn't really feel like drinking. I joined her, looking out. She took a pull straight from the bottle and kicked her shoes off. "It's almost a full moon," she said, "but not quite."

"I guess not." What would it be called? There were all sorts of names. A harvest moon? A salad moon? A lovers' moon? I'd never paid attention to those sorts of things in school.

Misty undid her hair and let it fall around her face, giving her head a little twist so that I could see her profile unobstructed in the moonlight. She was even more beautiful than she had been in high school, her cheekbones higher, her eyes darker. She shrugged her flannel shirt off and tossed it down beside her shoes and then dipped one toe in the water. "Not too cold," she said. I shivered just looking at her. Misty took another drink and looked around. Then she handed me the bottle. "Hang on," she said, "I just need a minute. Get yourself all set." She walked away, disappearing behind a large slab of rock, the sort that dotted the lake shore and reminded you that it had once been a quarry. She unbuttoned the top of her jeans as she went, running a finger along the inside of the waistline. The skin along her lower back was very white.

I set the bottle down, balancing it between two rocks, and took my own shoes off. April evenings in Ulster County were not particularly warm and the idea of stepping into the water at night was singularly unappealing, a proposal I would have shot down every time, but it had been almost three years since I'd been in a relationship and longer than I cared to remember since I'd slept with someone. Misty was drunk, very clearly drunk, and it would be wholly inappropriate to touch her or for anything to happen in any way, but I was not going to be the only one staying dressed if she wanted to go swimming in the lake.

I folded my shirt, which seemed stupid, and set it down on a rock next to the vodka, and then pulled my pants off so that I was standing in just my socks and boxer shorts. They were not the shorts I would have preferred, as they had polka dots and a tear along the seam, but I had not planned for this eventuality.

"Lukas," Misty said, "what are you doing? Do you want to go swimming?" She was standing by the rock, buttoning her jeans. She was fully dressed.

"Yes," I lied, "I love swimming. I love swimming at night."

She shivered and wrapped her arms around herself. She had been wearing a tank top beneath her flannel and though I was too far away to see I imagined she had goosebumps. "I don't know," she said, "it's a little chilly."

"Oh," I said. "I thought . . . well, you said to get 'all set' . . ."

"I thought you had to pee. You were fidgeting all around. That was what I was doing . . ." She gestured toward the rock. "I thought we should pee before settling in."

Of course she did. I was still holding my pants and I did not see any way out other than forward. "Well," I said, "I want to swim." I dropped the pants in what I hoped was a carefree but also masculine gesture and turned to the lake. There was literally nothing I wanted to do less than go in.

I walked straight ahead and the water was horribly frigid. I had no idea what Misty had been talking about when she said it wasn't too cold; it was likely that the vodka had numbed her extremities. The rocks were slippery under my feet and I realized that I had not taken my socks off but at that point everything was part of the act and I had to commit. "Come on," I called to her, "it's great!" The water was up to my knees and I took two, three strides and then dove, immersing myself and pulling away from the shore with a breaststroke. I did not like swimming but I was not necessarily a bad swimmer and I came up about twenty yards from shore in water that was over my head and turned to look back.

Misty was standing beside the water, looking at me. She had one hand on her hip and the other touching the side of her face. I wondered what my endgame was. I treaded water and turned in a circle. The lake stretched out behind me, small waves lapping around my neck, and by the time I had completed a 360-degree turn and was looking back at the shore I knew.

Of course, I thought. Of course this was the spot. I'd been in the hospital with Dad when Jason disappeared but I remembered the description from an article I read much later. The flat rock where I tossed my pants—was that where his belongings had been found? His watch, shoes, whatever it was? If not there, then someplace very close by. There wasn't a ton of lakefront at this spot. It had been a year ago, which meant it could have been a night like this. He would have entered the water just like I did, struck out to or past this spot. And his body had never been found. Regardless of my father's obsessive speculation it was obviously still here, somewhere, submerged for the last year.

I swam for shore in a freestyle that I hoped conveyed a relaxed, hearty sense of having had my fill of nighttime swimming, but really I didn't give a damn. I wanted out of that icy water. My foot struck rock and I stood, one hand gripping the waistband of my boxers so they wouldn't slide down around my ankles, and I stumbled from the water and up onto the lakeshore, stubbing my toes. "Invigorating," I said.

"It looks it."

"Yes."

Misty sat on a rock, looking out at the water. The wind was picking up and I was unhappy to be wet and nearly naked. I had an old blanket in my trunk, a faded wool thing, and I retrieved it and wrapped it around myself and then made my way back to where Misty was sitting, taking my place beside her. I was shivering and it was a relief to peel my wet socks off. She looked down at my bare feet. "You weren't actually planning to go swimming, were you?"

"It was sort of a spontaneous moment."

She laughed, then abruptly stopped. "You're unique, Lukas."

"Thank you?"

"No, you are. I never found anyone else like you after we were together."

"I remember, when we broke up, you said that I bored you."

"Did I?"

"Yes. It's not the sort of thing one forgets."

"God, I was awful. Well, to be completely honest, you did, but I was seventeen and everything bored me. Everything in Faith, anyway. I wanted to go to the big city. Everything seemed better there, more interesting, more real."

"Was it?"

"You tell me, you were there much longer than I was. And you were really living it; I was in a dorm in New Haven for four years."

I considered. I wanted to go back to the city, get my career back on track, but was life better there? "No," I said. "I mean, there was more happening, of course. There's more happening anywhere than there is in Faith, and no place has more happening than New York City. But it's also sort of the same, you know? More of the same, the same shit but faster. People are people. Crowding a few million onto an island in the Hudson River doesn't make them any better."

Misty was silent for a moment. "I still love it, though," she finally said. "It's the only place I want to be." She reached down and took a handful of pebbles and began flicking them into the water, one after the other.

I was finally warming up. She had stopped talking and I didn't know what to say, so I asked her: "This is the spot, isn't it?"

"Yes. It is."

"I'm sorry," I said, because I was.

"Can I tell you something, Lukas?" she asked.

"Sure," I said, "tell me anything."

"You'll think it's crazy."

"I can do crazy."

"I'm a little drunk."

"I know. It's cool. I'll . . . I'll just listen." I was ready. Whatever feelings she was having toward her high school boyfriend, whatever confession she had about how memories of me had followed her to college and beyond, I was there for it. I pulled the blanket tighter and sat up straight.

"Jason isn't really in this fucking lake."

I had not been ready for that. "You mean because we remember him?" I asked, hoping to clarify. "He, like, lives in our hearts?"

"No," Misty said, "I mean exactly what I said: He isn't here. He's somewhere out there." She tossed the last of the pebbles into the water and gestured in the vague direction of New Birmingham and the world beyond.

"Ah," I said. "Interesting. Um. Hmm."

"You think it's crazy."

"No," I said, "no, not crazy, just . . ." I trailed off, staring into the lake. It was totally crazy. It was as crazy as it was when my father questioned Jason Grant's fate. No one had seen him in a year and the circumstances of his disappearance pointed squarely to suicide. No one knew why he had done it, but that was true of lots of things. Who understands what someone else is actually feeling? People will always be mysteries, and our inability to crack them doesn't mean that we can make up whatever stories we want. "How do you know?" I asked. "Have you told anyone? Like, anyone besides me?"

"Well," Misty said, "that's the crazy part."

I thought we had already passed the crazy part so I braced myself for whatever was coming next. She reached for her backpack, rummaged inside, and took something out, turning back to me with it held close to her chest. "Will you promise me something, Lukas?"

"Sure."

"Promise me you'll keep this a secret?"

"Okay."

"I mean it. I don't want to sound overly dramatic, but this could be a matter of life and death."

It seemed like it would be hard to sound more dramatic but I nodded. "I promise."

"I think I'm being followed."

I looked at her, then felt compelled to twist around and look behind us. "By who?"

"I don't know his name."

"The guy you chased at the service?"

She nodded. "That's right. I'm an idiot. I should have hung back and taken a picture instead of running at him."

"He looked like an accountant. You think he's following you?"

She hiccupped. "I've had a lot to drink and it's a long story. Here." She held out the object she had been cradling. It was a small sketchbook.

"You've been drawing?"

"This isn't mine. This was Jason's."

I took it from her, holding it gingerly like it was some sort of artifact, and flipped it open. It was an ordinary sketchbook, about a third filled, the rest blank. The drawings were mostly in pencil, a few in charcoal. They were all drawings of the same woman. "Who is she?"

"I don't know. I've never seen her before. I've looked at pictures from his college class, his med school class, staff photos from the medical center. Nothing. I took pictures of some of these and ran them through Google Images. It wasn't helpful."

I wasn't surprised. Honestly, the drawings were pretty terrible. I doubted there was much resemblance to the model.

"I know they're no good," Misty said.

"There's a certain . . . um . . . something," I said. Actually, there was. The drawings were technically poor, the perspective and proportions off, no sense of texture to the woman's hair. There was feeling to them, though.

"She's the person I was looking for at the memorial," Misty said. "If she was someone Jason knew, someone important to him, I thought she might come and that she might have some answers."

"What does this have to do with the Accountant?" I asked. "And what does any of it have to do with Jason maybe not being . . . here?"

Misty hiccupped again. "I should go back to the beginning." She picked up her flannel shirt and wriggled back into it. "When Jason disappeared, I was still at Yale. I was in my last semester. I was basically done, I had all my credits, and when I stopped going to classes they pretty much just waved me through. Everyone was very sympathetic."

"Sure."

"They all assumed the same thing: that Jason had killed himself. The same as everyone around here. The same as you, probably. You just assumed that Jason had walked into this lake."

"I wasn't paying a lot of attention at the time, Misty. Dad was in the hospital. But yeah, to be honest, that is what I assumed. I mean, the facts all pretty much pointed to it."

"But you didn't have all the facts."

"What was missing?"

"That Jason called me, right before he disappeared."

"What did he say?"

"I was surprised he called. He never called; he texted, mostly. We hadn't been in close touch. I was busy, he was busy. You know how it is. But he called me; it was, like, ten o'clock at night and he said that he wanted to tell me something." Misty paused. She was no longer drinking the vodka but the nearby bottle was almost empty. "He said he got us tickets to Ibsen."

"You mean that revival at Circle in the Square?"

"Yes. My birthday was coming up and he said that he got us two tickets and he was going to come to town and would take me to dinner and the show. It was unlike him, Lukas. Very unlike him. Jason didn't like theater. He usually just texted on my birthday, or the week after."

"It was . . . nice of him." The tickets had obviously never been used.

Misty nodded, gazing out at the dark lake. "That wasn't all, though. I don't even think it was really why he was calling. I felt like maybe he'd had a few drinks; he told me about the Ibsen and said he was looking forward to it and then he kind of rambled for a bit about . . . well, sort of about nothing. About when we were younger, a couple family trips we went on, stories we both knew. Honestly, I had things to do. I told him I had to go. If I had known . . ." Her voice caught in her throat. I almost reached out to squeeze her hand but then she shook her head as if to clear it and went on.

"That was when he said it. At the end of the conversation, right before we got off the phone. He got quiet for a minute and then he said: 'You know, Misty, you're the only one who left.' And I asked what he meant and he said: 'Faith. You left. I'm back here, Garrett's back here. You got out. It makes me proud of you.' Which was, by the way, the first and only time he ever said he was proud of me."

"I'm not sure, Misty," I said, "I mean, what about all that makes you think he didn't . . . you know." I gestured awkwardly to the lake in front of us.

"It was what he said next. I felt awkward about the whole 'proud of me' thing and I told him that leaving home wasn't so tough, that he could do it, they need child psychiatrists in New York City, they need child psychiatrists everywhere. I was just kind of bullshitting but he took it seriously. He was quiet for a really long moment before he said: 'Nah. I've decided. I'm staying. I'm going to make this work.' And then he said: 'Maybe leaving home isn't so hard, Misty. Maybe going back is the hard part.'" She turned to me. "You see, don't you? He had so much conviction when he said he was going to make things work. And we had plans, plans to get together, and then . . . you see why I might not believe it, when they never found him. You see why I might think he wasn't here?"

"I see. I get it."

"But also, I know things change. I mean, there's some statistic that most people who kill themselves make the decision to do it, like, less than an hour before. I get that. He might have been determined when he spoke to me that night and then, I don't know, things could have fallen apart. And his car, his stuff. I mean, why would he fake something like that? He wouldn't. No matter what kind of trouble he was in, he wouldn't put our parents through that. He wouldn't put me through it."

"Right. So . . ."

"So, I started thinking maybe something bad happened to him. Maybe he knew something was going to happen and he was calling but he couldn't tell me exactly what was going on."

"Like what?"

"How should I know? I've been fucking sheltered, Lukas. I grew up here and had just spent four years at Yale. How should I know what kinds of things people get caught up in? I'll tell you what I did, though. I hired a private investigator."

"Like, a private eye?"

"Yup. A guy from Brooklyn."

"Weren't the police investigating?"

"I didn't think so. Not really. Everyone assumed he was here, somewhere under the water. I know my parents did. They just sort of collapsed in on themselves. Mom didn't get out of bed for weeks. Dad, Garrett—well, Garrett's always been a useless mess. No one was pressing on. No one was trying to figure it out. So, I found this guy. I researched him. Ex-Marine, former NYPD. Total professional. It was crazy, I know. I mean, when I met with him he told me straight up that people hire him all the time to investigate suicides because they can't accept that's what happened to someone they loved, and basically every single time it turns out to be suicide. I didn't care. I paid him three thousand dollars of my own money to find out what happened to Jason."

"And?"

"And he gave the money back a week later."

"He gave it back? Why?"

"He wouldn't say. He met me in Prospect Park and gave it to me in cash, like we were in a movie. He said he couldn't continue with the case and he wouldn't say why, but he told me that I seemed like a nice girl and that I should stop looking for my brother. I shouldn't hire anyone else and I shouldn't take large amounts out of my bank account. He said I should get on with my life and then he walked away before I could get any answers."

"That's bizarre."

"He almost seemed scared, Lukas. He seemed like someone who was scared and was trying to act like he wasn't."

"How long after the disappearance was this?"

"By the time I decided to do something and found that guy, it was about five months."

"So, seven months ago?"

"That's right."

"What have you been doing since then?"

"I didn't know what to do at first. I was sort of shocked. I tried to get in touch with the private investigator; something had obviously happened to scare him off and I wanted to know what. But he wouldn't return any of my calls. I waited outside his office and he went out the back way. He wasn't going to talk to me."

"Did you tell your parents?"

"No. I didn't tell anyone. I felt like I would sound crazy. And my parents . . . they wouldn't talk about Jason. That house became like some sort of mausoleum. Everything was just frozen, miserable. Plus, half the time Garrett was there. I stopped coming home. On one of my last trips before this one, though, I looked in Jason's old room. Searched it. I was home alone for an hour."

"Didn't he live in New Birmingham?"

"Yeah, they got rid of his condo. Had everything boxed up and taken away. His old bedroom at home was still there, though. They'd turned it into a guest room after he went to college, but it still had some of his old stuff. Including this." She held up the sketchbook.

"Is it from when he was in high school?"

"No, it's more recent. He dated a few of the sketches. It was tucked between books on a shelf. It's the one clue I have."

"The woman in the drawings."

"The woman. I have to find her."

"She's probably some random model from an art class, Misty."

"Maybe. I don't think so, though. I've come up for a few weekends without telling my parents. I checked all the community art classes in New Birmingham: the YMCA, the civic center, the art school. No one recognizes her or remembers Jason, and his life was too busy to go to classes in another town. I don't think she was a stranger, anyway. Not the way he drew her."

I didn't think so, either. There was something about those drawings, technically poor as they were. "So, she didn't come to the memorial?"

"No."

"And instead you saw that guy. The Accountant."

"I've seen him before. Back in the city. A few times. I first noticed maybe a month ago; he was sitting at a table near me at a café and I thought he looked familiar. Maybe I stared at him a little too long and he got up and left. But then, about a week later, there he was again, on the subway. And two days ago, when I went to pick up a rental car to drive up here, I swear he was across the street. He's following me." She looked at me. "You think the whole thing's crazy, don't you, Lukas? You think I'm imagining it. You think that guy looks like a thousand other plain white guys. You think Jason is out there, in the lake."

I spread my hands on my knees, still wrapped in the blanket. "You're not the only one who has doubts, Misty."

"No?"

I sighed. This was a conversation I was not eager to have. "Can you hold on just a minute?" I got up, collected my clothes, and swiftly dressed before sitting back down. "Can I have a nip of that?"

Misty handed me the vodka and I took a pull. Then I told her. I told her all about my father's preoccupation. His memory of a research proposal that was flawed in some way, a lost conversation he'd had with Jason just days before his brain injury. Dad's conviction, upon waking from his coma and learning that Jason was gone, that he had not died by suicide.

Misty listened, eyes locked on me. When I was done she reached out and took my hand. "Lukas," she said, "you are going to help me."

"I am?"

"You are. We're going to find out what really happened. We're going to find out where Jason is."

"That's an interesting idea . . ."

"And I'm going to stay around for a while."

"Stay around? Here?"

"Here, in Faith. At my parent's house."

"What about your auditions?"

"Screw the auditions. There will be more auditions. I'll have to get a job, a day job, something to use as cover. But what I'm really going to do is figure this out." She looked out over the water, still holding my hand. "Maybe this is fate. You coming back into my life like this, now. Someone I know I can trust, who knows me and my family."

"I'm not exactly super available, Misty. I told you, I'm only here because I have to take care of my dad. He needs me, and once he gets a little bit more stable I'm going back to Manhattan—"

"You don't understand, Lukas. Your father is the best part of this deal."

Dad did not seem like the best part of any deal. "You want my father to help?"

"You said it yourself. He's still smart. He's so smart, he always has been. And now he has this thing, what did you call it? No filter. Like, he saw every single one of the chairs, right? What else could he see? I bet he'd be a great detective. And, to top it all off, the two of you are free, which I very much need since the guy in Brooklyn told me not to try to pull funds out of my account."

Imagining my father and myself as cut-rate private investigators inspired a feeling equal parts hilarity and dread. "No offense, Misty, but it sounds like maybe a good deal for you . . ." I trailed off. She twisted around to face me, her back to the lake.

"You don't want to spend time with me, Lukas?"

"It's not that."

She studied me. "You are unique. And I was wrong about you being boring." She leaned forward, bracing herself on one arm, and her lips grazed my cheek. "Thank you listening to me," she said. "And thank you for keeping my secret. Obviously, I didn't mean from your dad. Talk it over with him and call me tomorrow." She climbed to unsteady feet. "It's late, and I don't want to keep you out too long. I know he needs you."

I got up and took her arm, helping her over the rocky shoreline to the car. I would drop her off at the top of the hill and would get home on time. I would tie myself to Dad, lying beside him on the living room floor. I would think about it all night: the phone call from Jason, the woman in the sketchbook, the man who might or might not be following Misty. I would wonder whether any of it was connected to Dad's preoccupation with Jason Grant's disappearance and his frayed memory of a conversation about a research proposal.

I would think about Dad lying on the pavement at Forty-Third and Vine with lilacs scattered beside him and I would wonder, for maybe the hundred thousandth time, who those flowers had been for.

I would think about my mother, far away in Montreal, and weigh my resentment for the burden she'd left me against my understanding of why she had to leave.

I would wonder what to do, whether to venture into what would likely prove to be a morass composed of my father's perseverative obsession and my ex-girlfriend's unresolved grief, and then as I finally closed my eyes I would think about Misty's lips brushing against my cheek and I would know that it had never been a question at all.

CHAPTER SEVEN

Having decided to solve a mystery, we immediately realized that we had no idea what we were doing. Dad set up my old bedroom up as a kind of headquarters. "You're not really using it," he pointed out. He peeled my old photos off the walls, neglecting one of Al Pacino in *Dog Day Afternoon*, and then he hung a giant dry-erase board, driving a screw right through Al's forehead.

Misty came at night. Worried that she was being followed, she walked down the hill from her house to ours through the woods behind, crossing our backyard and rapping on the kitchen door. On our third night meeting we all sat on my old bed, staring at the blank dry-erase board, Chinese food containers and a mostly empty box of red wine at our feet.

"We need a clue," I said.

I was familiar with mystery stories. I had played Dr. Watson in a dinner theater production of *The Hound of the Baskervilles*. That story had clues: footprints, cigar ash on the ground, a missing boot. Something to get it started.

"We have clues," Dad said, "we just don't know quite what to do with them." He stood and took a marker off my desk. "Let's begin with the premise that Jason was in some sort of trouble and he knew it was going to come out. It's why he called Misty, bought those tickets, mulled leaving town."

Misty nodded. "And then something happened."

"Whatever it was caught up with him and he had to disappear and didn't want anyone to come looking. Either that, or someone took him and didn't want people to search anywhere besides the lake."

"I think the latter," Misty said. "I just don't believe he would fake his own death. Whatever his problems were, having them come out couldn't be worse than making us believe he'd killed himself."

"Maybe," Dad said, tapping his chin with the marker. Then he stepped forward and wrote the first words on the blank board: *the secret.*

"Informative," I said. "Also, I hate to say it but we're skipping another alternative to suicide."

"Which is?" Dad asked.

I glanced at Misty. "Maybe it was someone else," I said, "but maybe they, you know . . . I hate to say it, but maybe they killed him and wanted people to think it was suicide."

Misty shifted her weight on my bed. "Possible," Dad said, "but put yourself in the killer's place in that situation. There's a certain amount of risk in staging that scene. It draws attention, gets everyone focused on finding him. Why not just bury him in a shallow grave and walk away? Let the fact of his disappearance slowly emerge over a week or so and be long gone, with no clues left behind? Why the theatrics?"

"I don't know."

"No," Dad said, "I agree with Misty. It was likely staged to draw attention to Lake Prout, and he's out there somewhere else."

"Well," I countered, "if someone abducted him, then I have the same objection you do. Why stage the suicide? Why not just take him somewhere far away? Same issue as the shallow grave, if you ask me."

"What if they weren't taking him far away?" Dad asked. "What if they were local, and they wanted everyone to focus on the lake? Maybe the risk of staging the suicide scene was outweighed by the risk of a wide search of Faith and New Birmingham."

"And they've been holding him for a year?"

"Maybe they brainwashed him," Misty said. "Maybe someone took him and interrogated him, got some sort of information, and then brainwashed him so that he doesn't even know who he is and doesn't know to come home."

"Nonsense," Dad said, with what I regarded as less empathy than one should bring to bear on someone clearly in denial. "They'd be more likely to wait until they got what they wanted from him and the search was called off, and then kill him and bury him somewhere. Or maybe incinerate the remains."

"Dad, please." I looked at Misty, who had gone pale.

"Regardless," Dad continued, "if we can figure it out, there will be some level of closure. I can finally stop thinking about that goddamn research proposal." He turned to the board and wrote *proposal* next to *secret*. He stepped back to study his handiwork. "There are a few more things," he said. "There was Jason's covert visit home a few nights before the disappearance, the one Emery saw. He walked up the hill and met someone, likely Garrett, in the woods, and one of them was smoking." He turned to Misty. "Who in your family smokes?"

"Garrett, sometimes. Uncle Frank smokes cigars constantly, but he rarely comes to visit. We always get together at his house on Lake George. Neither of my parents."

Dad nodded and wrote *nighttime visit* on the board. "And finally, we have these stray pieces. The girl in the sketchbook, who may well be some random model at an art class you haven't stumbled across, and the man you believe to be following you, although I have to note that your behavior over the last few nights smacks of paranoia and I view your report with skepticism."

"She thinks she's seen the man before, Dad. I saw him at the memorial. Why did he run from her if he wasn't following her?"

"She charged at him, for one thing. There are all sorts of reasons for him to retreat. Perhaps he had been Jason's secret lover? Was your brother drawn to other men, Misty?"

"Not that I know of."

"My point is that all delusions sound reasonable if you accept the premises of the deluded, Lukas. Misty is sneaking into our house through the back door after dark and insisting we keep all the shades down. I'm a researcher, not a clinician, but I saw this sort of behavior during my rotations at Bellevue."

"Just put the clues on the board, Dad." I reached over and awkwardly patted Misty on the shoulder. I imagined that she was starting to regret her choice to use the Moore Private Detective Agency despite our nonexistent rates. Dad wrote *sketchbook?* and *malicious accountant man?!??* next to the clues he had generated. Then he capped the marker and turned to the two of us, sitting on the bed.

"Do you know what I think?" he asked. "I think it's all about Garrett."

Misty straightened. "Garrett? What about him?"

"His situation isn't very good. I had coffee with your parents recently; they told me a bit about it. As a psychiatrist, people often look to me for counsel."

"I thought you weren't a clinician," I said.

"Nonetheless. Garrett is coping with serious addictive behavior, including abuse of prescription drugs. Pain meds, Adderall, benzos. And that's just what they know about. Jason was a psychiatrist, he had access. The last meeting, in the woods, was almost certainly between the two of them."

"You think he was giving Garrett drugs?" Misty asked.

"I think it's possible he was drawn into the drug trade and wound up over his head." He turned back to the board and in big letters wrote *Garrett Grant* over all the other clues.

"You're missing something, Dr. Moore," Misty said.

"What's that?"

"The investigator I hired in Brooklyn. The one who returned my money. Something scared him and he tried to warn me off too. I don't see my twin brother striking that kind of fear in a former Marine."

"Mmmm." Dad steepled his fingers. "Not him, maybe, but whoever he's involved with. That's the thread we have to follow. That, and the research proposal."

"Oh my God," I said, "that damn proposal."

"You're right about one thing, Lukas," Dad said. "We do need more clues."

"And where are you planning to find them?"

"I told you the other day, when we went in for my appointment: I want to go to the morgue."

CHAPTER EIGHT

"It's dark," I said. "They're doing construction all over the medical center, you'd think they could put new lighting in down here. Right or left?"

"Left," Dad said. "Didn't you ever visit me at work?"

"Once, in the third grade. There was a snow day and Mom had a deposition so she made you bring me."

"Ah, I don't remember that. Did you enjoy it?"

"You set me up with a coloring book and didn't notice when I wandered off to the morgue."

"That's one reason I wanted to keep my lab in the basement, even when they built the new facilities across the street. Mancini, the pathologist, was the only doctor in this place I could stand. We used to have lunch sometimes."

I remembered Dr. Mancini. Rail thin and barely taller than I was, even at age nine. He sat down with me at an empty table that I now realize was meant for autopsies and quizzed me on the math and science knowledge he felt I should have accumulated by the winter of my third grade year and, when he was satisfied and it became obvious that Dad was not going to notice my absence, he gave me two peppermint Life Savers and walked me back down the hall to the neuroscience lab. I remembered that there had been strange, lumpy objects under sheets along the walls, but I had been too young to draw any inferences.

The pathologist was, when we found him, exactly as I remembered. "Moore!" he said, looking up from a corpse. "You're not a vegetable."

"Not yet," Dad said, crossing the room and hugging the other doctor without regard for the body or the fluids on Dr. Mancini's apron. "I'm pleased you haven't up and quit in the last year. You remember my son, Lukas?"

The pathologist looked over to where I stood by the door. "Of course," he said. "You were a bright child. What are you up to now?"

"He's an actor," Dad said.

"I'm sorry to hear that," Mancini said. "Is that why he's here? You want me to talk sense into the boy?"

"I'm here because he can't drive," I said, "or do much of anything else." It was an unkind thing to say but I didn't appreciate the critique of my craft, and the smell of formaldehyde and sight of a hairy arm dangling from the table were making me woozy.

"Not surprising," Mancini said. "People don't recover particularly well from traumatic brain injury at your father's age. Lunch?"

"Delightful," Dad said. "Here?"

"Let's go up to the cafeteria," I said. The two doctors looked at me doubtfully but didn't seem to care. Dr. Mancini tossed a plastic sheet over the table and peeled off his apron. While he locked up I peered down the dimly lit hall. "Is that your lab?" I asked, pointing to a closed door at the far end. Dad nodded. "Do you want to go in and look?"

Dad paused for a moment. "No," he said, "I don't."

Lunch was terrible, but at least there were no cadavers present. Dad laid our situation out; we hadn't discussed confidentiality but I had assumed we were keeping the story to ourselves. It probably didn't matter, I thought, as I doubted Dr. Mancini had many other friends to tell and I knew that Dad didn't.

"Interesting, I suppose," Mancini finally said. "To a psychiatrist, at least. There's probably some level of psychopathology involved. I still think Dr. Grant is at the bottom of that lake."

"Likely," Dad said, "or dumped somewhere else. But, you know, rule out all alternative hypotheses and such. I'd like to clear things up."

Mancini looked at me. "What sort of actor are you?" he asked.

"A stage actor."

"A good one?"

"I try."

"He was cast as Stanley Kowalski in *A Streetcar Named Desire*," Dad said. "You know, the Brando role. The lead."

"I read something about that in the *Times*," Dr. Mancini said. "It's a big deal right now. Myrton something-or-other."

I wanted to put a plastic spork through my own eye socket, though I was surprised and touched that Dad had sounded something adjacent to bragging about me.

"So," Dad said, "the reason we're here is that I want to ask you about your boyfriend. You're still seeing him?"

"Derek? Yes."

"I like him."

"As do I."

"It shocked me that you found someone so charming, actually."

Mancini nodded and ate a scoop of potato salad. "I was as surprised as anyone."

"And he's still in medical billing?"

"Promoted to assistant director."

"Good for him. I wonder if he could get us some information?"

"Such as?"

"Jason Grant's HR record, and the location of his professional effects. His parents had his condo cleaned out, but the medical center must have done something with the contents of his office. His papers and such. In storage, perhaps?"

"I have no idea."

"Could Derek look into it?"

"I imagine he could. It will cost you, though."

"How much?"

"Not cash, you fool. A dinner. Have Derek and me over."

"Good lord," Dad said, "I'd rather just write a check." He turned to me. "What do you think, Lukas? Could we host a dinner party?"

"A small one," I said. "With a bit of notice."

"All right," Dad said, turning back to Mancini. "Deal. Now I'm tiring, I need to rest. Being back here is a bit much."

Mancini nodded and licked mustard off his thumb. It occurred to me that he hadn't washed his hands before leaving the morgue. "Good to see you, Moore," he said. "I assumed you were comatose. Come back around sometime."

"I will. I expect to be back at work shortly."

"I haven't examined a live patient in twenty years, but that seems doubtful."

"I tend to defy expectations."

"That's probably true. From what I heard about the accident you should have been dead. Regardless, good luck with this Grant thing. It sounds like a colossal waste of time but I suppose you don't have anything better to do. I assume your wife left if your son is taking care of you?"

"That's right."

Dr. Mancini nodded and I had the distinct impression it was in approval of Mom's decision. "Well," he said, "do come back around. There's no one decent to have a conversation with in this place, and my patients rarely talk back. I'll speak with Derek tonight; give me a call in a day or two." With that he walked away, exiting the cafeteria and leaving his tray of garbage for us to take care of.

"God, I miss that man," Dad said. "Lukas, I need a nap." He slipped his sunglasses on, apparently troubled by the overhead fluorescents, and waited for me to clear the table and drive him home.

CHAPTER NINE

Misty got a job, though not one I would have expected. I assumed she'd do some sort of office work or maybe wait tables at one of the many high-end restaurants popping up around New Birmingham. Instead, she went to work at our old elementary school.

Alice Quinlan, Emery's little sister, was supposed to have an aide, but that person had quit a few months before and the district hadn't been able to fill the position. "Are you qualified?" I asked Misty. "Do you know anything about education, or disabilities, or kids in general?"

"I'm terrible with kids," she confessed. "I once got cut as Mary Poppins because the director decided I couldn't be maternal enough. I read the Wikipedia entry on Down syndrome and also googled some stuff. Honestly, the people at the school didn't seem to care. The woman in HR said they just needed a warm body. And Mrs. Quinlan seemed so excited and appreciative. Ever since her husband left it's been just her and those kids and they're both handfuls, though in different ways. I feel like I'm doing something good. I feel like I'm making a difference."

"Better you than me."

"You can't see yourself working in a school?"

"Jesus, no. Did you see Mr. Jollett at the memorial? He looks like he's aged about a hundred years."

"High school drama teacher is a tough job."

"I guess so. I mean, I want to be onstage, or directing, in the city or in LA."

"You always were going to be a big star, Lukas. You still will be."

I thought I had a chance at it, if I could ever get out of Faith and back to the city. Jules Pierre was still texting me audition notices and I was still putting him off and promising to return with as vague a timeline as possible. My extrication seemed to have become caught up in the Jason Grant mystery; I had the sense that, if Dad could find resolution to his nagging questions and in the process flex the remaining 93 percent of his frontal lobes, then more might be possible, including a life without me tied to his wrist at night.

It was therefore with a sense of cautious optimism that I found myself sitting in our car on a rainy night, four days after our meeting with Dr. Mancini, outside an off-site storage facility on the outskirts of New Birmingham. Derek had come through with the location of Jason's office effects. "What do we tell the guard?" I asked.

"Leave it to me," Dad said. Before I could reply he stepped out of the car and started toward the building. Misty hopped out of the back seat and followed him.

"Shit," I said, putting the car into reverse and backing into a spot by the curb. By the time I reached the lobby Dad was in a heated discussion with a bored, irritated guard behind a Formica desk.

"Grant," Dad said, "Jason Grant, MD. I'm a colleague of his. I'm told his papers are here."

The guard tapped the screen in front of him and shook his head. "Sorry," he said, "you're not on the list of authorized—"

"Listen," I interrupted, "we understand the protocol but we don't have time. Myself, along with Dr. Hill and Dr. Paroo, have a very complex case and we need to access Dr. Grant's files. Are you familiar with River City Syndrome?"

The man shook his head.

"Neither are we, but we have a case and we believe it to be highly contagious. Highly contagious, and very lethal. We need the information in Dr. Grant's files if the child is going to have a chance."

"A child?" The man pushed his rolling chair back a bit, allowing more air between him and us.

"Six years old. And he doesn't have much time."

The guard shifted back and forth and then tapped the screen again, taking a Post-it note and jotting a series of numbers down. "Unit eighty-seven Q. Here's the combination. It's on the third floor. Elevator's over there."

I took the note. "Thank you."

"That was well done, Lukas," Dad said in the elevator.

"Dr. Paroo?" Misty asked.

"Marian Paroo. From *The Music Man*."

"I caught the reference, Dr. Hill."

"It was what came to mind. We did it together, freshman year."

"I remember."

We stepped out into a hallway on the third floor, lights coming on in response to our movement. Unit 87Q was at the other end of the building. I tapped in the combination and opened the door. "Here we are."

The room was full of boxes. Some of them were neatly labeled—"Archives of General Psychiatry," "dopamine references"—but most were blank. "Where do we begin?" I asked.

"We'll divide it up," Misty said. "I'll start in that far corner; Lukas, you work right here, and Dr. Moore, you take the other corner. We'll sort of converge in the middle."

We set to work opening boxes and sifting through the contents. Dad reminded us, three times, to keep an eye out for anything referring to Garrett or for a research proposal dated a bit more than one year before. I wasn't sure that I would recognize a research proposal if I saw one, but I didn't want to bring that up.

We worked in relative silence for almost an hour, Dad occasionally grunting. I found nothing of interest and sustained two paper cuts. At one point I stood to stretch and glanced over at Misty. She was crouching over a box, holding a framed picture in her hand. I walked over. It was a photo of her and Jason, apparently taken at Yale. She was dressed in a toga, he in a suit with an arm around her. They were both beaming into the camera.

"*Antigone*," she said. "Sophomore year."

"I'm sure you were great."

"I was very mediocre, but he came to see it twice."

I nodded, unsure of what to say.

"I can't imagine he would get involved with drugs," she said. "I can't imagine he would give Garrett pills. He was a good doctor. He was a good person."

"You took geometry?" Dad asked from where he was sorting through a file box in the other corner.

"Tenth grade," Misty said.

"Do you know the term TBI?"

"Traumatic brain injury?" I asked.

"In geometry it's 'true but irrelevant.' My teacher used to write it in red next to unnecessary steps in a theorem. 'TBI.' Applies in life as well. Maybe Jason was an ethical doctor and maybe he wasn't. Maybe he was a good person, whatever that means. It's irrelevant. All that matters is what he was doing and who he got involved with." He paused and held up a paper. "Ho ho, what's this? The Mullens Center?"

"What's the Mullens Center?" I asked.

"Total nonsense is what it is. Lucrative nonsense. It's a carve out within psychiatry. The Mullens Center is separate from the old child psych unit; cash only, something like fifteen grand for a two-week program."

I whistled. "People have that kind of money?"

"Some do, and more of them are moving to New Birmingham. They launched the program with much fanfare two years ago, and it looks like Grant was stepping into the director position. I don't remember any announcement, but I wouldn't be surprised if they kept it quiet. Giving the chairman of the board's son that sort of prestigious post at such a young age . . ." He glanced at Misty. "Did you know anything about this?"

"I've never even heard of the Mullens Center."

"Hmm."

A knock at the door made all three of us jump. The guard was standing in the hall, as far back as he could, probably worried that River City Syndrome could be airborne. "Sorry," he said, "but I found something else. Another unit for Jason Grant."

"Another unit?" Dad asked. "Are you sure it's the same Jason Grant?"

The man nodded. "I didn't notice at first because it's a different account. This one, the one you're in, was paid for by New Birmingham Medical Center. The other one was opened by Dr. Grant personally, eighteen months ago." He looked from Dad to me. "Do you think it might be important?"

"It might be," I nodded. "Thank you. I think we're going to be able to save that child."

I took the new Post-it from the guard's outstretched hand, allowing him to beat a hasty retreat. The number for the second unit was also on the third floor. "Go take a look, Lukas," Dad said. "It's probably just furniture he couldn't fit into his condo or something like that. I'll keep looking here."

Misty and I followed the unit numbers until we arrived at Jason's second storage locker. I entered the code and opened the door. The first thing to strike me was the smell. I reached in and flipped on the light.

The room was full of art. It smelled of paint and clay and charcoal and eraser rubber. There were a few boxes, but one wall of the unit was covered with metal shelving and the shelves were covered in ceramics. Canvases and framed photos leaned against the far wall. Misty and I stood in the doorway. "It looks like that sketchbook was just the tip of the iceberg," I said.

We went inside.

"Did you have any idea he was doing all this?" I asked.

Misty shook her head. "I don't know where he found the time. I don't know where he had the space. I didn't . . . no. I had no idea."

I crossed the room and started flipping through the prints leaning against the wall while she picked up the ceramics one at a time, examining lopsided coffee mugs and misshapen bowls. The largest canvas, and the only one framed, was covered with one word, written in green paint against the backdrop of a snowy birch forest. The letters looped in and out of the trees, wrapping around them: *INTEGRITY.* I studied it for a moment and then shifted it to one side to examine what lay behind.

"Misty. Look." I held up a photo. The drawings from the original sketchbook weren't good but there was no doubt: it was the same woman. She was nude, stretched out on a couch, propped on some cushions with an open book covering the lower half of her face. Even with her mouth and nose obscured there was no doubt as to her identity "Do you know where that is?"

"His condo. That was his sofa."

"So, probably not an art school model."

"Apparently not." She took it from me.

"I have it!"

Misty and I spun around. Dad stood in the doorway, a binder held triumphantly in his hand. "This is it! The proposal." He looked around the room. "What is all this shit?"

"Um, it appears to be Jason's work," I said.

"These were his . . . hobbies?"

"I guess so."

Dad walked in, peering at the ceramics before turning to the oil paintings on the floor. "He couldn't find one he was good at?"

"Look," Misty said. "The woman from the sketchbook, taken in his condo."

Dad studied the photo. "Hypothesis revised," he acknowledged. "He obviously knew her personally. Possibly TBI, however."

"But you think the proposal is relevant?" I asked.

He held the binder in both hands. "Something in it is," he said, "and when I read it I'm hoping I'll know what. Shall we?"

"I'd like to look around here a while longer," Misty said.

"Why?" Dad asked. "We have what we came for."

"You have what you came for," I said. "Let's take some time with this second room."

Dad looked around once more, shrugged, and then retreated to the hallway to sit and read the proposal. I stepped to one side and let Misty wander, sorting through coffee mugs and oil paintings, charcoal sketches and black-and-white photos, holding each piece in her hands for a moment before setting it back where she found it, as though through the array of flawed but carefully preserved pieces she could find the brother who had created them.

CHAPTER TEN

Dad did know it when he saw it, but it got us nowhere. "What the hell is 'Lotus'?" he demanded. "What in the actual hell is it?"

I had no idea. It had been a week since our visit to the storage facility. Dad read and reread the proposal for funding. Jason Grant had been looking for a lot of cash, more than two million dollars. Most of the sixty-three-page funding proposal was unintelligible to me, to say nothing of deadly boring. It had been a draft and various suggestions and corrections were scribbled into the margins, including several in Dad's handwriting. Then, on page forty-seven, in the middle of an interminable section on funding sources, in between a paragraph on the National Institute for Mental Health and another on the State University of New York, someone had written "Lotus!" with three stars next to it.

"That bothered you?" I asked.

"Lukas, I've written well over two hundred research grant applications. I know every conceivable source of funding for psychiatric and neuroscientific proposals. I have never heard of anything called 'Lotus.'"

"So, did you ask him?"

"I did. I think I did. I'm not sure. It was too close to the accident."

A search for "Lotus" pointed to the British car company, and there was lots about the flower. There were numerous sites relating to

Buddhism and a few Chinese restaurants, including one a few miles away. Nothing that would appear on an application for mental health funding. Dad stewed.

Misty started getting up early and walking Emery and Alice to school, spending her day there as Alice's aide. I stood in the window on the third morning of her employment, sipping coffee and following the action. Emery marched down the hill, back straight, head held high, his sister trailing behind. Alice was struggling with her backpack and their mother was standing by the front door in her bathrobe shouting at Emery, telling him to wait, telling him to help, and he turned and looked back, took a few steps toward his sister, then spun and walked away again, heard his mother, pivoted, on and on. He looked like he was on some invisible elastic string, stretching away and rebounding back and falling away again.

Misty came down the hill, moving quickly. She trotted up to Alice and helped get her backpack closed and situated. Then she walked over to Emery, said a few words to him, ruffled his hair with her hand, and they all turned and walked toward school with Emery slightly in the lead.

Mrs. Quinlan stood in front of her house. In addition to her bathrobe she was wearing bright red sweatpants and slippers with the stuffing coming out the side of the left one. She was one of those neighbors who was always around but whom I never really noticed. She usually seemed rushed and harried, slightly overwhelmed by her kids. Since Dad's accident I'd sometimes see her peering across the street, as though trying to gauge how disabled he had become. She never came over or said anything, though. She was no more help than anyone else.

"I'll be back," I told Dad.

He grunted his assent from the spot where he was doing his core exercises, crunches and planks. I took my coffee, poured some more into a travel mug, and hurried outside. Mrs. Quinlan was still in her doorway, watching the children go. She looked very lonely. I waved, then jogged down the street to catch up.

"So, you'll just hang out with Alice all day?" I asked Misty, handing her the coffee. Alice was walking a bit ahead of us with her brother, who seemed to be doing his best to ignore her.

"I think so," Misty said. "This is my first real day. I've just been filling out forms and showing them my CPR certification and stuff like that."

"You're CPR certified?"

"I auditioned for an off-off-Broadway production of *A Midsummer Night's Dream* that was set in a contemporary ER. All the fairies were nurses and Puck was the head of the billing department, or something like that. It was supposed to be a commentary on managed care and I was going through a method acting thing."

"Interesting."

"I didn't get the part." She sipped the coffee. "This is good."

"I made it myself."

"My family has this expensive shit from Italy. It tastes awful."

"So, you're going to keep on living with your parents?"

"Well, I don't make enough as an aide to get my own place."

I decided not to point out that her parents owned a fair chunk of the real estate in Faith and New Birmingham and could likely spot her a condo. She'd said that she paid for Yale on her own. She was probably stuffing cash in a jar on her parents' kitchen counter to reimburse them for the Italian coffee she didn't like.

"I don't think I just hang out with Alice," Misty said. "I'm going to help teach her. Her mom gave me a copy of her special education plan, which has a ton of goals and benchmarks, and she says most of them aren't being addressed or anything. The teacher just doesn't have time. So I'm, like, working on all that with her."

"That's cool," I said. "That's great."

"Alice, your shoe is untied!" Misty called.

"She doesn't know how to tie her shoes," Emery called back. "I keep telling Mom to get her the ones with Velcro straps but she won't."

Alice stopped until we caught up and Misty knelt to tie her shoe. Emery kept walking.

"Is it weird being back at the school?" I asked.

"It's so run down, Lukas," Misty said. "Everything's beat-up."

"It was beat-up when we went there."

"It wasn't new, even then, but this is different. There's a leak in the ceiling in Emery's classroom. You can't use half the gym because the floor is damaged."

"Sounds depressing."

"There you go, Alice," Misty said. "Double-knotted."

Emery was half a block away. Alice set off after him, leapfrogging down the sidewalk. "Hey Emery, wait for me!" she called. He sped up.

"It is depressing," Misty said, "and you know what? People are depressed. The staff, I mean. The teachers. And they can't get new people; they hired me on sight and I'm totally not qualified."

"Alice," I called, "don't go through the puddles. Your socks will be wet all day."

"See?" Misty asked. "You're better at this. I would have let her jump in every puddle between here and school." Misty trudged through a puddle of her own.

"Why don't they build a new school?" I asked. "And hire new people?"

"Money, I guess."

"They're rebuilding everything else in Faith. Your father's doing most of it. All these people moving up from the city and from New Jersey, they have to send their kids to school somewhere. No one will be happy if they buy a huge house for a ton of money and then have to send their kids to a school with a leaking roof and burned-out teachers."

"There are three private schools that weren't here when we were kids," Misty said. "The new people are probably sending their kids to those."

We caught up with them, Alice now veering around puddles in her path. Emery spent the rest of the walk delivering a detailed and difficult-to-follow explanation of rocket dynamics and his harrowing plans for the next launch. I said goodbye in front of the school. Misty handed the coffee mug back to me. "This was good," she said. "Maybe a little stronger tomorrow?"

"Sure," I said. "I'll make it stronger tomorrow." I watched as she escorted the children inside.

I walked home, arriving to find Garrett Grant digging a hole in our lawn. It appeared to be his third. His back was to me as he leaned over a shovel, digging into the grass. "I never had you pegged for a landscaper," I said. "You know you're supposed to put plants in those holes, right?"

Garrett turned to face me, unsteady on his feet and leaning a bit too hard on the shovel. He was in jeans and a flannel with sweat stains under his arms, even though the morning wasn't that warm. His pupils were dilated. "Lukas. Hello."

"Hi."

He glanced over his shoulder at the holes, still holding the shovel for balance. "You're probably wondering what brings me here."

"I was curious."

"The Matchbox cars."

"Ah ha."

"You remember?"

"I absolutely do not."

He grimaced, spit to one side, and again gripped the shovel, plunging it into the hole. "We were six. Maybe seven. No, six. Definitely six."

"Go on."

"We used to trade Matchbox cars."

"I remember that."

"Well, we decided one day . . . it was definitely when we were six, because I remember we were in Mrs. Loci's class at the time . . . we decided that I would take my three favorite and you would take your three favorite and we would bury them in your yard."

"Why would we do that?"

"Hell if I know, Lukas. We were six, it made sense at the time. The point is, I want my cars back." He scooped out another shovelful, tossing it on the small pile beside the hole.

"Garrett, are you seriously going to dig up my lawn to find six worthless toy cars?"

"Three cars. The other three are yours. And I don't have to dig up the entire lawn, I remember where we put them."

I glanced at the two other holes. "You do?"

"It was six paces in from the tree. Six paces. I'm just not sure which tree."

It was true; the first two holes were about six steps from two trees on the edge of the yard, and the one Garrett was working on was a similar distance from a third.

"I could have sworn it was that first tree," he muttered, "but no dice."

I walked over to what was apparently the first hole. "Garrett, come here."

He joined me, shovel in hand.

"You paced it off?"

"Of course I paced it off. Watch." Garrett went to the tree and then took six steps, heel to toe, bringing him to the edge of the empty hole.

"We were six," I said. "Our feet were about half as big." I walked midway back to the tree and made an X in the grass with the toe of my shoe. Garrett stared at me for a long moment, then came over and viciously dug into the spot I had indicated. I stepped to one side to watch. "I think I vaguely remember this," I said. "Now that you're bringing it up."

He grunted and dug.

"Is there a particular reason you want these cars now?"

He muttered something indecipherable.

"Are you planning to fill in these holes when you're done?"

No response to that one.

Garrett excavated a hole about two feet by two feet and eighteen inches deep. The ground was soft and he worked quickly, sweat streaming from his face. Finally, he dug the blade into the ground and we heard the sound of metal on metal. He tossed the shovel to one side and dropped to his knees, clearing dirt away with his hands. I was eager to see what he found in spite of myself.

It was a tin box. Garrett set it down at the edge of the hole and wiped the top clean. Fletcher's Cookies, with a picture of a cascade of butter cookies plunging into a cup of milk. I hadn't eaten Fletcher's in years. Garrett pried the top off and peered inside. "Well?" I asked. I was standing behind him and couldn't see inside when he hunched over.

He set them one by one on the ground beside the hole. A fire truck. A Jeep. A Corvette convertible. A motorcycle with sidecar. A yellow sedan. A VW bus. Garrett shifted his weight to one side, sitting in the dirt beside the hole, contemplating the cars. I walked around to the other side and sat facing him. I felt tired, even though I hadn't done any of the work. I looked at the cars. I had no idea which had been his and which had been mine.

"What do you remember," he finally asked, "about my family?"

"What about them?"

"What were we like? When I was young?"

I picked a blade of grass out of the lawn and twirled it between my fingers. "Rich. Fascinating. Glamorous, maybe, though I wouldn't have known to use that word. You went places, did things."

"Were we happy?"

"I don't know if you were happy. You were cool. Your dad was . . . confident, I guess is the best word. Firm. Your mom was kind of perfect. Jason was totally perfect. And Misty was always beautiful."

Garrett nodded, looking at the cars. "God, you had a crush on my sister."

"I did."

"I think you still do."

"Maybe."

"You were like a puppy dog with her."

"Let me have some pride."

He chuckled. "When the two of you finally got together in high school I thought your head was going to explode, and when she dumped you I thought . . ." He trailed off. I knew he had been going to say that he thought I would kill myself. "Do you want to know what I remember about your family?" he asked.

"Not particularly."

He looked up, squinting at the facade of my house. Dad was likely going over notes up in my room, which did not face out onto the front yard. "Why not?"

"What is there to remember? My mom worked a lot, my dad worked even more."

"I wasn't surprised when I heard they broke up," Garrett said. "And I wasn't surprised that she was the one to do the leaving. She always seemed a little, I don't know, ambivalent."

"Hm." I did not want Garrett's remembrances of my mother.

"Your dad did try, though. I'll give him that."

"He tried? Dad? When?"

"A few times. He tried to show us how to throw a boomerang; that thing must still be on the roof. And the kite, for third-grade science fair. And that really rainy spring, when we were nine or ten, all kinds of weird-ass mushrooms came up and he took us for a walk and told us what they all were."

"I don't remember any of that."

"The mushroom thing was boring as shit, but he was trying. I just don't think he really knew how to talk to kids. I don't think he knew what to do." Garrett pushed himself up with a grunt, climbing to his feet. "Mine, mine, and mine," he said, grabbing the Jeep, the motorcycle, and the convertible.

"Are you sure?" I didn't particularly care, but I was curious.

"I remember everything, Lukas. It's a goddamn curse."

"So is the opposite, I'm finding."

He again spit to one side. He was sweaty and pale and unsteady. He half turned away, cradling the three cars in his hands. "I'll, uh, come back later and fill these holes in."

"Sure. Do you want the tin?"

He nodded. I stood and handed him the Fletcher's box. Garrett carefully placed his cars inside and tucked it under one arm. Then he looked down into the palms of his hands, scrutinizing them for so long that I wondered whether he was going to pronounce some sort of fortune. "No one's too good to get their hands a little bit dirty, are they, Lukas?" he finally asked. Then he walked away without waiting for a response, across the lawn to the street, turning up the hill toward his house.

I watched him go. I didn't remember a boomerang or a kite, and I didn't remember anything about any fucking mushrooms. What I remembered was feeling clueless and lonely. I remembered a golden family at the top of the hill who I could visit, could bring my Matchbox collection to make trades, could even stay for dinner sometimes, but could never, ever be part of. And standing there, seventeen years after the fact, I could just barely remember agreeing to bury my three favorite cars with Garrett's three favorites in what we took to be a grand gesture of friendship. For six-year-olds, it probably was.

I reached out with one foot and nudged the three remaining Matchbox vehicles into the hole. Then I picked up the shovel Garrett left behind and filled it back in.

CHAPTER ELEVEN

"Here's what I think," Dad said. "And I feel this very strongly, so please listen: the Balthus is the proper knot to use for a formal occasion."

"This isn't a formal occasion," I said.

"I thought it was a banquet? I thought it was a date?"

"It is a banquet," I told him, "but it's not a date. At least, I don't think it is."

"Best to use the Balthus if you're not sure."

Misty had given me very short notice. She asked that afternoon, in fact, stopping at my house after dropping the Quinlan children off across the street. "It's a fundraiser," she explained. "Alice wants me to come. It's the Ulster County Down Syndrome Foundation's annual dinner. They asked this morning and it turns out I get a plus one."

"It's a dinner?" I asked.

"It's a fundraiser. But yeah, we eat. I put you down for chicken."

"I didn't say I would come, and I didn't say that I like chicken."

"Everyone likes chicken though no one likes it very much. And what else do you have to do? We'll get you back for your dad by one A.M.; I don't think these things go very late."

I thought about it for a moment and it occurred to me that she wasn't looking at me like someone who assumed I would come and quietly eat a dry chicken breast. She was looking at me like someone who hoped I'd say yes. "Sure," I said. "Sounds fun."

"It won't be fun," she told me, "but Alice will appreciate it and so will her mother. Pick me up at seven." Then she walked away. I watched her all the way up the hill, but she never looked back.

"My chief resident, Dr. Goldberg, used to knot his tie in an Eldridge," Dad said. "Now that was a man who knew a thing or two."

"I'm just going to tie it the way that I tie it." I studied myself in the mirror and then knotted the red tie in a few swift motions.

"A half Windsor," Dad said sadly. "That's all you know."

I pulled my only blazer on. "Well," I said, "you had eighteen years to teach me the Balthus." I took a paper bag from beside the door. "I won't be late."

"Lukas," Dad said.

"Yeah?"

He stepped close and reached behind my neck, adjusting my collar. Then he stepped back and clapped me on the shoulder. "You look good."

"Thank you." I stood for a moment, holding the bag, not sure what else to say. Then I nodded again, turned, and left.

"A scone?" Misty asked when I picked her up. "You brought me a scone?"

"It's orange almond," I said. "You like that kind. I remembered that you like it, and it occurred to me that the chicken could be awful so you might want a snack beforehand."

"Is there a piece missing?"

"Well, all that occurred to me after I took a bite. But look, I broke off the piece where I'd touched it so it's just, like, three-quarters of your favorite kind of scone. Maybe two-thirds."

Misty studied the scone, the empty bag in her lap. "I got myself the salmon," she finally said, "but thank you." She took a bite. I pulled out of her driveway and drove to the Marriot in New Birmingham where the dinner was being held. "Is this the hotel?" Misty asked as I parked.

"Of course it is," I said. "It's on the invitation you forwarded."

"No," she said, "I mean *the* hotel. The one where your father was going when he was hit."

"Oh. No. That's on the other side of town." I told her the name.

Misty brushed crumbs off her lap. She was wearing a red dress and her hair was piled on top of her head. She looked like she'd pulled it together three minutes before I knocked on her door. She looked amazing. "Do you wonder about it?" she asked. "About what he was doing there?"

"It seems pretty clear what he was doing there," I said.

"I mean the whole story, though. Who he was meeting, how long he'd been seeing her, how serious it was. No one came to see him in the hospital? No one's come around or called in all the months he's been home?"

"No."

"It can't have been that serious then. If I was meeting a guy at a hotel and he got run down in the street outside I'd at least send a get-well card."

"I guess that would be the decent thing to do."

"You don't want to talk about this?"

"Not really."

"All right then, let's get it over with." Misty got out, shut the door, and started toward the entrance. I sat in the driver's seat for a moment. It seemed like an inauspicious start to a maybe date. I grabbed the empty paper bag from her seat, crumpled it up, tossed it over my shoulder, and then got out and hurried to catch up.

The chicken, it turned out, was delicious. We were seated at a table with Alice, her mother, and two sets of parents with their children. I didn't say much, just ate my dinner and ignored a few speeches. When no one was at the podium I listened to Alice and her friends tell us about school and the after-school program they were in through the foundation. It was an arts-based program and they were coming up on a unit on theater. Alice was excited because she knew Misty had gone to theater school, and they spent a few minutes talking about ideas for a musical theater revue before Misty turned to me and said, "You know, I went to drama school and all, but Lukas is a real actor. He's been in the city for the last five years, auditioning and really living the life, working in the professional theater."

All eyes swung to me. My mouth was full of chicken and it took me a moment to respond. "Uh, well," I said, "yeah, that's true. I mean, I have worked in the professional theater. Most of the time I was waiting tables, though."

"But you're an actor?" one of the mothers asked.

"I'm an actor."

"We'd love to have you involved," she said. "We have so few male volunteers."

I glanced at Misty. "Well," I said, "I mean, I don't know how long I'm going to be in town. I'm helping my father out with some things, but I'm going to be heading back to the city before too long. To audition, and . . ."

"The program ends in a few weeks," Misty said. "Are you heading back in the next few weeks?"

"No," I admitted. "That seems unlikely."

Misty and the five parents at the table all nodded in unison, as though something had been settled. Alice clapped her hands but a boy sitting to her left shook his head. "No," he said. "No."

I wasn't sure what his criteria for rejection were but I tended to agree with him. His father dipped his head, spoke with him for a moment, then looked back up. "Brian doesn't like the idea of being onstage," he said. "It scares him."

Everyone looked back at me as I prepared to take another heaping bite of chicken. I froze, fork halfway to my mouth. *Holy shit*, I thought, *they want me to say something*. I lowered the food to my plate and looked across the table at Brian, a variety of possibilities running through my head. Assuring him that he would be fine seemed flip, and frankly went against the grain of my assessment of his odds as a performer. I always hated it when people told me things would be fine, anyway. How would they know? Things often were not fine. It basically translated to "calm down and shut up."

"It is scary," I said. "It's very scary. Being up onstage with everyone watching is one of the scariest things you can do. You have to be brave."

"But I'm scared," Brian said.

"Right. That's why you have to be brave. Being brave doesn't mean you're not scared; it means you're scared, but you do it anyway." We looked at each other for a moment. "You look brave to me," I told him.

"All right, folks," a man at the front of the room said into a mike, "the silent auction is going to begin, so please make sure you have your number and turn your attention to the side door, where Mrs. Hernandez will be reviewing the ground rules."

Everyone dug around for their silent auction number and turned their attention to Mrs. Hernandez. Everyone except Misty. Misty kept looking at me. I wasn't sure how to read her expression and I didn't plan on doing the silent auction, so I finished my chicken.

We drove back to Misty's house two and a half hours later. She'd bought a ceramic lamp at the auction. It was made by Alice, though Misty pretended not to know. It was painted green and yellow and purple and Misty said that those were her favorite colors and that the lamp would go in the middle of the living room and she'd read beside it every night. It made Alice very happy.

"Mets tickets?" Misty asked as I drove up our hill. "I didn't think you liked baseball."

"I've never really had a chance to check it out," I said. "And they seemed like a good deal. They're in the bleachers."

"The bleachers are the cheap seats, Lukas."

"Oh."

"Dad's company has a box at the stadium."

"That must be nice."

"I only went once. I didn't like it, actually. You can't really hear the game, you can't feel the sun and wind, you can't smell the ballpark."

"How does a ballpark smell?"

"Terrible, usually. That's not the point, though. If you're going to watch from a luxury box you might as well watch on TV from home. It's just a stupid status symbol."

"Well," I said, "I got two tickets so maybe you can come. I bet you can smell things in the bleachers."

"Maybe."

The tickets had been an impulse buy at the silent auction. I justified it to myself as being for a good cause. I wasn't sure I really wanted to go but in the moment I'd had an irresistible urge to have them. I suspected that I'd prefer a luxury box to the bleachers.

"Wait, Lukas, pull over here."

I slowed and pulled to the side of the road. We were past my house but still about fifty yards from her driveway. "What is it?"

Misty was quiet for a moment. She fidgeted with the hem of her dress and then folded her hands in her lap. "I'm not ready to go home."

"Oh. Do you want to come over to my place?"

She shook her head. "I need a break from the dry-erase board, you know? And your father. He's great, but he tends to . . . say things."

"He certainly does."

"My house is pretty miserable. My parents are miserable. Dad drinks too much. Mom is so fragile. Sometimes I think that a loud noise could shatter her like glass. Garrett's usually up in Boston, not that I particularly like having him around, but at least he's a living, breathing person. At least he makes noise and says things, even if most of them are pretty mean."

"What does he do in Boston?"

"Who knows? He's staying with Uncle Frank, who's a contractor. Supposedly he's working construction and learning the business, but I can't imagine anyone would let him near power tools. Frank's a tough guy; hard worker, no family. Old-fashioned. He's supposed to be helping my brother stay clean. Garrett will be home Sunday and your father wants me to talk to him when he gets back."

I thought about Garrett's dilated pupils as he manically dug up my front lawn. Uncle Frank would have his hands full. "Dad still thinks Garrett's in the middle of all this."

She shrugged. “Maybe he is, somehow. I don’t know. Like I said, I need a break.”

“What kind of break?”

“This kind.” Misty leaned over and kissed me. When we were younger her lips tasted like bubblegum. She didn’t taste like bubblegum anymore. She tasted like salt and like sadness; she tasted like some vestige of our youth and like a cheap plate of salmon. When we stopped kissing she twisted around and looked into the back seat. Apart from her new lamp it had an assortment of food wrappers and empty coffee cups. I wished I had cleaned it out. “Let’s go somewhere,” she said, turning back to me.

“Where do you want to go?”

“Anywhere. Somewhere quiet. Anywhere but the lake.”

“All right,” I said, “we’ll find a place.” I turned the car around and drove back down the hill.

CHAPTER TWELVE

"You got in late," Dad said.

"You were asleep. I was back before one."

"Twelve thirty-five, I'd say."

"How do you know that?"

Dad nodded toward the front door where my dress shoes had been kicked off before I inflated the air mattress, tied the cord, and dropped into a deep sleep. "Clay."

"What are you talking about?"

"It started to drizzle at eleven twenty-five last night. Not much at all. Not enough to saturate the ground before about twelve fifteen, maybe twelve twenty. Regular dirt, that is. Soil with a high concentration of clay is much more absorbent. And that on the side of your shoe is clay of the color found at the old Nelson quarry. There's not much of it and it's not smeared; you didn't clean the shoes and you weren't hiking around. You had a car but only stepped out of it for a brief moment, presumably to get back into the front seat. The clay was likely damp enough to leave that mark by eleven fifty and the quarry is thirty-five minutes away if it's dark but there's no traffic, putting you back at twelve twenty-five, or twelve thirty-five if you dropped someone off and paused to say goodnight."

"You can do all that but you can't remember how to fill the coffee maker?" I asked, lunging toward the counter where the carafe was gurgling and overflowing. He was dead right, of course. It had been 12:37, but I wasn't going to argue the point. I mopped up the coffee and made two mugs, returning to the living room and giving him one. "How was Dr. Mancini?" Dad had seen the pathologist the afternoon before but we hadn't time to compare notes in detail before my dinner out.

"Outstanding. He and Derek picked me up for afternoon tea. Isn't that quaint?"

"Yes," I said, "charming. What did they tell you?"

Dad cleared his throat and rummaged in a briefcase beside the couch, withdrawing a bundle of papers.

"What are those?" I asked.

"Data on the psychiatry department, and particularly on the Mullens Center. Derek works in billing."

"I know. He just gave it to you?"

"I'm still on staff. I told them that I am interested in trying to transition to a role in administration and before I pitch it to the chairman, I have to get up to speed on the financials. Mancini doesn't give a damn and Derek seems like he'd do anything for Mancini. At any rate, we do owe them a dinner as thanks." Dad flipped through the papers, muttering to himself. "I looked it over last night and then I got a headache. These are expenses, very boring, and staff salaries, which frankly Derek shouldn't have shared with me but fortunately for him I don't give a shit, and this seems to be an accounting of referral sources, which they've tracked for some time."

I looked at the sheets in his hand, printouts with dense lists of names and numbers. I thought it would give me a headache too, even without a brain injury. "What did Derek think about the Mullens Center?" I asked.

"He said it was a winner from a financial point of view. Payment is almost entirely out of pocket. The facilities were expensive to build but the staffing doesn't cost any more than it does in the rest of psychiatry. The nurses, the therapists, they're all paid the same, which is not very much. He called it a cash cow."

"Who is it for?"

"Children, ages six to seventeen. A range of diagnoses: depression, anxiety, autism spectrum, bipolar and its variants. They have thirty beds."

"That seems like a lot of beds to keep full."

"I suppose there's a need. As you know, I'm not really a clinician."

"Yes, I know." I sipped my coffee and scanned the page. "Wait," I said, "there: Lotus Consultants."

Dad seized the paper. "Where?"

"Right there." I pointed.

"My God, I must have been blind last night."

"You were tired."

"These are referral sources."

"So, Lotus Consultants sends patients to Mullens?"

"Apparently so. Lukas, look through the rest of this. I fear that my sustained attention isn't what it used to be."

I took the papers and my coffee to the dining room table. Ten minutes later I summoned him. "Here." I pointed. "The list of donors. Second from the top: Lotus. So, they give money and also send patients to the center?"

"I suppose so. Hold on." Dad took out his phone. "Dr. Moore for Dr. Kwan," he said. "Well, page him please. I don't care if he's not on call, I need a consult." He waited, drinking his coffee and sorting through the pages. "Kwan," he said after a moment, "I need some input. Do you know Lotus Consultants?" He listened for a moment. "Ah," he said. "Well, how do I get in touch with them?" He grabbed a pen from the table beside the couch and scribbled a number in the margin of one of the pages. "What's that? No, I'm fine, for once you've actually been a help." He hung up. "They're some sort of private educational consultants," he said, "whatever that means. I have their number."

"Dr. Kwan could probably have told us what it means," I said.

Dad snorted. "He would have said some nonsense about meeting children's needs and supporting families and matching them with blah blah bullshit. We'll figure it out for ourselves."

It was surprising that it had taken so many years for someone to run my father over with a car.

"How was your night?" Dad asked. "Other than the quarry?"

"Fine. It seems that I'm going to be doing some directing."

"Really? Of what?"

I told him about the plans for the revue. To my surprise, he didn't roll his eyes or call the idea absurd. "That's interesting, Lukas," he said. "There's a surprisingly reliable literature on the utility of artistic participation for children with developmental disabilities."

"That's good to know, I guess."

"You don't seem excited."

"I just . . . you know, I've always seen myself onstage more than behind the scenes."

"Stanley Kowalski."

"Yeah." We didn't talk much about the role I'd given up.

"I know how you feel."

"Do you?"

"Not about the acting, but about the glory. Do you think when I was top of my class at Yale Med that I saw myself running animal trials on adenosine agonists at a regional medical center?"

I stared at him across our dining room table, my coffee cup halfway to my mouth. Dad's career seemed fused to his personality, inseparable.

I had never imagined that he could be dissatisfied with it, because I had never imagined that it could be another way. "Where did you see yourself?" I asked.

"Nebraska."

"Nebraska? The state of Nebraska?"

"Right. Specifically, Professor Irving Gupman's lab at the Institute for Neuroscientific Progress at the University of Nebraska."

"Never heard of it."

"Of course you haven't. But for someone in my field, it's the equivalent of Broadway and Hollywood rolled together. It's the absolute pinnacle. Gupman is world-renowned. So are his associates."

"So, what happened?"

"This happened," Dad said, gesturing at the dining room we were sitting in and the house around us and the greater town of Faith surrounding the house. "You happened."

"Sorry to derail your dreams."

I meant it sarcastically but Dad didn't smile. "Don't be. You want to be on Broadway, Lukas. I wanted to be at the Institute. What do you think that's all about?"

"Wanting to be the best."

He shook his head. "Wanting to be famous. Which, unless you have some unfounded faith in group judgment, you have to acknowledge is not the same thing at all. Fame is not about quality, it's about immortality."

"I'd take that."

"So would I, but the immortality of fame is a mirage. It's the illusion that, if you are recognized by others, you can transcend the limitations of your own life. Do you know Marcus Aurelius?"

"No."

"Ancient Roman emperor, Stoic philosopher. He said that fame is mere vanity, and following after it is oblivion."

"Although I notice you're quoting him, what, a few thousand years later?"

"And he's been just as dead for just as long as the millions of his fellow Romans we've forgotten. In any event, I'm not telling you that teaching kids with Down syndrome to sing and dance is intrinsically better than acting on Broadway. All I'm saying is that I think you'd be good at it."

"You do?"

"I do. You know, when your mother left and you decided to move home I thought I was going to die. I told the staff at the rehab hospital. I said: 'My son, Lukas, is thoroughly incompetent to provide any sort of care for someone with residual neuropsychological deficits, and he will likely inadvertently kill me.' But your support has been surprisingly competent."

I was stunned and a little disoriented by this type of encouragement from my father. This was the man who once hid my tap shoes when I was training to be a triple threat onstage; who responded to a line drive I took to the sternum during a brief, untutored effort to play Little League by suggesting that I find a sport that didn't require speed, strength, coordination, or good reflexes. "Thank you, I think."

He nodded curtly. "Now, about dinner."

"With Dr. Mancini and Derek?"

"No, with the Grants. I understand that Garrett will be home from Boston. I'd like to go over for Sunday dinner."

"Um, yeah, Misty said she was going to talk to him . . ."

"I'd like to do it myself, Lukas. I find Misty to be a bit paranoid and prone to primitive defense mechanisms such as denial. She thinks an accountant is following her and that we're going to find Jason wandering around brainwashed."

"I just called him an accountant because that's what he looked like," I said. "I don't think he's literally an accountant."

"My point is, she's lovely but unreliable."

"So, you want to go to dinner?"

"We'll both go. Sunday dinner."

"We're not invited."

Dad glanced at me. "After last night, I'm sure you can wrangle an invitation from Misty."

I felt myself color. Dad and I had never talked about my dating life. Not once. It was profoundly uncomfortable. "All right," I said, "I'll see what I can do."

"I'm sure you will," Dad said. "And pick up some decent wine."

CHAPTER THIRTEEN

Dad had been right: the air mattress helped, though I was prone to roll too close to the edge. I felt it give way beneath me. Cursing before I opened my eyes, I slid off and onto the living room floor.

I peered at my watch: 4:14. I needed to go to the bathroom. I started to stand, and then froze. I'd slid away from the couch, on the far side of the mattress, and nothing had tugged back. I looked down and then over. The line was slack and the couch was empty.

I climbed to my feet. The bathroom? No. Maybe the kitchen? Not there either. I headed for the stairs, wondering whether Dad might have performed the extraordinary feat of going to his own bed, and then I saw it: the front door, open a good six inches.

Of course. It had happened before. I threw the door open and ran onto the lawn wearing nothing but my boxers and a ratty undershirt. The grass was wet and cool beneath my feet and the neighborhood was silent. Three bare patches of dirt covered the holes Garrett had made.

The last time Dad left, before I started tying him to me, he walked downhill in what I assumed was the path of least resistance. I started in that direction and made it ten or eleven steps before I caught a movement from the corner of my eye and turned left, looking across the street.

Dad was standing by the side of the Quinlans' house, hidden in the shadows. His back was to me. I wouldn't have seen him if he hadn't moved at the right time, bending over with his head close to the bushes.

"Dad!" I whispered. He didn't turn. I hurried across the empty street. All the lights were off in the Quinlans'; the last thing I wanted was for Emery to wake up and come outside for a conversation.

"Dad," I said again as I crossed their front lawn and approached him, keeping my voice low. "What are you—"

He swung around to face me. Even in the dark I could see that his eyes were wide and confused. One hand shot out and seized me by the forearm in an iron grip. "Help me," he rasped. He pulled and I almost fell over, stumbling beside him in the damp grass.

"Fuck's sake, Dad, let go!"

"Look," he said, "look, goddamn you!" He dropped to his knees and began burrowing in the mulch under a hedge like a deranged gopher.

I looked up and down the silent street but the cavalry wasn't coming. Why would it? As far as the world knew we were doing well, or well enough, and there were many needier cases. I'd seen them in the rehab hospital and even if Dad were willing to admit permanent disability and apply for benefits, the social worker had made it clear we would be at the end of a long line. The only person with both an inkling of our situation and some capacity to help was in bed three hundred miles to the north getting some shut-eye ahead of a big deposition.

I knelt beside the shrubs. "Your name is Richard Moore," I said evenly. "You're recovering from a traumatic brain injury. You're agitated. You're confused. You're safe."

A handful of mulch hit me between the eyes. He had reached the roots of the plant and shifted to his right, cursing and beginning a new excavation. The moon came out from behind some clouds and in the new light I could see tear tracks furrowing the dirt on his face. I reached out and placed a hand on top of his arm. He tensed and I flinched, remembering the first time I'd tried to intervene when he was confused and been rewarded with a slap to the side of the head, but I didn't take my hand away. "Do you know who I am?" I asked.

He looked at me in the moonlight. His pajamas were torn. He wiped the back of a wrist against his running nose. "You're my son," he finally said.

"That's right."

"Lukas."

"Yes."

He looked me up and down. "You're in your underwear."

I sighed. "Silly me."

He looked down toward the hedges. "It's not there."

"No."

"It hasn't been in a long time."

"Probably not." I had no idea what he was talking about and I doubted that he did either. After his last nighttime expedition Dad confessed to having hallucinated a chocolate owl. He'd probably been out here digging for candy treasure. "I can't tell you how much I have to pee," I said.

"So do I."

"Let's go." I took Dad by the arm and helped him back across the Quinlans' yard. We both used the bathroom and washed the dirt off. Then we returned to the living room, where Dad situated himself on the couch. I tied myself firmly to him and lay down. Minutes passed and I drifted. Then, he stirred. "Are you okay?" I whispered, hoping he wouldn't answer.

He wasn't really awake. His eyes were closed but he murmured, just barely decipherable: "Do you know how beautiful your mother was, Lukas? My God, do you know how much I loved her? Do you know how much I wish . . ." He trailed off, head tilting farther to the side.

I wanted him to say more. I wanted to know when he stopped loving her, or at least loved her little enough to go sneaking off to a rendezvous with some mystery woman on the west side of the city. I wanted to know how it happens, if love leaks away in a steady, constant trickle or if it's gone all at once like some magician's trick, the sheet whisked away to show that there's nothing where you thought there was something.

He was asleep, though, a low snore escaping from his mouth. I turned away, waiting for my own sleep to come.

Misty had placed the lamp right in the middle of the living room, just as she'd promised Alice. The loud colors were out of place in the tastefully appointed space but it beamed on an end table just the same.

Dad and I stood in front of a wall that was covered in framed photos, the Grant family participating in a dizzying array of sports, trips, and community activities. Venice, Paris, Mexico. Sailing, kayaking, tennis. Our family had never traveled or been into sports. Sporadic family vacations had been trips to see extended family who, in retrospect, were probably less than thrilled by our descent.

Owen Grant waved us to seats on a couch that seemed never to have been used before; it was a pristine, unblemished white with plumped-out cushions. "None for me," Dad said in response to his offer of a drink. "Not a good idea on top of a brain injury. I'll just have some water." Owen turned to me. "Yes, please," I said.

Owen sat in a massive leather armchair across from us. He was dressed in gray slacks and a blazer over a crisp pin-striped shirt. Garrett slouched in a companion chair next to his father's, separated by a small table with a vase of fresh flowers and a pile of papers on it. He was dressed in torn jeans and work boots and appeared to be having a triple shot of scotch, neat. As diminished as Owen had been by grief, Garrett was still dwarfed by his father's massive frame.

We all raised our glasses, though it wasn't clear what we were toasting. The scotch was very peaty; it tasted like I was drinking a cigar. "The ladies will be here in a moment," Owen said.

"We were admiring your photos," Dad said, nodding toward the wall.

Owen blinked and squinted as though he had forgotten the pictures were there. "Ah, yes. Our little collection."

"You travel quite a bit."

"We used to, especially when the kids were younger and more portable."

Dad settled back on the couch and drank his water while I remained perched on the edge, ill at ease. The room was too quiet. A white cat appeared from around the couch and regarded my father and me. We both stared back. "Say hello to Carmine," Owen said.

"Hi, Carmine," I said.

"She belongs to Lucia," Owen went on. "Lucia's always had cats, since before we were married. That was her one condition when I proposed: that we would always have them."

"How many do you have?" I asked.

"Just this one, at the moment. He's young. Lucia will be ready for another kitten soon." He reached out with one foot and poked Carmine with the toe of his shoe. "I don't mind. They comfort her."

I watched Owen Grant play with the cat. Carmine crouched and swiped at his shoe. I'd worn a lot of shoes; an acting coach had advised me that, if I wanted to find my way into a part, the best first step was to figure out what shoes the character would wear. In the time I'd been preparing to play Stanley Kowalski I had stomped around New York City in a pair of worn work boots I'd found at Goodwill.

Owen was wearing Gucci loafers, worth at least nine hundred dollars. One of Carmine's claws stuck in the brown leather. Owen wiggled his foot and then brought the other one up, delivering a sharp kick to the animal's ribs. Carmine leaped away, hissing. Owen chuckled and sat back in his armchair, taking another drink.

"You're not an animal lover?" Dad asked.

"I grew up with animals but they weren't the loving kind. Dogs, mostly, though my brother Frank kept a pet snake."

"Where was that?"

"South Boston. You ever go up to Boston, Richard?"

"I've presented at a few Harvard conferences."

"Probably didn't get down to Southie."

"I can't say that I did."

"What about you, Lukas? You like the Sox?"

"I like the Mets," I said.

He snorted. "The Mets. I have a box, but it's just for business. You have pets when you were growing up?"

I shook my head. In addition to not being travel or sports people, we hadn't been pet people either.

"That's too bad," Owen said. "A boy should have a pet. It teaches responsibility, discipline. It teaches you how to project authority. Those dogs . . . well, if they didn't know me and Frank were in charge they would have torn us to pieces."

"What kind of dogs were they?" I asked.

"Pit bulls. Three of them."

"You had very understanding parents," Dad said, "if they let you have three pit bulls in South Boston. I can't imagine there was a tremendous amount of space."

"They didn't let us have anything. Those were my father's animals; when he left it fell to me and Frank to take care of them. And no, there wasn't a lot of space but what there was, the dogs had. Pit bulls have a way of getting what they need."

"You've come a long way," Dad said. "From South Boston to this."

Owen looked around his living room. "I have indeed. It's been a long road. I started with nothing. I never went to college, barely made it out of high school. I think they gave me a diploma because they wanted me gone. No money, no connections, at least not around here. I got into the real estate game in New Birmingham when it was cheap and I did it with borrowed money, and I can tell you that if I had not been able to pay that money back it would not have worked out well for me at all." He chuckled into his glass as he drank.

"New Birmingham seems like a strange destination," Dad said. "You could have stayed in Boston."

"Like I said, it was cheap." Owen studied my father over the rim of his glass. "What about you, Richard? You didn't grow up around here. I've always detected a bit of a Brooklyn accent."

"Park Slope," Dad said, "though like New Birmingham, it was cheaper in those days."

"You come from a long line of doctors?"

"No," Dad said, "I was the first. First to go to college, in fact."

"Is that right?"

"It is."

"That's a lot of pressure. A lot of eyes on you. A lot of shoulders to stand on."

"I'm sure you felt the same, starting out in business."

"Ah," Owen said, shrugging his broad shoulders, "business is very simple, compared to something like medicine." He leaned forward and studied Carmine, who had crept back closer to his feet. "People think, to succeed in business, you need to understand what people want, and you do." He extended one Gucci-clad foot. Carmine stiffened and reached out with a paw. The cat seemed to love good leather. "That's only half of it, though," Owen continued. "You also have to understand something else. You have to understand what they fear." He stomped his other foot, the one he had used to kick Carmine. The cat hissed and scurried away. Owen weighed his now mostly empty glass and watched him go. "That's it, though," he said thoughtfully. "Want and fear. You understand those two things, and you will succeed in any business."

Garrett, who had been steadily working on his drink, rolled his eyes. Owen noticed and turned to him. "Sick of hearing your old man talk?"

Garrett didn't respond, just stood and made his way to the side cabinet where the bottle of scotch was waiting. "What are you doing in Boston?" Dad asked him.

Garrett poured himself another stiff drink and then turned, theatrically spreading his arms to display his torn pants and paint spattered shirt. "Construction."

"Commercial? Residential?"

Garrett took a long sip. "A bit of both," he said when he was done. He leaned back against the liquor cabinet. "And how are you, Dr. Moore? Recovering nicely?"

"Very nicely, thank you."

"Will you be able to release Lukas from his servitude sometime soon?"

"I expect that I will, yes."

"You doing some acting, Lukas?" Owen asked.

"I was."

"You skipped college altogether, didn't you? Right to the stage."

"Yes, I tried."

"Well, you were a hell of a Hamlet, I remember that. I'm not much of a theater buff myself, that's more Lucia's department, but I've seen my fair share of Shakespeare what with Misty's performances and all, and I never saw a Hamlet as good as the one you did right over there at Tricounty High."

"Thank you, Mr. Grant."

"Owen, please!"

Garrett snorted, drank again, and turned for another top off. "Slow down, son," Owen murmured. Garrett ignored him.

"Lukas," Dad said, "let me have a taste of that whisky."

Dad had never been a drinker but I handed him the glass. He made a show of sniffing it and holding it up to the light and then took a sip. "Outstanding."

"Laphroaig. Eighteen years," Owen said.

"Will you write it down for me? My memory's not what it used to be."

"I'll take a picture of the bottle, Dad."

He dismissed me with a wave of his hand and gave me back the glass. "I don't trust phones, Lukas."

"A man after my own heart," Owen commented, taking a pen from his shirt pocket and scribbling on one of the papers next to him. "All that shit winds up in some cloud and then who knows where?" He leaned forward and handed the paper to my father, who examined it with some interest and then tucked it in his coat pocket.

"About that construction," Dad said to Garrett, who was refilling his drink, "what's your specialty? Are you learning electrical? Carpentry?"

Garrett spun around, sloshing some of the whisky over the edge of his too-full glass. "What's your interest, Dr. Moore? Are you thinking of getting into the building trades?"

"Easy, Garrett," Owen said, extending a hand with an outstretched palm. "Our neighbor is just making conversation. He hasn't really caught up with you in years." He turned to us. "Garrett's overtired," he said. "Frank's been working him too hard. My brother is old-school: up before the sun, no breaks, no off days. Kids from this generation aren't used to it, am I right, Richard?"

Dad nodded judiciously. "They're very soft."

"Soft is right. Not that I wanted my kids to grow up like me and Frank, mind you. We had nothing and we expected nothing. Everything we have, we took for ourselves. And look!" He waved his glass at the spacious room around us. "I'm proud of this, to be sure, but Frank . . . Frank's the real success story. You can't spit in upstate New York or southern New England without hitting something the man helped build. One of his subsidiaries has done a good deal of work on the medical center, you know."

"Hopefully not the fountain in the lobby," Dad said. I remembered how water sprayed the marble floor on our last visit to the clinic.

"What? Oh, that. Yeah, I saw that when I was over for the board meeting the other day. Fountains are finicky pieces of shit, but people love them. We'll get it adjusted." He sipped his drink. "I'll tell you something though, Richard. It comes at a price. For all the good work he's done, all the money he's made, all the jobs he's created, Frank never had time to slow down and have a family of his own. It's a damn shame." He glanced over at the wall of family photos. A portrait of Jason was especially prominent. It looked like a staged publicity shot from the medical center; he was dressed in a white lab coat, making a note in a medical chart.

"He tied a wonderful knot," Dad said after a moment. "Is that a Prince Albert?"

"A what?"

"Jason's tie. A Prince Albert knot?"

Owen shrugged. "Who knows? I hate ties."

"Ties? Really? Are you boring these nice men?" Lucia Grant asked as she entered the room, Misty close behind.

We all stood. Misty and Lucia both wore black dresses, though Lucia had a red scarf and pearls while Misty was unadorned. They carried glasses of white wine. Lucia was in very high heels and she teetered as she started across the room, carefully balancing her drink and giggling. Misty put a hand out to steady her mother and they made their way to a love seat set at right angles to the couch. Dad, Owen, and I resumed our seats. Garrett returned to his armchair.

"Dinner will be ready soon," Lucia said. "We're so pleased the two of you were able to come."

"Thank you for having us," I said. It was hard not to stare at Misty and her low-cut dress. I made a mental note to take it easy on the scotch. Carmine came forward and leapt into Lucia's lap.

"Our cats have never seemed to care for me," Owen said, "but they love Lucia. They loved Jason too. He had a way with them. I remember, in seventh grade, he did a project on animal training. Something about conditioning."

"Operant conditioning," Dad said.

"That sounds right. Anyway, he used it to train our cat at the time, Miles, to do this whole routine. He built it, one step at a time, giving Miles treats when he followed directions but then giving the treats less, you know, less consistently. There was a whole science to it."

"Yes," Dad said, "it's called psychology."

"It sounds amazing," I chimed in, eager to cover my father's disparagement. "He was really talented. Jason, that is. I mean, medicine, psychiatry, and the animal stuff, and, he did ceramics, right? Pottery, and, um . . ." I grasped for actual talents and glanced at the wall of pictures. "And it looks like he parasailed?"

"It was unbelievable," Owen continued, "he made the cat do a little dance to a song that was real popular at the time. What was it?"

"'I Don't Want to Miss a Thing,'" Misty said. "Aerosmith."

"That's it!" Owen said. "Yes. We had a video of it, didn't we? We should—"

"Oh, he was such a Renaissance man," Lucia said, "he was just amazing. I've never understood how he could fit all those things in his head in school. Why, Richard, you're a doctor too . . . How do you do it?"

I braced myself for another of Dad's sharp responses, but instead he quietly regarded Lucia for a moment and then said: "Just as Lukas observed, your son had a surprisingly wide range of talents."

Misty shifted closer to her mother and lay a comforting hand on her arm. Lucia looked small and fragile. She turned her head to the side for a moment, brushing against her daughter's shoulder and then taking a long drink of her wine.

"We should watch that video," Owen said. "I loved seeing that cat dance."

"No," Lucia said. Her voice was surprisingly sharp. "The past is past."

The group fell into an awkward silence. Owen finished what was left in his refilled glass.

"Lukas, it's wonderful what you're doing," Lucia finally said, turning back and seeming to gather herself.

"Yes," I said, "Umm . . ." I took a large sip of my own drink, wondering what she was talking about.

"With the Down Syndrome Foundation," Misty said, "Their theater program."

"Right, yes," I said. "I'm looking forward to it."

"Owen and I have been donors forever," Lucia said, "but we've never really been involved. And you'll get Misty's input as well, of course. You can't have a graduate of Yale Drama up the street and not ask for her support."

"Lukas will do a fine job, Mom . . ."

"Misty coming home and going to work in the school was such a surprise, a pleasant surprise," Lucia continued. "She's been out in the world for the last five years, insisting on this nonsense about paying her own way and taking out absurd loans to pay for Yale when we would have been more than happy to pay outright, wouldn't we, Owen?"

"More than happy," Owen said, standing and making his way once more to the bottle of scotch.

"Mother—" Misty began.

"In any event," Lucia continued, "we're happy she's here, and we're delighted to be involved in this cause!"

"Mom wants to hold a fundraiser," Misty said.

"Didn't we just go to a fundraiser?" I asked.

"Not that kind of fundraiser. Not the kind with cheap chicken and a silent auction."

"Misty, please," her mother said, laying a hand on her arm. She turned to me. "I'm sure it was a lovely fundraiser and that it generated important, um, streams of revenue . . ."

"We got this lamp," Misty reminded her.

"Yes," Lucia went on, studiously not looking at Alice's lamp. "But as with anything, there are tiers of fundraising. To access high net-worth individuals you need to have the right connections, hold the right events." She smiled at me, and the vacant, slightly medicated look I was becoming used to sharpened. Talking about money seemed to focus her. "Owen and I would be honored to organize a few occasions in the coming months."

"Honored," Owen agreed, burping and pounding his chest with the side of his fist. "Lukas, you golf?"

"No," I said, "never been."

"Never been golfing? Tennis? You look like a tennis player."

"No."

"Basketball?"

"I used to play horse with the guys on the playground. In, like, seventh grade. I won once."

"Come to think of it, I don't remember you as the sporting type when Misty and Garrett were kids and you used to come around," Owen mused.

"I never seemed to be good at sports, though I can't say I really tried."

"We always used to pick Lukas last for any team," Garrett commented. "Once, when I was captain of the kickball team in fifth grade, I traded him away for half a bag of gummy worms."

"Well," Lucia said, "I'm sure you'll be more successful in the disability support space. Misty says you're very empathic."

"I said he was nice," Misty said, draining the rest of her wine.

"Quite similar. Oh, I think it's time; let's move into the dining room. And Garrett—go get changed and wash. You're not coming to dinner looking like you just walked off a construction site."

"I did just walk off a construction site, Mother."

Misty snorted. "I know Uncle Frank is supposed to be straightening you out, Garrett, but I wonder if he could work just a little goddamn faster?"

"Misty! Please!" Lucia stood, wavering on her heels. "We have company. Lukas, Richard, please forgive us. Our family is still a bit . . . unsteady. Garrett, go change. Misty, you've had quite enough wine. Now, please follow me."

We made our way down the hall and into a formal dining room with a table that could have seated two dozen but was set for six. It had been years since I visited the Grant home, but I remembered always being very impressed by that table. Owen took the head, with Lucia to his right and Misty beside her. Dad and I sat across from them. A woman entered from the kitchen and silently distributed plates of salad. "Thank you, Claire," Lucia said. She turned to me as the woman left. "I think it's Claire," she whispered. "She's new. I can't keep track!"

There was something brittle about Lucia: she was immaculate and when the conversation was on her turf she seemed formidable, but she was like an overinflated balloon and Misty, if not Owen, seemed acutely aware of the possibility that she could pop.

Silence again fell as we ate. I glanced across the table at Misty, who was midway through a refilled glass of wine in defiance of her mother's directive.

"You seem well, Richard," Lucia said. "I wasn't sure what to expect when you came over for coffee a few weeks ago. We hadn't really seen you since before your accident."

"Thank you," Dad replied. "By the way, you should take your cat to the vet. Not the regular one, a veterinary ophthalmologist."

The Grants stared at him. Lucia reached down to touch the white cat, who had been nuzzling her foot. "A cat eye doctor?" Misty asked.

Dad bit into a cucumber. "Right."

"Why?" Lucia asked.

Dad chewed, swallowed, drank some water, and said: "Iris melanosis."

Lucia scooped her cat up as though Dad had threatened to skin it. "What is that?"

"Discoloration of an iris due to excessive proliferation of melanin. It's not unusual and it's typically benign, but it can become cancerous and that's more common in a younger animal such as . . . um . . ."

"Carmine," I said.

"Yes," Dad said. "Carmine."

Lucia turned Carmine's head with one hand to stare into her eyes. "I don't see anything," she said.

"It's subtle. The left eye, superior temporal quadrant," Dad said.

Lucia frowned at her cat. "Maybe?"

"Aren't you a psychiatrist?" Owen asked Dad.

"I am," he said, "that's why I'm referring you to a veterinary ophthalmologist."

That, plus the fact that his medical license was suspended and his bedside manner was so bad he would alienate even a cat. "Dad's usually right about these things," I said grudgingly. I wasn't an animal person, but I didn't want their cat to die of eye cancer.

"Just get it checked out, Mom," Misty said. "Dr. Moore picks up on things other people don't."

"Typically benign," Owen said, echoing Dad's prognosis with a slight slur.

Lucia stared at her husband, then at the cat, then back at her husband. "Well," she said, "we'll take him to see the best cat eye doctor on the eastern seaboard. You'll find him, won't you, Owen?"

"Of course I will, my dear."

"It could be a her," Misty said, taking a drink.

Lucia shrugged as though a female ophthalmologist were a theoretical possibility never actually glimpsed in nature and then giggled and set the cat down. Claire, if that was her name, interrupted to refill glasses and begin removing salad plates and Garrett arrived in fresh pants and a shirt. He took a seat next to Misty but did not look at any of us. He was calm, dissipated, and I wondered what he'd taken upstairs.

Lucia seemed to buoy, launching into a long, enthusiastic, somewhat disorganized account of past fundraising successes and concepts for events to support the Down Syndrome Foundation. She had an elaborate social strategy, and as soup emerged from the kitchen, was consumed and cleared, followed by plates of prime rib, she explained the architecture, which seemed to revolve around increasingly exclusive events with higher and higher expectations for donations. She was theoretically incorporating Misty and me into the plan, but we were basically accessories after the fact. I had the impression that we were expected to show up and look nice at a series of coffees, which was more than I had in mind when I sort of agreed to help with a summer musical theater revue. Owen worked his way through his steak and his scotch. Misty listened silently, a gloss of what struck me as well-practiced polite indifference on her face.

Dad, on the other hand, seemed strangely intrigued by Lucia's philanthropic strategizing. "So, the donations are tax deductions," he finally said. "The donors know that they're tax deductions, but they knew that already. And they already knew what the Down Syndrome Foundation is, so really they could just write a check today if they cared to. But you go through this complex ritual of wooing them in order to create the emotional effect of particular exclusivity and virtue, the illusion that they, and only they, can help and that it is their privilege to do so? In effect, your job is to create a series of elite experiences that will make them feel good about their tax deductions."

Lucia, who had been detailing plans for a golf tournament, stared at him.

"It's fascinating," he said. "It really is." He turned to Owen. "Speaking of donations," he said, "I've been thinking about my role at the medical center."

Owen sat back, glass in hand. "Interesting. Tell me."

"Well," Dad said, "I've been thinking about how I can be helpful, how I can best contribute. Now, I've spent years down in the basement with my lab rats and I think that I've made significant contributions. Fifty-seven peer reviewed articles, to be precise, to say nothing of the seventy-nine presentations at national or international conferences, and I would have been elected to the National Academy of Sciences if it weren't for that ass, Edelman."

"Focus," I whispered, nudging him under the table.

"That is neither here nor there," Dad continued, waving his hand in the air. "What is important is that I have reached a new stage in my career and I believe that I can bring my experience and expertise, my training—Yale Med, as you know—to bear on some higher-level problems. I am ready, in other words, to go into administration."

This was the first I was hearing of this and I wasn't sure whether Dad was deploying some secret strategy or whether he was having a stroke. Owen stared at him and hiccupped.

"What I really need to understand," Dad continued, "is how all this works." He waved his hand again, gesturing across the table in Lucia's general direction and seeming to encompass nonprofit institutions, philanthropic giving, and personal wealth as concepts shortly to be grasped.

Lucia cleared her throat. "Well, that's wonderful, Richard. I'm sure that Owen and I can help to make some connections."

"The connections are there," Dad said, "I just don't understand them. Lotus Consultants, for example. I understand that they're very important to the hospital, particularly the Mullens Center."

Owen, who had been raising a forkful of mashed potatoes to his mouth, froze and lowered it back to his plate. He sat back in his chair and looked at Dad, and despite the amount of scotch he had drunk his vision seemed crystal clear. "Lotus?"

Dad nodded. "You know them?"

Owen cocked his head to one side and considered. "They're major donors," he said. "They've been very supportive of child psychiatry in particular. When we were building the Mullens Center they really stepped up."

"They're educational consultants?"

"If you say so. All I know is that they cut generous checks."

"Jason must have known them."

"I'm sure he did. We didn't really talk about his work."

"No? You're chairman of the board."

Owen shrugged and spread his hands. "I'm a simple man, Richard. I never had the benefit of the education you and my children enjoyed. Yale, you said? Just like Misty. Garrett went to Cornell, though he hasn't finished yet. Jason went to Dartmouth, then Stanford. I barely made it out of South Boston High. I'm good at building things and I've been blessed with success in doing so. My job at the hospital is to do just that: keep building. My son was brilliant. I couldn't have understood a tenth of the things he did in the course of his day."

"Speaking of dessert, I should check on the crème brûlée," Lucia said, ignoring or oblivious to the fact that no one had spoken of any such thing. She rose from the table and left the room.

Owen stood and moved to the sideboard, retrieving the almost-empty bottle of whisky he had brought from the living room.

"Here's something curious," Dad said. "The bylaws for the medical center indicate that any donations in excess of ten thousand dollars shall be personally reviewed and approved by the chairman of the board. Lotus made no fewer than four such donations in the last five years, maybe more before that. Statutorily, you must have discussed them."

Misty and I reached for our glasses at the same time. I finished mine and wished I'd accepted more. Garrett remained oblivious, wrapped in the haze of whatever he was using.

"I may only have a high school education," Owen said, "but I know when someone is calling me a liar."

"I'm not calling you anything," Dad said. "I'm observing that your statement doesn't make sense within the context of what we know to be the reality of the situation."

"That sounds like a dressed-up way of calling it a lie."

Dad shrugged.

"You seem to notice a lot of things," Owen said, gesturing at the cat, curled up on a chair in the corner. "Have you noticed that we're in mourning? Have you noticed that my wife and I recently attended a memorial service for our eldest child?"

"Yes," Dad said. "I did."

"If you did, and you were a decent man, then you wouldn't be sitting in my house, eating my meat, accusing me of lying about some obscure, bureaucratic nonsense that I probably signed off on in an elevator, or while walking down the hall, or with my son over a . . . a . . . over a drink after a board meeting . . ." His voice broke. My father sat impassively, watching him. Seated at Owen's left elbow, they were maybe two feet apart.

"Dad," Misty said. "Dad. He didn't mean anything. He's just . . . he's . . ." Her eyes turned to me. I wasn't sure what word or phrase to supply her with. "Brain injured" seemed like a blunt description, "neurologically disabled" too vague.

Owen regained his composure. "You seem well-acquainted with the bylaws and the donor history," he said quietly. "I'm sure you would be an asset in an administrative position."

"Thank you," Dad said.

"Keep in mind, beyond a clerical level all such hires need to be approved by the board."

"Noted."

"You should go."

Dad stood and left the room without hesitation. I stood as well, but paused. Misty and Owen remained sitting. So did Garrett, who looked up and wiggled his fingers at me in a vague acknowledgment of our departure. His mouth creased in a smirk, and I wondered whether he was more aware of his surroundings than he let on. I turned to Owen. "I'm so sorry," I said. "He hasn't been himself since his accident. Or, he may be a bit too much himself. He's unfiltered. He didn't mean anything by it."

Owen rubbed his jaw. "You're the one taking care of things now, Lukas?"

“I am.”

“Then my advice to you is this: get them taken care of and leave.”

“I’m trying.”

“I grew up with people who were trying to leave. You know what happened to most of them? They never did. Their families and friends bound them in place, and one day they woke up and were one foot in the grave and it was too late to be anything other than what they were.”

I glanced at Misty, but she wasn’t looking at me. I nodded to Owen and then left the room, joining my father on the front porch. I turned to close the door and as I did so I spotted a subtle movement halfway up the stairs. It was Lucia Grant. She was standing on the landing, tapping a pill from a brown plastic bottle into her hand, and it struck me that she looked like a frightened animal waiting for a storm to pass. I wondered how it was to live with a man like Owen, year in and year out, gauging his moods and his whisky consumption on a nightly basis. She tilted her head back to swallow whatever it was she’d been prescribed and our eyes met for a moment. Then, not knowing what to say, I pulled the door shut and followed my father down the stairs, into the dusk.

“That was a lot, Dad,” I said as we walked down the hill. “You blew up that dinner because you thought he was lying, all on the basis of some stupid bylaws no one else probably even reads?”

“He was lying,” Dad said, “and that dinner had run out of utility. Neither Owen nor Garrett were going to tell me anything else, and Lucia had already been helpful.”

“I’m not sure how helpful she was,” I said, “and I don’t understand how you can be so sure Owen was lying.”

Dad reached into his pocket and withdrew a scrap of paper, handing it to me. I peered at in under a streetlight. *Laphroaig, 18*. “It’s the *L*,” he said.

"What about it?"

"It's the same as the *L* in the word "Lotus" where it's written in the margin of the research proposal. It has a very distinctive loop, common among people who had the misfortune of an early Catholic education. As the Grant boys likely did, up in Boston."

I handed the paper back to Dad. "So, he lied about Lotus. Or he forgot about it. It's been over a year. He's been through a lot. He's drunk."

Dad tucked the paper back in his pocket. "He was lying, Lukas. He's a good liar, far better than you, but the man has about five different tells. He was lying about one of the largest sources of referrals and donations for a flagship profit center at the hospital where he's chairman of the board."

"You think I'm a bad liar?"

"I think you're a terrible liar," he said. "Whatever we do next in our little investigation, it should not involve you lying."

"I'm a professional actor, you know."

"I know. And I largely agree with Owen in his assessment of your Hamlet, although I did see Ralph Fiennes on Broadway in the mid-nineties and, needless to say, he completely eclipsed your adolescent interpretation. Still, you were quite good. But taking on a role is one thing, lying as yourself is another. You may have too much integrity for it." He turned, still standing under the streetlight, and looked back up the hill at the Grants' home. I stood beside him.

"Sad," I said.

"What's sad?"

"All of them. Owen's a drunk, Lucia's half unraveled and on pills, Garrett's a drugged-out loser. It's a sad place for Misty to find herself."

Dad shrugged and clapped me on the back. "Who's to say, Lukas? The game is still afoot and things aren't always what they seem. What's been said has been said, what's done is done. I'm tired and still have work to do."

We turned up the front path of our house as my phone vibrated. I took it from my pocket and swiped the screen. Misty: Be down in an hour. Find something to drink. I was tired too, but apparently the night was not yet over.

CHAPTER FOURTEEN

I looked for vodka but found only tequila. Misty didn't seem to care. We sat on my front steps and drank together. The night held some of the warmth of the day and we were both in short sleeves.

"Aren't you worried about being seen?" I asked. "What happened to sneaking in the back door?"

"Fuck it," Misty said. "If they want to know that I drink with you at night, let them know it." She drew a deep breath of night air. "I love this time of year. You can feel spring coming. Another week or two and all the buds will explode. Can you feel it?"

"Yes," I said, "definitely." I was impressed that she was making such rapid progress with the tequila given that I'd counted four refills of her wineglass during dinner, and that was assuming she'd had no more in the time since Dad's and my unceremonious exit.

"What's your favorite time of year, Lukas?"

I'd always hated questions like that. I wasn't the sort of person who had a favorite time of year, or a favorite color or number or character on *Sesame Street*. (Although, come to think of it, I'd been partial to Oscar the Grouch. He was a kindred spirit.) "Fall," I said, because it wasn't currently fall and if she asked why I could say something about foliage. "Now can I ask you a question?"

"Of course. Fair is fair."

"Are you glad to be here?"

"Sure. Drinking with you is better than drinking alone."

"No, not here. Here, here. Faith. Working with Alice."

"Oh." She nodded, as though reflecting that it was, in fact, a good question, and took another pull on the bottle. "Well, that's harder to say. I saw Alice one morning and knew that she needed help, her mother needed help. The dad keeps up his child support but he's not coming to see them anymore, the prick. He barely even calls."

"Good fathers are hard to find."

"Tell me about it. Do you want some of this?" She held up the bottle.

"I'm good."

"I don't know if I can finish it."

"You probably shouldn't."

"Judge much?" She took another drink, apparently determined to try to see it through. "That's not all, though, the bit about Alice and Mrs. Quinlan needing help." She turned her head to look up the hill, toward her house. "My mother too. You see what she's like. She's never been strong, but now she's basically held together with meds and duct tape. I don't know if it helps having me there, if I take a little bit of Dad and Garrett's edge off, but I try."

"I know something about that."

"I bet you do."

"You can't stay around for them forever," I said, channeling my inner Jules Pierre. "You have a life waiting for you back in the city. A career."

"I know. So do you."

"Yeah. I guess we both have some things we have to deal with here first. Speaking of which, I'm sorry about the way my father behaved tonight."

"Don't apologize—he was wonderful! The thing with the cat's eye? That was amazing. And catching my father fibbing about those consultants! I mean, I can't imagine that means anything; Dad must have cut corners on every building code in New York state, so I doubt he'd be lying awake worrying about the hospital bylaws. Still, it was perfect. I told you he'd be a great detective."

"I don't know that we accomplished anything."

"What does your father think?"

"I don't know."

"Where is he?"

"Inside." I'd left Dad pacing in my converted bedroom, tacking up papers from the portfolio Derek had given him. They stretched all the way up the wall, and when I'd left he was taping one to the ceiling in order to maintain the symmetry of a column. All he needed was some of our yellow cord to connect the dots and he would look like a proper lunatic.

"Can I tell you something?" Misty asked.

"Sure."

"I went to the hotel."

"What hotel?" I asked, though I already knew.

"That hotel."

"Oh. Why?"

"I met a guy."

"Um . . ."

"No, not like that. An assistant manager. I figured out ahead of time that he was the older brother of someone I was in community theater with and I went down there and pretended I was going to this terrible convention, something about dental hygienists, and I got into a conversation with him."

"You posed as a dental hygienist? That might be illegal."

"I said I was interested in the field. Do you want to know what I found out?"

I really did not but I nodded anyway.

"He was on duty when it happened."

"How do you know?"

"I mentioned it, the accident. I didn't say anything about you, just that my neighbor had been hit by a car right outside and that it had been really dramatic and he said that he remembered the ambulances and fire trucks, how they arrested the driver. There was something else too. There was a woman."

"What woman?"

"A woman who had been waiting in the lobby and ran outside when it happened. She was really upset and he assumed she must have been the wife, but then at the last minute, when they were loading your dad into the ambulance, they offered her a hand up and she stopped, looked around, and then ran away. That's what he remembered, that it was so weird she ran away instead of going to the hospital with this guy who she obviously knew and cared about."

I finished my drink and poured some more. "Huh," I said. "Interesting."

"You know what the kicker is, Lukas?"

"Jesus, there's still a kicker?"

"There is. There's video. Security footage of the lobby. It goes onto this server and it's held for eighteen months. They still have it!"

"Did you look?" I asked, a sinking feeling in my gut.

"No, he couldn't just show it to me. But he said that if I came back when he was on night shift and no one else was around he could make it happen. I think he sort of likes me."

At some level I understood that Misty thought she was doing me a favor, that she was reciprocating. I was trying to figure her brother out and she was going to do the same with my father. That was why, instead of smashing the tequila bottle on my front steps and telling her to stay the fuck out of my family's business, I controlled my voice and said: "No. No, thank you. I appreciate it but . . . no. And please don't go back to that hotel."

"Really? Why not? It's so easy. We just go down there, maybe we have to pay the guy off, who knows, I'll cover it, and then you find out who your dad was meeting. I mean, Lukas, if I could figure Jason out that easily I'd do it in a second."

I shook my head. "It's easy but it's not easy."

"What's that supposed to mean, Yoda?"

"I mean, maybe I don't want to know. Did you ever think about that? Maybe not everyone sees their family as a mystery that has to be solved. Maybe I want to let it rest."

Misty stared into the night. "That," she said after a moment, "is something I will never understand."

There were lots of things I would never understand either, starting with the girl sitting next to me and what the status of our relationship was and whether I might propose a dinner for later on that week with the possibility of a return visit to the quarry to follow, though I yearned for more chivalrous wording and it was eluding me. I opened my mouth, hoping that something workable would come out, but before I could speak Misty interrupted. "There," she said. "Look!"

A rocket rose across the street, from behind the Quinlan house. It rode a plume of fire and ascended into the night.

"Should we move?" Misty asked. "Should we take cover?"

I shook my head. Emery's latest creation flew straight and unbending into the clear dark of the sky. "I think he did it," I said. "I think he worked it out. Did you ever get him an altimeter?"

"No. Now I wish I did."

We sat together and watched the rocket, waiting for it to fall, but whenever and wherever it did was too far away for us to see.

CHAPTER FIFTEEN

The line pulled taut at three in the morning. It took me a moment to sit up. "It's all right," I said. "You're home."

"Shh," Dad said. He was sitting on the couch and the lamp was on. He held his cell phone to one ear. "Go on," he said to whoever was on the other end. He was fully awake and his eyes were razor-sharp as he looked into the middle distance. A pause. "When?" He nodded. "All right. We'll be there soon." He hung up and lowered the phone to his lap.

I rose and sat on the couch next to him. "What is it?"

"They found Jason Grant. That was Mancini. He has him on his table now."

"Where was he?"

Dad turned to look at me. "He was in the lake, Lukas. They found him washed up on the edge of the lake."

"I like the night shift," Dr. Mancini said. "It's quiet. Life Saver? I have peppermint and wintergreen."

I figured that the morgue must always be quiet and the last thing I wanted was a snack, though Dad helped himself to a wintergreen and loudly bit it in half.

"Did they tell the family?" I asked. "Has the family been notified?"

Mancini and my father both looked at me. "What does that matter?" Mancini asked.

"I'm friends with his sister."

"Oh. Yes, probably. The police should have notified them."

I wished I could have been there with Misty when the cops came to the door instead of in this cold basement room with a couple of ghouls eating candy.

"There was an interesting feature," Dr. Mancini said, "which is why I called and didn't wait for morning."

"We appreciate it," Dad said. "Lukas, look over there."

I turned toward a blank wall just in time to hear Dr. Mancini whisk the sheet off the table, and I understood that for once my father had done something truly considerate. There was a moment of silence behind me.

"Are we sure it's him?" Dad asked.

"I already matched the dental records, and a wallet with his license was still in his pocket."

"It's been a long time since my pathology rotation," Dad admitted. "I'm a bit out of my league on this one."

"Of course you are. There's no question about drowning as the cause of death; I've already determined that his lungs are full of fresh water. He sucked a fair amount of lake down before he expired."

"Is that a ligature mark, there on his wrist?"

"Yes. Sometimes suicides do that, when they want to be sure not to come back up. He tied a line to his wrist and attached it to something heavy, but not too heavy to carry or perhaps swim a short way with. Line finally decayed and broke a year later, and back he comes."

"Mm," Dad said, "there's something I don't like about that."

There was a lot not to like. Even with my back turned I was feeling shaky. Mancini had a metal desk with a rolling chair in one corner. "I'm going to sit down," I announced and walked over to it. The smell in the room was terrible. Chemicals mixed with lake smell and the odor of rot.

"Lukas," Dad said, ignoring my distress, "there's something that's bothering me, but I can't quite put my finger on it."

"I'm sure it will come to you," I said, sitting and lowering my head between my knees in what I vaguely remembered was an antidote to fainting.

"What did you find interesting?" Dad asked Dr. Mancini.

"These discolorations, here . . . and here."

"Ah. I wouldn't have spotted them among the general decomposition."

"Naturally. Even most pathologists would not have."

"What causes them?"

"In my opinion, chemical burns."

"What does that mean?" I called.

"Is he all right?" Mancini asked Dad.

"He's fine."

"Do you want a Life Saver?" Mancini asked. "Your blood sugar might be low."

"No, thank you," I said. It didn't look like anyone had vacuumed under the desk in decades. The linoleum was dirty and cracked and dust lay thick against the wall.

"Chemical burns are burns caused by chemical exposure," Dad helpfully said. "Perhaps from the lake water? There could be high concentrations of pollutants from runoff."

"I don't think so," Mancini said. "No. I've never seen that, and I've seen a fair number of bodies brought up from underwater. The pattern doesn't fit."

"What, then?"

"To be honest," Mancini said, "it looks less like he was floating in the chemical he was exposed to than that he was lying in it."

The two men were quiet for a moment. I raised my head so that I was sitting straight but did not turn toward them.

"Can you be sure of the duration?" Dad asked. "That he was down there for a year?"

"Not really," Mancini said. "He was certainly there for a significant period of time, months, but seven months, eight, nine, twelve . . . it's very difficult to say. It's been getting hotter, you know, year by year. The water out there was warmer last summer than it's ever been since we've kept records. It throws off what I expect about rate of decomposition at this latitude. I'd have to research it a bit, and even then I'm not sure I can be as precise as I'd like."

"Ah."

"It's not anything I'll put in my report," Mancini said. "It's not definitive; I'm really just speculating. I've simply been asked to confirm identification so that the family doesn't have to see him. But I expected you'd be interested in my thoughts."

"We are," Dad said. "Your thoughts are worth more than those of the entire psychiatric department put together." Mancini seemed to accept the compliment as a matter of course. I heard rustling and the clink of metal on metal. "Will you keep looking into it?" Dad asked.

"I will, if you'd like me to. I can hold on to tissue samples after the body is released. Hair; skin from there, there, and there; and perhaps that right thumbnail. Hand me the large tweezers, will you?"

"That's it!" Dad said. "The right thumbnail. Lukas, think about the portrait of Jason on the Grants' wall, the one where he was all dressed up in his white coat, writing in a chart."

"Yeah," I said, "I remember."

"He was writing with his right hand."

"If you say so."

"I do. But his tie was that wonderful Prince Albert, and I suspected from the lie of the knot that he had tied it with his left hand."

"So? Maybe he was ambidextrous."

"Or a natural left-hander who had been trained to write with the right hand as a child."

"Or that. What does it matter?"

"This ligature mark is on his left wrist. He tied it with his right hand, but if his left was truly dominant then it would have been more natural to do it the other way around."

"Seems thin," Mancini said, and I heard a squishing sound.

"No," Dad said. "I don't think it is. Lukas, when we were looking at the photos on the Grants' wall, do you remember any of Jason playing baseball? Tennis? Something like that?"

"I can't say that I do," I said, "though I'm having a hard time thinking clearly right now."

"Blood sugar," Mancini said to my father. "It happens on the night shift. His body isn't metabolically attuned to being active at three o'clock in the morning."

"You should extract that fourth fingernail too," Dad said. "It's intact, but particularly discolored."

The squishing sound intensified and I bolted from the chair and from the morgue, making it down the hall to the bathroom before emptying what was left of my dinner into the toilet. Afterward I stood in front of a mirror and rinsed my mouth in the sink. I looked at my reflection. Mancini was partially correct; it's hard to face three o'clock in the morning under most circumstances, and a morgue is a particularly difficult place to try to do it. My method-acting friends liked to talk about sensory and emotional memories, things they could draw on to produce authentic emotions in a performance. I told myself that I was developing a generous supply, though in reality all I'd ever done onstage was pretend to have feelings, and standing in that bathroom I was just hoping to make it through the night.

I took another few minutes and then returned to the corridor. A fluorescent was flickering overhead. My father stood at the far end, outside the closed door to his old lab. I walked down the hall to him. His head was bowed slightly as though he were listening. He had one hand raised, fingertips pressed against the wood.

"I guess this is it," I said. "I guess we have our answer."

"What answer is that?" he asked.

"Where Jason was. He was in the lake the whole time. We're finished."

Dad raised his head and studied the door. RICHARD MOORE, MD, DEPARTMENT OF PSYCHIATRY, CLINICAL NEUROSCIENCE LAB was printed on a black plastic sign. For a moment I thought he might try the handle but then he dropped his hand and turned away. "No," he said, "I don't think that we are."

"Don't fucking feel sorry for me," Misty said. "Don't you dare feel sorry for me."

"Do you want vodka or do you want tequila?" I asked. "I picked up a bottle of each." I was sitting on the stoop, the sun was going down, and Misty was standing midway up our front walk.

"I'm not drinking tonight," she said.

"All right," I replied. "I'm sorry, Misty. I don't feel sorry for you, but I am sorry. I truly am."

"Is your father home?"

"Yes."

"Is he busy?"

"I doubt it."

Misty walked up the path, around me, and through the front door. I scrambled to my feet and followed.

Dad was sitting on the couch with his sunglasses on. The early morning had been tough, and he'd been fighting a headache. Julia Roberts was on the TV, running across an impossibly wide and green lawn. Why were people always running in these movies, I wondered. Why were they always hustling after love?

"Hi, Dr. Moore," Misty said.

"Hello, Misty."

"Do you think it was suicide?"

"I don't know."

She sank onto the couch beside him. "He was so young," she said. "He was beautiful and young and brilliant. He didn't deserve this."

"TBI," Dad replied.

"Can you help me?"

"Help you how?"

"With this," Misty said, "with all of this. You're supposed to be a brilliant psychiatrist. Don't you know anything about grief?"

"He's not really a clinician," I noted from behind her.

"At least answer one question," Misty said. "Will it get better?"

"I don't know," Dad said again.

"Can't you offer me anything?"

"Did Lukas offer you a drink?"

"She didn't want a drink," I said.

Dad paused the movie and sat for a long moment, looking beyond the frozen screen. "I don't know if it will be better," he finally said, "but it will be different. You won't always feel the way you do right now."

"That's not comforting," Misty said softly.

"I wasn't trying to comfort you. I was trying to tell you the truth."

I walked around so that I could see Misty's face. Her eyes bore into him. I almost stepped between them; I imagined that her intensity would be more than he could bear, but Dad seemed unphased. "It's not good enough," she said.

He barked a short laugh. "It rarely is."

"Are you laughing at me?"

"Misty, he's—" I began.

"I don't know what you think we've been doing here," Dad interrupted. "I don't know what you think this investigation has been about. Was it supposed to be therapeutic? Go make an appointment with one of my former colleagues. We've been after the truth. It was never going to make anyone feel better. If you can't take it, then you can leave."

"Jesus, Dad, she just . . ."

"She just what? Found out that her brother is dead? That he wasn't brainwashed and living some alternate life? Spare me. This story was never going to have a happy ending."

"You want to talk about truth?" Misty asked, rising from the couch. "Why don't you tell your son the truth? Tell Lukas where you were going, the night of your accident. Tell him who you were meeting. We know there was a woman waiting at that hotel. There's video, for Christ's sake, but Lukas is too scared to go and look at it. You're okay with stories that don't have happy endings? Tell your son what happened to his family."

No one moved for a moment. Dad gazed at Misty, his chin slightly elevated, as though appraising an interesting specimen. "Lukas knows what happened to his family," he finally said. "He's a smart boy, even if he never bothered to go to college, and he's been a raw nerve since the day he was born. I was what happened. If he wants specifics, then he is more than welcome to look at that video."

"You're a fucking psycho," Misty said. "I don't know if you were like this before you got brain damaged, but you are the last person I should have looked to for help." She glanced at me, opened her mouth to say something else, then turned and marched out the front door, slamming it behind her.

Dad and I were silent for a moment, him sitting on the couch and me standing beside him. Then he picked the remote up, pointed it at the screen, and restarted his movie.

CHAPTER SIXTEEN

"Lukas?"

"Hi, Mom."

"Are you all right?"

"Yeah, I'm sorry, I know you're at work. I just wanted to let you know, since you're probably not seeing local news: they found Jason Grant's body in Lake Prout."

"Oh, that's right, he was never found, was he? Oh dear, that's just terrible. Honestly, though, I'd half forgotten that he wasn't recovered."

"Yeah, um, he washed up and they found him, I guess."

"Just terrible. I'll send a basket of jam to Owen and Lucia. She's always been so delicate."

"That would be nice."

"Are you back in the city, Lukas?"

"No, I'm still here in Faith."

"I thought you were heading back after the last doctor's appointment."

"Well, I was hoping that appointment was going to help, but things didn't go exactly the way I'd planned . . ."

There was a rustling noise on the line, muffled voices, then: "I'm sorry, Lukas, I have to go, we're heading into an important deposition."

"Sure, Mom, no problem, I just thought you'd want to know. I love you."

"You too. I'll send the jam." The line went dead.

Al Pacino was screaming "Attica!" in the photo, but it looked to me like he was pissed off at having a screw through his forehead. I sat on my old bed, drinking coffee, watching as my father paced back and forth in front of the dry-erase board. It was covered in his scribbles, and the wall next to it was papered in documents from the Mullens Center. The sketchbook with the mystery woman lay on the dresser beside the photo of me as Hamlet.

Dad had taken to spending almost all his time in this room. Pizza boxes and Chinese food containers were piled beside the trash can. There were multiple wrappers for spicy falafels, which he insisted broke through the dulled sense of taste resulting from his brain injury. The overall effect did not smell good.

"Frankly," he said, "death changes nothing. Death was always the most likely outcome. What I want to know is whether he was truly right-handed. You spent time at the Grants' house when you were young. What did you see? How did he use a knife, for instance?"

"I don't know."

"You never saw him chop onions? You never saw him play Ping-Pong?"

"I don't know, I'm sorry. I can't remember."

"What about school? Where did he go to elementary school?"

I flipped open a notepad where I had compiled as much of Jason Grant's life story as possible, drawing on Misty's recollections and on material Mancini had passed to Dad from human resources. "East Faith Elementary from third grade on. He went to Our Lady of Peace until the second grade. Misty said that their father started getting building contracts for the public schools and he thought it would look bad if his own children weren't attending."

"Yes," Dad said, tapping the side of his face with a dry-erase marker he had failed to cap. "That makes a good deal of sense. The nuns hate lefties. The sinister hand, and all that."

"Sounds a bit medieval," I said. "This is the twenty-first century. Also, you're coloring your chin green."

"Religion is intrinsically quite medieval, Lukas," Dad said, "and so are many of its modern-day adherents. I wouldn't be at all surprised if they forced young Jason to write with his nondominant hand."

"I think you're getting too stuck on this, Dad. I think you're perseverating."

"Just because I've had a brain injury doesn't mean that everything I do is a symptom of the brain injury. The issue of lateral dominance is significant. If Jason was a true left-hander, then I find it doubtful that he would use his right hand to tie a knot at a moment of extreme stress. And if that is the case then it means that the knot was tied by somebody else. Unfortunately, we've made precious little progress in determining who might have done such a thing, or why. As to the latter, I continue to suspect that the answer lies with Garrett. He's an addict, and I don't for a moment believe he's doing construction when he's up in Boston. Jason had a secret meeting with him shortly before his disappearance. Yes, there is certainly something there, something having to do with the drug trade. There are plenty of ways a young physician can be drawn in."

"You're speculating," I said.

"I'm hypothesizing. We need to continue our investigation if we are to test our hypotheses. The girl in the sketchbook remains a dead end." He waved at the book on the desk. We had run a Google search of the framed photo of her on the couch, but with a book covering half her face we came up with nothing, other than a lot of porn. "We must pursue Lotus." Dad set the marker down and opened a fresh carton of spicy lo mein, launching into a rambling discourse that, punctuated by the intermittent slurping of noodles, converged on a set of propositions. First, that Jason Grant was head of the Mullens Center despite his junior status in the department of psychiatry. Second, that shortly before his death he had been drafting a proposal to apply for a great deal of funding for Mullens from a range of government and nonprofit institutions and asked Dad for help. Third, that Jason's own father, in his capacity as chairman of the board for the medical center, had also reviewed the proposal and suggested including among the funding sources a for-profit company that was a source of both patient referrals and donations to the center. This had set some sort of alarm bell off for my father, but it had been silenced by his unexpected meeting with a Toyota sedan.

"What's the big deal?" I asked. "So you weren't familiar with Lotus as a funding source. So what? They'd been giving money to Mullens, buying tables at galas and bricks in patios. Why not go back to them for another check?"

"I asked Jason about them," Dad said, "because I wasn't familiar. I don't think he wanted to include them. I think he was actually quite adamant."

"Why?"

"I have no idea."

I sighed and picked at my beef with broccoli. "What about the storage unit full of artwork?"

Dad snorted. "He should have stuck to psychiatry. A good residency program doesn't give its doctors time for hobbies. At any rate you're welcome to search for that girl, though I have no clue where you'd look. Meanwhile, we have an appointment in the morning."

"We do?" I asked. "Where?"

"Lotus. How better to learn more about the nature of their operation than as prospective clients? Don't look so distressed, Lukas. You're an actor and you need to practice acting. How is your little project going, by the way?"

"The revue? Fine, I guess. I actually need to get to rehearsal in a bit. We're working on blocking. The kids can be a little bit . . . challenging."

"Keep at it. It's good work. It has integrity."

Integrity. Just like the painting in Jason Grant's storage locker. Maybe it did have integrity, I didn't know. I didn't know a lot of things, including whether humoring my father's preoccupation with the ligature mark on Jason's arm and the now-defunct funding proposal would yield any insight into our former neighbor's death, or whether it would just prolong his sister's process of mourning.

I hadn't tried to walk Misty to school that morning. I wasn't sure whether she would go, but watching from our front window I saw her appear at the Quinlans' house right on schedule, Alice and Emery joining her on the sidewalk, Mrs. Quinlan drawing her aside for a moment to speak quietly and then giving her a hug and watching as she walked away with the children. I sensed that Mrs. Quinlan knew something about grief.

"Snap out of it, Lukas. I'm the one with the brain injury and you have sauce on your shirt. Get changed and go to work."

I set the Chinese food down and nodded. "All right. What will you do while I'm at rehearsal?"

"Where else would I be?" He gestured to the piles of empty food containers, the dry-erase board, the papers climbing the wall. "I'll be right here."

CHAPTER SEVENTEEN

"The problem is my son," Dad said. "I'm here to do something about my son."

"They know why we're here, Dad," I told him. "Just let her know that the Moore family is checking in and that we're ten minutes early."

The receptionist smiled up at us. "Please have a seat," she said. "Coffee, tea, and hot chocolate are on the sideboard."

I guided Dad to a chair across from a boy who looked to be sixteen or seventeen, seated between his parents. All three were on their phones and none of them looked up as Dad and I sat. The chairs were unusually comfortable for a waiting room, but everything about Lotus Consultants seemed to be comfortable.

"Maybe I'll have coffee," Dad said.

I rose and went to the Keurig, made two cups, then returned and handed one to him. I sat and studied the family across the room, wishing I could perform one of Dad's tricks and draw a brilliant inference or render a stunning diagnosis. Was there geographically specific mud on the boy's shoe? A vocationally telling rip in his pants? A medically significant blemish or scar somewhere on his exposed forearm? I had nothing except that he was probably high, and that was a slam dunk given that everyone in the waiting room could smell the weed.

They called us after five minutes. We were shown down a long hall into a large, sparsely furnished office and seated on a couch that looked too spindly to bear our weight. A handsome, well-dressed, early middle-aged man came in a moment later and introduced himself as Rafael, one of the codirectors. We shook hands and he sat across from us, crossing his legs and resting a slim manila folder on his knee. His black hair was slicked back and his clothes were extremely well tailored. "So, Dr. Moore," he said, studying the intake sheet. "Psychiatry at New Birmingham Medical Center. I would have thought we'd have collaborated before now."

"They keep me in the basement with the rats," Dad said.

"Ah, I've never been to the basement."

"What would we have collaborated on?"

"Our staff often works with the mental health professionals at NBMC, particularly in the Mullens Center."

"What are your qualifications?"

"Oh, we're not clinicians ourselves. We serve as consultants, connecting families with the right resources at the right time. Sometimes the Mullens Center is one of those resources; at other times patients who are already there need a next step."

"You're educational consultants," Dad said. "What does that have to do with psychiatry?"

"A heavily overlapping Venn diagram. Many of our clients struggle with mental health challenges. Sometimes these are causal, undermining their education, and sometimes they are downstream of a poor school match."

Dad leaned toward me. "A Venn diagram—" he began.

"I know, Dad."

The man smiled and turned to me. "Lukas."

"Hello," I said.

"Tell me about yourself."

"Well," I said, "I'm an actor."

"I see."

"Lukas didn't go to college," Dad said. "I'm a single father, on sabbatical from my research, and that has given me time to appreciate just what a miserable failure he has made of his life."

"Ah ha." Rafael raised his eyebrows and made a note in the file. I sipped my coffee. Dad and I had planned our story, though I didn't remember "miserable failure" from that conversation.

"I was referred by my colleague, Dr. Kwan," Dad continued. "He tells me that your firm is the best with situations like this, but I've never heard of you. How long have you been around?"

"I've personally been in the educational placement industry for fifteen years," Rafael said. "Lotus itself is a relatively new venture; we're coming up on our six-year anniversary. Our parent company has a tremendous amount of experience in the health care consultative market space, however."

"I see," Dad said.

"At Lotus, we don't use terms like 'failure,'" Rafael said.

"What if someone fails?" Dad asked.

"Define 'failure.'"

"Trying and not succeeding. Missing your mark. Coming up short. Not being good enough."

"Yes," Rafael said, "but what if there was a more useful framework?"

"It seems pretty useful," Dad mused.

"Lukas," our consultant said, wisely giving up on Dad and pivoting to me, "tell me about your goals."

"Well, I think I should go to college."

"Should?"

"Yeah. I mean, to get a job and all. It's hard to make a living as an actor."

Rafael glanced back at his file. "Your father went to Yale," he said. "Undergrad and med. That's quite a lot to live up to. And it looks like your mother was an attorney?"

"She still is," I said. "She's not dead."

"Of course."

"He doesn't have to go to Yale," Dad said. "Even with legacy, you have to be very talented to go to Yale."

I felt that Dad was leaning a bit too far into his role, but Rafael was up for it and I appreciated his efforts. "Everyone is talented," he said, "we just have to find out how, and how their talents are being obstructed. What is obstructing your talents, Lukas?"

"Um . . ." I said, waiting for Dad to pounce on the everyone-is-talented hypothesis. He apparently decided to let things play out. "Anxiety, I think?"

Rafael nodded and made another note. "Let's take a history."

Forty-five minutes later I had fleshed out my story and I was pretty damn proud of it. It felt good to flex my creative muscles again. I told Rafael about my background as an only child with unhappily married parents. I told him about a long history of anxiety and chronic stomach pain and the way that smoking pot made both problems go away when the doctors couldn't do anything about either of them. I told him about declining grades and getting busted for having a dime bag in tenth grade. I said that my grades had dropped and that I'd barely graduated from high school and I made my efforts to audition seem less like the serious artistic pursuit that they were and more like a hobby I used to pass the time between parties. I didn't include the bit about being cast as Stanley Kowalski because it made me sound too successful. The story was made up, mostly. There were elements of truth, though, more in the tone than in the facts. Enough that the telling of it bordered on being therapeutic. Dad sat listening, sipping his coffee and occasionally nodding.

Rafael took notes and when I was done speaking, he capped his pen and looked at me. "We can help you," he said.

"Oh," I said. "Good."

"How?" Dad asked.

The how turned out to be a plan that promised to be complex and detailed and ultimately withheld until we wrote Lotus a check. Rafael talked about the need for individualized assessment, which would be with a psychologist Lotus sent us to; and then for tutoring to get me in shape for the SAT, which would likewise be with a Lotus-connected tutor. He said they would produce a list of colleges that were compatible with my interests and my strengths and they would help me complete the applications and "strategize and optimize my responses to the essay prompts," again with college admissions coaches they could connect me with.

"It seems like you have quite a network," Dad said.

"We do," Rafael replied. "It's one of the chief benefits Lotus offers: frictionless transition to the services you need, in real time."

"What about the anxiety?" Dad asked. "What if Lukas needs more intensive treatment on that front?"

"We have those connections as well. Therapists, neuropsychologists, psychopharmacologists."

"Inpatient treatment?"

"If that were necessary."

"Where?"

"We have a relationship with the Mullens Center."

"He's too old."

"We can make arrangements. He'd have a private room."

"Is there someplace else? I work at the medical center."

"We have an exclusive arrangement with Mullens. We can arrange for your privacy, if it came to an inpatient admission."

"What does an 'exclusive arrangement' mean?" Dad asked.

Rafael shifted in his seat. "It means we have an excellent relationship with them. Open lines of communication. We know the staff there and they know us. We trust them to take care of our clients."

"And you won't send your clients anyplace else?"

"We're low on time," Rafael said, glancing at his watch. "This has been an outstanding conversation and I appreciate your coming in. I'll be writing up a proposal for a management package for Lukas and emailing it over within the next few days. Please stop at the front desk on your way out to take a packet outlining our cost structure." He leaned forward and looked at Dad. "Dr. Moore," he said, "we are always interested in psychiatric consultants. It's easy work. Per diem; you review files when you're available, flag the high-need kids who are most likely to be our cost centers. Work when you like, make very good money. Any interest?"

"I'll give it some thought," Dad said, in a tone that I recognized as indicating he would absolutely not be giving it any thought.

Five minutes later we were standing on the sidewalk. I paged through a glossy brochure and folder with papers outlining costs for packages that stretched well into the six digits. "That was sort of a waste of time," I said.

"What makes you say that?"

"I mean, what did we learn?"

"We learned what Lotus does."

"We knew what they do."

"I mean the service they really provide."

"Which is?"

"Access, Lukas. They sell access." He looked over my shoulder, taking in the menu of services. "Fuckers," he said. "Absolute sons of bitches."

"Easy there," I said as a woman walking by jerked her head up, looked at Dad with alarm, and gave us a wide berth.

"I've never seen such pure bullshit."

"I appreciated the part when he said I wasn't a failure."

"What's that? Oh, well yes, that's his job, isn't it?" Dad looked around, stepping off the curb to peer at a street sign a half block away. I grabbed his arm and pulled him back onto the sidewalk as the light turned and traffic started moving.

"What's your problem with them anyway?" I asked. "They're helping kids. They're helping people with stories like the one I told him."

"They're exploiting vulnerable people," Dad said. "They have no clinical credentials and they're taking ungodly sums of money to tell people with real problems that they're not failures, they're just obstructed, like psychiatry was some branch of gastroenterology. I mean, look at this! Just look!" Dad grabbed the folder from my hand, opened it to the sheet with price points, and shook it in the air. Other people were making sure to pass on the far side of the sidewalk. One man crossed against traffic to the other side of the street.

I took the papers from him and replaced them in the folder. The night before had been a hard one. Dad woke up three times: once to use the bathroom, twice with agitation. I was tired and my performance for Lotus had made me more tired still. I rubbed my eyes. "You should think about consulting," I said. "I mean, not with them, maybe, but there are probably other places, right? And you don't need your medical license if you're not seeing patients and you're not on staff at the medical center. You could keep busy, make some cash." It wouldn't hurt; his disability insurance was fairly generous, but nowhere near to what he and Mom used to make.

"Easy work?" Dad muttered. "Psychiatry should never be easy work. If it's easy you're doing it wrong. 'Cost centers'? My God."

My phone rang. I looked at the caller ID and answered. "Misty?"

"Lukas." She was out of breath.

"Where are you?"

"Out for a run. I just stopped at the Starbucks on north Main."

"What the matter?"

"Lukas, I'm being followed."

"By who?"

"I can't tell, but it has to be him. The Accountant. He's back."

CHAPTER EIGHTEEN

Early in *The Hound of the Baskervilles* Sherlock Holmes and Dr. Watson, determining that their client was being followed, decided to do the same, trailing him until they spotted the shadow. In the dinner theater production, we staged the scene in the audience, with me and the other actors dodging between tables and hiding behind waiters. It was supposed to be fun, though one night I got a plate of fettuccine Alfredo spilled in my lap as I tried to blend in with a family at table five.

Dad and I tried to do the same, minus the fettuccine. I drove back to Faith as quickly as I could. I'd told Misty to take the long way home and breathed a sigh of relief when I finally spotted her up ahead, jogging on the sidewalk. I slowed down and scanned the street, looking for a brown Volvo.

She had passed it three times before calling. She noticed it once because it was parked illegally but it really caught her attention the second time, when it pulled away from the curb as she passed and then seemed to idle beside her a bit too long. The third time it was parked across the street in a handicapped spot. She hadn't been able to see the driver's face, but the fender was dented in the rear and there was no question it was the same car.

Not seeing anything, I passed Misty and circled the block, reemerging behind her and driving as slowly as I could without seeming suspicious.

Still nothing. The third time, though, I saw it. The Volvo was parked along the side of the street beside a fire hydrant about a block and a half ahead of Misty, who was continuing at a steady pace. I slowed and pulled into an open spot on the right. Dad and I watched as Misty passed the brown car. Once she was half a block farther on it pulled out and followed. I gave it a moment and then did the same. "Jot down the plate number," I told Dad.

As I spoke, Misty, apparently tiring of the game, suddenly accelerated to a sprint. She turned off the sidewalk into a playground and dashed underneath a sprawling play structure, reemerging on the edge of a vacant soccer field and crossing it at an impressive pace. She was moving in the general direction of our homes. The Volvo wavered, as though the driver was considering following her off-road, and then sped away.

"Follow it," Dad urged.

"I'm trying," I said through gritted teeth. "I don't want to be obvious."

I managed to tail the car out of Faith. I lost him once as we entered New Birmingham but picked him up again and watched as he drove into a newer neighborhood and past a set of partially completed condo complexes.

"I hate this part of town," Dad said. "They're ruining the character of the whole city."

I had recently wondered whether he might downsize from the house in Faith to one of these units when I moved back to Manhattan. "They're not so bad," I said. "Some of them are attractive."

"Ticky-tacky," he replied. "Horrendous."

"Maybe keep an open mind? Wait, look, he's stopping."

The driver of the brown Volvo had pulled up in front of one of the buildings. A sign out front advertised rental units as available. I pulled over and we got our first sight of the driver as he climbed out of the car.

He was slightly built, as I remembered the Accountant being, and was wearing a knit hat despite the warmth. "I can't see his face," Dad said. The man bounded up the stairs and into the building.

"Come on," I said, getting out of the car. I jogged down the sidewalk, Dad right behind me.

"What are we going to do when we get to him?" he asked.

"I don't know," I said. "I've never done anything like this before."

Dad and I entered the lobby just in time to see the elevator doors close. We watched as the floor indicator rose to two, three, and stopped at four. We waited for the car to return and then rode it to the fourth floor, stepping out into a silent, empty hallway. "What are we going to do?" I whispered. "Knock on every door and ask if they were—"

"Shh." Dad held up a hand. There was a faint noise down the hall, the sound of a door closing and a lock sliding into place. "Come on." He hurried midway down the corridor, stopping at number 22B.

"Dad, I'm not totally sure—"

He pounded on the door. There was silence for a long moment. "I'm not sure this was the one," I murmured. Then the lock clicked and the door opened, and we found ourselves face-to-face with the woman from the sketchbook.

CHAPTER NINETEEN

She had been crying. Her eyes were red and she sniffled a bit as she reached up and took the knit cap from her head, the curly hair that was familiar from Jason Grant's sketches and the framed photo spilling down around her face. In her other hand she held a small gun, pointed directly at my father's chest. "Come in," she said softly.

I thought about running. I figured I could pivot and dash down the hall, maybe making it to the stairs beside the elevator before she could shoot me in the back, but I didn't think Dad would have the presence of mind to follow. It was a moot point anyway as he had already strolled into the apartment as though accepting an invitation for coffee. I clenched my fists and followed behind. "Close the door," she said. I obeyed.

The entry hall led directly into an open space that consisted almost entirely of paintings in various states of completion. They stood on easels and leaned against walls and milk crates and ranged from realistic depictions of New Birmingham and what I recognized as surrounding towns, parks, and nature scenes to works that were considerably more abstract, blocks of form and color taking up canvases that were at least as long as I was tall. Light spilled in from a floor-to-ceiling window on the far wall. There was no TV. The room opened to a kitchen on the right and a hall led away. The only place to sit was on a pair of sofas facing each other across a coffee table. Dad proceeded to one and settled himself, continuing to act as though he were on a simple social call. The woman sat across from him, gun still raised. I cautiously sat beside my father. He crossed one leg over another and looked around.

"Why are you following me?" the woman asked.

"We weren't following you," I said, "we were—"

"You've been following me since Faith," she interrupted, reeling off the streets and county highways we'd traveled together in the correct sequence.

"Why did you let us in?" Dad countered. "You could have kept the door locked and called the police."

The woman studied him. "I'm not interested in involving the police," she finally said. "What I'm interested in is finally getting some fucking answers."

Dad nodded. "About Jason Grant."

Her eyes widened and I flinched as the gun trembled. "Maybe let's go slow here, Dad," I murmured. "Let's not drop any bombshells without—"

"How did you know Jason?" she asked.

I cleared my throat, resting my trembling hands on my knees. "He was a neighbor," I said. "He was a friend. Well, sort of. I was more friends with his younger sister, Misty. And with Garrett, when we were younger. We've been, um, sort of looking into his disappearance."

"What's your name?"

"Lukas Moore."

"Jason never mentioned you. Who's this?"

"This is my father."

"Hello," Dad said, "I'm Dr. Richard Moore."

"You brought your dad?" the woman asked me.

"He has a condition," I said. "I have to keep an eye on him."

"What sort of condition?"

"Not a contagious one."

"Why were you following me?"

"Why were you following Misty Grant?" Dad replied.

"I told you, I want answers."

"And you think Misty has them?"

"I think Garrett Grant does but he left town again. If he knows things, then maybe his twin sister does too."

"Ah," Dad said. "That's actually very interesting. I assume you and Jason were lovers?"

"Dad," I said, "please." I turned to her. "Look, do you mind putting that gun down?"

"She's not going to shoot us, Lukas," Dad said. "It's a prop gun."

"What do you know about guns?" I asked.

"I did a bit of sport shooting when I was younger. My chief resident, Dr. Goldberg, came from a family with a big spread upstate. He had me up a few times. Have I mentioned the gorgeous Cavendish knots he used?" He turned his attention back to the woman. "By the way, did you ever see Jason shoot a gun? Play tennis? Kick a soccer ball? I'm very interested in establishing lateral dominance."

The woman stared at him and then turned to me, eyebrows raised.

"I promise it's not contagious," I said.

"Jesus Christ." She tossed the gun onto the table between us. "I'm not going to shoot anyone. I'm a goddamn medical student."

"Where do you go?" Dad asked.

"Harvard. I'm on a leave of absence."

"I'm a Yale man myself. College and medical."

"I knew I'd heard your name before. You're a psychiatrist at New Birmingham Medical Center."

"I am."

The woman nodded and considered for a moment. "My name is Joanna Bartlett," she said. "I spent a summer interning in psychiatry. Do you want coffee?"

"Yes," Dad said, "black."

Coffee was served in ugly, lopsided mugs that I recognized as Jason Grant originals. While it brewed Dad showed himself around, examining the canvases. "These paintings are terrible," he said. "Just terrible." Joanna and I both stared at him. "The still lifes are good quality," he continued, "but these abstract pieces? Nonsense." He turned his back to us and wandered to the window.

"I'm sorry," I said in a low voice. "You worked in psychiatry, right? He has a brain injury. A seven percent reduction in frontal lobe volume, according to the doctor. They had, like, scans from before, from an Alzheimer's study, though he doesn't have Alzheimer's. It's his brain. It's complicated."

"Are you sure he isn't just an asshole?" Joanna asked.

"That may be part of it too."

We resettled ourselves on the couches with our coffee. "Well," Dad said, "we know you and Jason were lovers. We've seen some very amateur sketches and a half-decent photo." I felt my face redden at my recollection of Joanna on Jason's couch with nothing but a book covering half her face, but she didn't seem to mind. "We know you were following Misty. I assume you were making an effort to gather information because they finally found the body." She did flinch at that but Dad plowed on, oblivious. "What I don't understand is why you don't simply speak with his parents or with the Faith police if you want information. Following his sister on her run seems like a poorly thought-through and frankly desperate strategy, even for a Harvard student."

"His parents don't know about me," Joanna said, "and I don't trust the police." She wrapped both hands around her mug. "If I tell you about my relationship with Jason, will you tell me what you know about his disappearance?"

I turned to Dad, setting a hand on his knee in warning.

"Don't worry, Lukas," he said, "she didn't have anything to do with his death. If she had, then the last place she'd want to be would be near his home and family, particularly so soon after the body turned up."

"You think someone killed him?" Joanna asked.

"We think it's possible," Dad replied.

"We don't know," I added. "We're sort of investigating."

"You're private investigators?"

"No. Well, sort of. We're not professionals."

"No shit." She took a deep breath and sized me up. "You don't look like him."

"Like Jason?" I asked, confused.

"Like the man he told me to be on the lookout for."

Dad leaned forward. "Slim, well-dressed, blond, with glasses?"

Joanna's eyes widened. "You've seen him?"

"At the memorial. Were you there?"

She shook her head.

"We call him the Accountant," I said. "What did Jason tell you about him?"

"That if I see him I should run the other way."

"I think it might be very valuable for us to share information," Dad said, his fingers drumming on the table, coffee forgotten. He was getting excited. He leaned back, body taut, and briefly sketched out the events of the last several weeks, beginning with the memorial service and Misty's pursuit of the Accountant; continuing to what Misty had revealed about her brother's last phone call and her aborted effort to hire a private investigator to look into his disappearance; our discovery of Jason's sketchbook and later his storage locker full of art; Dad's recovery of the fabled funding proposal and our undercover visit to Lotus.

"I share your suspicions about Garrett," he concluded. "I think Jason got in over his head and that it had to do with his brother. I don't know exactly what it was; my guess is that one of the Grant boys wound up owing the wrong people a good deal of money and they couldn't go to their parents for a loan. Fortunately for them Jason was assuming control of the Mullens Center, which as I understand it is essentially a big piggy bank. A lucrative, for-profit mental health program; more than that, he was looking to obtain much more funding. The two strands have to be connected. Some of that money must have been headed into his own pocket."

"How does Lotus fit in?" Joanna asked.

"I don't know yet, but I know I don't trust them. Owen wanted them added to the funding proposal. Maybe they let their father in on it, or at least part of it, and he suggested Lotus as a firm that could be helpful in moving money from one place to another."

Joanna thought for a long moment, sipping her coffee. "The thing about your theory," she said, "is that the Mullens Center would have been the solution to a problem for him. If he owed people money, or if his brother did, then you're saying that embezzling from Mullens might have been a way out."

"Precisely."

"But you're dead wrong," she continued. "He hated the Mullens Center. He thought the profit margins were obscene. He felt pressure to take the helm but he preferred the old, half-broke child psychiatry unit. The whole thing, the idea of working there, of running it—he despised it."

Dad leaned forward, picked his coffee up, and then set it down without drinking. "That doesn't make sense," he muttered. "It doesn't fit."

I cleared my throat. "Maybe you should tell us more about Jason and, you know, how he felt about things," I said to Joanna.

"I don't know where to begin."

"When did the two of you meet?"

They met the May before his disappearance. Joanna was originally from New Birmingham and returned from her first year of medical school to take a summer internship at the medical center. She wanted to be a surgeon and had a spot in orthopedics; when that fell through at the last minute, the only option was an opening in behavioral health. She thought she would hate it, find it boring and full of hopeless cases, but on the first day she met a young doctor who made child psychiatry seem like the most interesting and heroic thing in the world. Jason was her direct supervisor, and they kept the relationship, which was strictly against hospital policy, a secret. But at night he came to her apartment, and they sat on the rooftop and looked at the stars or lay in bed and talked about the lives they were changing. Jason told her that the right treatment, the right words at the right time, could make all the difference. He said that mental illness was like a river: at full strength you were rarely able to change its course, but if you met it at its source, where it is just a small creek, you could have a profound effect on everything that comes downstream.

Dad shifted in his seat beside me. "So he was a good clinician?" he asked.

"He was the best. We started seeing each other almost immediately. It was like a chemical reaction. He inspired me and I inspired him. Jason was interested in art but he had no experience. I've always painted, drawn, worked with ceramics. I actually went to the New Birmingham High School for the Arts. I encouraged him to try his own hand at it."

"You didn't meet his family?" Dad asked.

"No. Like I said, the relationship was a secret. He could have been fired, even though his father was chairman of the board."

"Did he talk about them? About Garrett?"

"Hardly ever. But I think something happened with them over the July Fourth weekend. They all went away together, to his uncle's place on Lake George."

"Uncle Frank?"

"Right. Jason went, and his parents and his brother and sister, and he was different when he came back."

"Different how?"

"Distant. Preoccupied. Upset, sometimes. They wanted him to take over Mullens, there'd been some sort of big talk with his dad. He was pissed. He threw himself into his art. He wanted me to show him everything I knew."

"Did you ask him what happened? What was bothering him?"

"Jason was a doctor, not a salesman. He liked talking to people, spending time with families. He went to meetings at kids' schools to help them understand his patients as they went back to their lives after the hospital; he didn't get paid for that part but he went anyway, on his own time. He didn't like the new center. It was too new, too . . . I don't know, ostentatious. He was always doing the math. That place is crazy expensive, almost all cash. Jason was constantly figuring how many new cases needed to come in. He had to have lunch with high-end community therapists and with these educational consultants, people who could refer cases. He hated it. He hated the consultants."

"It sounds awful," Dad agreed.

"Why didn't he quit?" I asked. "I mean, couldn't he have refused to be director of the center and just worked as a regular psychiatrist, if that's what he wanted?"

She shook her head. "I told him that too. He just said that he was under a lot of pressure, I assume from his father. And then, at the end of the summer, it went away."

"Went away how?" Dad asked.

"Like July Fourth, it was a trip to Lake George. His uncle had a Labor Day thing up there and off they all went again, and when he came back it was like a weight had been lifted. I was done with my internship, there were just a few days before I had to go back to Cambridge, but they were the best days of the whole summer. He was light, happy. It was like he'd been freed."

"Did he quit Mullens?" Dad asked.

"No. He was still talking about it but he had new plans. As I said, he thought the center was too lucrative, the profit margins too large. He said that if they were making that much money it meant they were catering exclusively to rich people. He wanted to reach underserved populations, kids who weren't getting care, people with shitty health insurance or no insurance at all."

"And he could do that?" Dad asked. "Take the center in a radically new direction?"

"That was the problem. He needed the board's approval."

"His father is chairman," Dad pointed out.

"I don't know where he stood. I just know that Jason needed to find an independent source of revenue. He was working on a big proposal. It must have been the one he showed you. That fall and winter he was in touch with me all the time, asking me to connect him with public health researchers at Harvard, people who have data on mental health service delivery. He was obsessed; as the fall went on it got more intense. He came up to Cambridge between Halloween and Thanksgiving, sort of to see me but mostly to have meetings with a group of statisticians who were working on an analysis of how the availability of psychiatric services impacts child and adolescent mortality."

"I know that work," Dad murmured. "It's reputable."

"So you were still together after you went back to Harvard?" I asked.

"We were. I came down to visit when I could, which wasn't as much as I would have liked. And he came up, though like I said he was obsessed with the center and with this proposal. He was still painting though. Not as much as he did the summer before, when I was in New Birmingham with him, but maybe a new piece every month or two. He did a piece that winter that I really liked. It was called *Integrity*."

"I saw it," I said. "I liked it too."

Dad stood, bumping the table and spilling his coffee. "This isn't right," he said, turning on his heel and pacing behind the couch. "It doesn't make sense. You're telling me that he was looking to make less money, not more."

"Maybe different money?" I suggested. "Maybe he wanted funding that was just his, not hospital revenue, so he could siphon off what he needed."

"Maybe," Dad said. "It's not a bad point, Lukas, though those sorts of grants are usually closely audited. If he wanted to embezzle then he would have been smarter to stick with clinical revenue."

"I don't think he wanted to embezzle anything," Joanna said, dabbing at the spilled coffee with a paper napkin. "Jason was a wonderful clinician. He was devoted. He wanted to help children who were slipping through the cracks. Even with him gone, some of his initiatives are still in place at Mullens. They're still doing good."

"True but irrelevant," Dad said. "Good people do bad things all the time. They trust the wrong people, make the wrong decisions, and before they know it they're in over their heads and have nothing in front of them but bad choices. If Jason was afraid for his life, or for his brother's, embezzlement may have been the only move he saw open to him." He stopped pacing and leaned over the back of the couch, eyes locked on Joanna. "You said you suspected Garrett," he said. "Why? And when did Jason warn you about the Accountant?"

She set the damp napkin to one side and studied her clasped hands. "The last time I saw him," she said softly. "A few days before he disappeared. He showed up in Cambridge without telling me he was coming. And an hour after he left, so did his brother."

Dad dropped a hand onto my shoulder, squeezing it so hard it hurt. "You've buried the lede here," he said. "I'll take another cup of coffee, and then I think you'd better tell us the rest of the story."

CHAPTER TWENTY

Jason Grant appeared at Joanna Bartlett's door in late March. It was freezing cold in Cambridge and there was a foot of snow on the ground. She hadn't known he was coming and she had a pathology seminar that afternoon, but she welcomed him in anyway. Almost a year after they'd met, what was supposed to be a summer fling had transformed, for her, into something more.

The weight that had been lifted from his shoulders at the end of the summer was back. Jason was distracted, anxious. He paced back and forth in her small apartment off Mount Auburn Street, sitting down and standing up, looking at her latest canvases without really seeing them. He said he was just there for an hour, on his way to a neuropsychiatry seminar in Portland. He stood by the window, peering out at the street, and when he left his last words to her were a warning about the man we referred to as the Accountant. "He didn't tell me the man's name," Joanna said. "I don't think he knew. But he described him just the way you did and he said that if I saw him—which I never did—I should get away, and he told me that if I was back in Faith or New Birmingham when I saw him, under no circumstances should I call the police."

"That also doesn't make any sense," Dad said. He was sitting next to me again and was as tense as a bowstring. Just being near him was making me nervous. "If he wanted to warn you about someone, he could have called. He didn't have to come all the way to Cambridge. Was there even a neuropsychiatric conference in Portland that day?"

"There wasn't," Joanna said quietly. "I checked. Later."

"So?" Dad continued, "Why come? There's something you're not telling us."

"I don't know," she admitted. "I never saw him again." Her hand trembled as she raised her mug to her lips. "What I can tell you," she continued, "is that Garrett arrived half an hour later and he had precisely the same questions: Where was Jason going, what was he doing, what had he told me?"

"You said his family didn't know about you," Dad said.

"They didn't. I recognized Garrett from photos in Jason's condo. I think he just assumed I was some random girlfriend."

"Did you tell him about Jason's warning?" Dad asked.

"No . . . I just, I told him Jason was on his way to Maine. I hadn't yet checked on the seminar story. I made it sound like it was casual, you know? Like he just dropped in to see me for, you know, a hookup or something." She shrugged. "He scared me."

"Garrett? Why?" I asked.

"Because he seemed scared. Scared, and angry."

"At you?"

"At his brother. He was only in my apartment for a few minutes; he clearly didn't buy the Portland story and he left when it was obvious I didn't know where else Jason might be going. He said something, though, that I remembered. I asked him why he was following his brother and he said that someone needed to explain to Jason that 'no one is too good to get their hands a little dirty.'"

We all sat quietly for a long moment. I felt that we were much closer to understanding Jason's movements than we had been when we arrived, but Dad was clearly dissatisfied. “The money still doesn’t fit,” he said. “I don’t like it. I don’t like it at all.” He stood. “Lukas, we must be on our way. We have friends coming to dinner.”

“We do?”

“Indeed, and we need to pick up some wine.”

I rose. “Dad, you really need to give me the heads-up about these sorts of plans.” I turned to Joanna. “May I use your bathroom?” I asked.

“Down the hall.”

“What kind of paints do you use?” Dad asked.

I walked down the hall, letting the two of them chat about the chemical properties of oils versus acrylics. The bathroom door was open on the left and there was a closed door on the right. It was, I realized, the only closed door in the place. It was probably her bedroom, though why close your bedroom door when you’re home alone? I glanced back over my shoulder and then opened the door, slipped in, and froze. It might be a cliché to describe the hair standing up on the back of my neck, but that is exactly what happened.

The paintings were all the same. I mean there were differences, of course. Some were at night and some during the day, some in the fall with foliage in full glory and some in the dead of winter, the trees stripped bare. A few were in the rain, it seemed, and in one the world was frozen. But they were all of the same place. I recognized it from my visit with Misty, from my ill-fated swim. I saw the rock where she had peed and I had changed. The room was full of painting upon painting upon painting of the spot where Jason Grant had disappeared.

“Do you see one you like?”

I jumped. Joanna had come in behind me.

“The bathroom is across the hall.”

"I like that one," I said. It was leaning against the wall, a nighttime scene with a full moon over the water. It looked the way the lake had looked the night I had been there.

"Ah." Dad also came into the room, squeezing behind us. "Now, these are very good. You shouldn't keep them in the back." He looked around for a moment, lips pursed. "Well," he finally said, "I suppose there are some things that can't be left behind."

"If they can, it hasn't happened yet," Joanna replied.

Dad nodded. "Lukas, you're the frontal lobe of our operation, but I believe we are running late."

I followed him out, Joanna closing the door to the room with the paintings and trailing behind us, silent. I wasn't sure what to say.

"Get a cat," Dad suggested, pausing in the doorway. "This building has mice. *Peromyscus leucopus*, or the white-footed mouse. A few of your canvases are good quality and it would be a shame if they were chewed on. Also, the paint thinner by the toaster has been recalled because it's carcinogenic in sixty-two percent of adult rabbits, and the radiator closest to the kitchen is going to start leaking next winter. Put some of the abstracts over there; don't let the good stuff be water damaged." He walked out into the hall.

"Thanks for talking to us," I said. "I hope you, uh, get a lot of good painting done. I'll give you my phone number, in case you think of something else." I jotted it on a scrap of paper and then turned and hurried after my father, trying to catch up with him before he reached the street.

CHAPTER TWENTY-ONE

Dad charged past the chardonnay, past the merlot and the malbec and the cabernet. He paused when he reached the mezcal, apparently realizing he had gone too far, and turned back. He stood in the center of the aisle staring down at the cracked and peeling linoleum.

"What are we serving?" I asked.

"It's wrong, Lukas," he said. "Something's wrong."

"Maybe I'll get a white and a red?" I suggested. "Just to cover the bases. Everyone likes merlot, right?"

Dad's mood had steadily deteriorated since leaving Joanna Bartlett's apartment. He sat silently in the car, chewing on a knuckle, one knee bouncing at a steadily rising frequency. I selected a bottle of merlot and a bottle of pinot grigio more or less at random, paid, and ushered him back to the car. "Look," I said, getting in behind the wheel and driving out of the liquor store parking lot, "you said it was a hypothesis, right? I mean, I'm not a scientist or anything, but I thought the whole concept was to test hypotheses, prove or disprove them, and then come up with a new theory. Isn't that how it works?"

Dad looked out the passenger side window, his fingers drumming on the door handle. It was starting to rain. "I don't know," he said. "I don't know if I can do it anymore."

I knew exactly what he meant. He couldn't shift gears. He couldn't get off one track and onto another. He'd had a theory, a way of looking at things, and Joanna's story had disrupted it by suggesting that Jason Grant wasn't interested in easily accessing a large pool of money; quite the contrary, in fact, and Dad couldn't cope.

"Try to relax," I said. "Maybe some of the deep breathing they had you practice at the rehab hospital? We'll be home in ten minutes. It will be good to have people over."

I hoped it was true. We hadn't hosted a thing in the months since he got home from the hospital, but we had to start somewhere.

Derek towered over Dr. Mancini. While the pathologist was a slender Italian who was five foot six at most, Derek was a Black man who had to be six four, maybe six five. He was wearing gray slacks with a red blazer and he had a diamond stud in one ear and I immediately aspired to dress like him and knew that I could never pull it off. "Welcome," I said, "please come in."

The two bottles of wine sat on our table next to a pile of empty plates. I'd ordered Chinese from the nicer of the two options in Faith. Mancini and Derek brought two bottles as well, and while Mancini brought them to the kitchen and Dad looked for a bottle opener, Derek walked along the bookshelves lining the far side of our living room. "Well, well," he said, "look at you."

I walked over to join him. I didn't spend a lot of time looking at the framed pictures on the shelves and they hadn't been touched or rearranged since Mom left. There was her and Dad on their wedding day, looking like different people who had not yet encountered the pressures and dissatisfactions life would bring. A picture of me as a baby in a bassinet. The three of us captured sitting on a park bench by a forgotten photographer. My school pictures up until sixth grade, the onset of the clunky years. Derek was looking at one of me, alone, holding a massive chocolate ice cream cone with a dab of the stuff on the tip of my nose, grinning at the camera. "I was a cute kid for a minute there."

He chuckled. "You were." He turned his attention to the rows of books. "I figured your dad for a science reader, maybe popular histories, but there are quite a few novels here."

"Those were Mom's."

"And plays."

"Mine."

"Angelo says you're an actor."

It took me a moment to connect Angelo to Mancini. "I am. On hiatus right now, though I guess I am doing a little bit of work with the Down Syndrome Foundation."

"Oh yeah? What kind of work?"

"A summer showcase. Sort of a musical theater thing. I'm just helping to direct a couple of numbers. It's a fundraiser."

"That's wonderful."

I shrugged.

"You have a gap."

I followed Derek's gaze to a space on the fourth shelf, like a missing tooth in a smile. "Mom took those when she left."

"What were they?"

"*Anne of Green Gables*. The whole series, first edition."

"I read those books when I was young," Derek said. "I loved them."

"So did she." I remembered when she bought them. It had been a birthday when I was too young to get her anything myself but old enough to know what was going on, and Dad had forgotten and hadn't bought her a gift. I think he came home from work with a card he'd picked up on his commute and Mom didn't say anything, but a week later a package came in the mail and she unwrapped those books and said that if she had to take care of her own birthday then she was going to get something she really wanted. I don't think he even noticed.

"Wine," Dad announced behind us, appearing with two glasses of red and pressing one into Derek's hand and one into mine.

"The food will be here soon," I said. "I'm sorry it's running late."

"Not at all," Derek said. "It gives us time to talk."

"And drink," Mancini said, emerging from the kitchen with his own glass. Derek and I moved away from the shelves and sat on the couch. Dad and Dr. Mancini came in and sat in the armchairs flanking the TV across from us.

I was surprised to see that Dad had a glass of wine in his hand. "This is very good," he said, sipping.

"Derek chose it," Mancini said.

"We had to be together for two years before he would let me select the wine," Derek said. "It almost broke us up."

"He's pigheaded," Dad said, "but he's no fool. Now, Mancini says you had a chance to look into the question I had?"

"I did," Derek said. "It's actually very interesting. This firm you're interested in, Lotus, seems to be a subsidiary of Burned Stone partners, a corporation registered in the Cayman Islands that has additional subsidiaries, including Hiring Consultants, the firm that manages personnel and HR for the medical center." Derek went on for a few minutes about the intricacies of the corporate structure.

"You really think this is interesting?" Mancini finally asked him.

"What do you know?" Derek said, "You think decomposition is a kick. I haven't gotten to the interesting part anyway."

"Yes," Mancini said, "I know."

The doorbell rang. I stood and collected the bags of food, bringing them to the dining room. I threw away the chopsticks that came with the meal and brought forks to the table, not wanting to exacerbate Dad's frustration with fine motor skills. We rearranged ourselves, pouring more wine. Mancini caught me staring at Dad's second glass. "Merlot pairs well with neurological injury," he said with a wink. I wasn't so sure. We sat and passed the food.

Derek turned back to Dad. "All right now," he said, "the part I'm coming to is speculative, and it's sensitive. Angelo knows what I think, but I wouldn't be saying it if I wasn't among friends whom I could trust, okay?"

Dad set his fork down and nodded. I did the same.

Derek rubbed his hands together and glanced at Mancini, then back at us. "Have you noticed the lines in the lobby?" he asked.

Dad frowned. "The hospital lobby? I've noticed the malfunctioning fountain. I suppose the line was a little long when we were there for my last appointment. The front desk seemed understaffed."

"Everything is understaffed," Derek said. "Understaffed and mis-staffed. Unqualified people in jobs they should not be in. I have a master's in health administration; there are people higher than me in the organizational hierarchy now who haven't finished college. There isn't enough staff at the front desk or in the cafeteria. Custodial is shorthanded too; there are bathrooms that only get cleaned once a week, if that."

"Derek's unhappy about the bathrooms," Mancini said through a mouthful of egg roll.

"I'm unhappy about all of it. I've spent my career at NBMC. I care about it. I'm not a doctor like you two, but I do my part. No margin, no mission, you know?"

"How long has it been like this?" Dad asked.

Derek considered. "Hiring Consultants started taking over personnel operations about six years ago, shortly before the big expansion. That was the start of it. That's what's interesting; I've had a bad taste in my mouth about them for some time and now it turns out you have questions about this other firm, Lotus, which is owned by the same parent company but has nothing to do with the medical center."

"Not nothing," Dad said. "Lotus seems to have been sending both clients and donations to the Mullens Center. So what do an incompetent HR subcontractor and an educational consulting firm have in common, other than ownership?"

"I'm not sure HR is just incompetent," Derek said. "Over the last few months there have been a few cases that may spill over into actual fraud."

"Such as?" Dad asked.

"Michael Porter."

"Who?"

"One of the three night watchmen."

"Oh. I wouldn't know him."

"Neither would I," Derek said. "I'm a nine-to-fiver. You know who might? Angelo. There was an incident a few months ago, nothing terrible, but a vagrant who'd been in the ER, high on something, walked out into the hospital at two A.M. and wound up wandering into the morgue and threatening Angelo."

Mancini waved his fork. "It was nothing. I calmed him down and walked him back up to emergency medicine. I probably would have been a good psychiatrist, Richard."

"Doubtful," Dad grunted.

"The point is," Derek said, "Angelo mentioned that the security seemed light during the night shifts and I was pissed and looked into it. And you know what I found? One of the three men on the payroll, Michael Porter, a man with a full HR file—photo, Social Security number, everything—does not seem to exist outside of our records and certainly has never reported for work at the medical center."

"Have you told anyone else about this?" Dad asked.

Derek shook his head. "Angelo didn't want me to. I work in billing, not HR. We're still our own department, for now. I stay in my lane. The only reason I'm telling you is because you wanted background on Lotus."

Dad nodded. "They, in contrast, seem to be legitimate. Lukas and I went, posing as clients. I find them obnoxious, elitist, and full of crap, but they are charging real money and, as far as I can tell, providing real services."

"Who knows, though?" I asked. "To me it was all corporate BS. I mean, companies say things all the time. It's their job to make it sound good. They talk a good game while dumping chemicals in some poor person's backyard, or shit like that." I'd had two glasses of wine and was speaking freely.

Derek nodded. "You're right. So, you know who can tell you the real story?"

"Who?"

"The person with a backyard full of toxic chemicals."

"Which is who in this case?" Angelo asked.

"A dissatisfied customer," Derek said. "Someone who gave Lotus a lot of money and then got pissed off with their service, like a customer at an expensive restaurant who finds a hair in the soup."

"How do we find someone like that?" I asked. "I've looked online; it's scrubbed clean. There are no complaints, no bad reviews."

"You said they're sending kids to the Mullens Center," Derek said. "I'm sure it's great up there, but not all those kids get better, right? Some probably get worse. Seems like a question for the psychiatric department." He looked at Dad.

Dad turned to Mancini. "I like him," he said. "I'm sorry we haven't spent time much together before. When you said you were seeing someone in billing I was skeptical because they're mostly idiot trolls, but I approve."

"Yes," Mancini said, "I'm quite in love with him. Lukas, pass the soy sauce, please."

Derek, Mancini, and Dad spoke for a few more minutes about the expansion at the medical center, the noise and the endless lines of trucks clogging up the roads, the frustration of new doors that didn't close and roof leaks in the wintertime, the general trend of the discussion being that they didn't build things like they used to. It then drifted even further, into department financing, and I was bored and poured another glass of wine. A few minutes later, as we were clearing the table, I looked across at Dr. Mancini. "Do you think you'll stay together?" I asked.

"Who, me and Derek? Perhaps. Why do you ask?"

I shrugged. "Someone has to. I'd like to see somebody live happily ever after, just to know it's a possibility."

He laughed and picked up a stack of dirty plates. Dad and Derek were in the kitchen. "You're a romantic, Lukas. That's my diagnosis, and unfortunately it's untreatable. You are a romantic."

"I suppose maybe I am."

"I'll tell you a secret," he said. "I am, too." I looked at him, and he chuckled. "You think that a man who stands over dead bodies all day can't be a romantic? Just because I see how every story ends doesn't mean that I can't have hope for the earlier chapters. Hope for love, hope for integrity."

A plate broke on the kitchen floor; Dad and Derek howled with laughter. "We're okay!" Derek called.

"Don't worry," Mancini said, "I'm driving home." He winked at me and carried the rest of the dishes out of the room.

We hadn't planned for dessert. I searched the freezer for something passable, but Mancini and Derek said it was all right and that they needed to be going. Dr. Mancini had some lab results he wanted to show my father and while he struggled to bring them up on his phone and the two of them spoke in low voices in the kitchen, I stood with Derek in the front hall. "Your father is a decent guy," he said. "He's a good friend."

"Really?" I asked.

"Really. When Angelo and I were first together we didn't have many friends at the hospital who we felt that we could tell. Not many friends anywhere, really. And I didn't want him to tell your father, but you know what he said?"

"What?"

"He said: 'Richard Moore is a giant pain in the ass and he is the only doctor in this hospital more arrogant than I am, but he is a good man all the way through.'"

Dad and Mancini emerged from the kitchen, Mancini tucking his phone into the inner pocket of his jacket. "It's interesting," Dad said. "You'll continue to look into it?"

"Yes," Mancini said. "It's nothing definitive. It's nothing that anyone could swear to under oath. But it's a fascinating little side project and I'm doing some digging on the biochemistry of it. I'll let you know."

My father clapped him on the back.

"Angelo," Derek said, "I'm drunk. Take me home."

Angelo smiled and turned to me and Dad. "Thank you for having us," he said. "Next time at our place."

We all shook hands and then the two of them headed for their car and I shut the door. I went to the bathroom and when I returned Dad was standing in front of the bookshelf. "What are you doing?" I asked.

"Nothing. I don't read as much as I used to. I can't focus well enough." He turned away, kicked off his shoes, and collapsed on the couch.

"How much wine did you have?" I asked him.

"Too much," he said, stretching out. He shut his eyes. "Maybe it fits after all, Lukas. Maybe it's drugs, not cash. Maybe Jason and Garrett calculated that it would be easier to funnel drugs through a center serving a high volume of poor patients than through a boutique clinic for a smaller number of rich ones. I should go upstairs . . ." He started to sit up, then wavered.

"Maybe give it a rest for the night?" I suggested. He lay back and almost immediately started to snore.

I put the leftover Chinese food away and stepped into the hopelessly cluttered garage to drop the empty wine bottles into recycling. I slid the door open and maneuvered the bin down to the curb for morning pickup and then I stood by the street for a moment, enjoying the air and the silence. Emery, for once, did not appear to be launching anything. Mrs. Macarthur was not out walking her semi-incontinent dog. I looked up the hill, toward the Grant home, and saw a pinprick orange flare in the trees off to the left. It was the spot, invisible to the front door camera, where Garrett and Jason had presumably met just days before Jason's disappearance.

I glanced over my shoulder to where Dad lay sleeping in the house. I would just take a moment. I walked up the street and across the Grants' lawn to the trees. The ember flared every few moments ahead of me.

"Hello, Lukas."

"Hello, Garrett."

He stood under the low branches of a sapling, one hand in his pocket, the other holding a cigarette. He was dressed in his construction clothes. He took another drag, studying me. The wind picked up a bit, rustling the leaves overhead.

"I'm sorry," I said, "about Jason. I haven't seen you since . . . well, I'm sorry."

"I've mostly been in Boston."

"Ah."

"It wasn't exactly a surprise, you know."

"I know. It still seems hard."

"So's life."

"Yeah."

Garrett continued to smoke. He continued to look at me. It was unnerving.

"So, you're doing okay?" I finally asked.

"Here's the thing, Lukas." Garrett half turned, grinding his cigarette out against the trunk of the sapling and flicking it into the darkness. "The thing about having a brother like Jason, and I know you won't appreciate this, being an only child and all, but take my word for it: He sucked the air out of every room he was in. Ever since he was a kid. If Jason had a basketball game, we were going to watch basketball. If it was hockey, we were going to watch hockey. If Jason didn't feel like pizza, we were getting Thai. That's just the way it worked. And the problem wasn't that no one cared what I wanted for dinner; the problem was that, after a while, I couldn't have told them what I wanted if they had asked. Whatever was going on inside was useless information. So, am I doing okay? I don't know. I never fucking know." He tapped another cigarette out of a box and studied it, rolling it back and forth between his thumb and a finger.

"You know how you asked me what I remembered about your family?" I asked. "The day you dug up the Matchbox cars. I remember that Jason was always good at everything. Sports, school; he was popular. He never made anyone laugh though. That was always you. You made everyone laugh. Especially me."

Garrett nodded, eyes on the cigarette. "It's been a long time since I made anyone laugh."

"Yeah. Well, hit me up if you ever want to try."

Garrett glanced at me, then flipped the cigarette into his mouth and drew a lighter from his pocket. The breeze was in his face and he turned his back to strike a flame, but he did not turn back. I left him and walked back down the hill to my house, letting myself in and locking the front door. I changed and inflated the air mattress and turned out the lights. I lay down and tied one end of the cord to my left wrist and then reached out to tie the other end to Dad's right.

Maybe it was all beside the point, I thought. Maybe all my father's suspicions about the research proposal and the Mullens Center and Lotus, the detailed machinations taking shape on the dry-erase board up in my room, maybe it was irrelevant. Maybe whatever happened to Jason Grant had been rooted in something far more basic. Dad said it, standing in the back room of Joanna Bartlett's apartment, looking at painting after painting of Lake Prout: there are some things that can't be left behind. Maybe jealousy was one of those things. Resentment. Emptiness, or whatever feeling Garrett was trying to channel when he said that he couldn't have told his parents whether he wanted pizza or Thai food.

Was it worth killing for? Maybe it was. Maybe if a story went on long enough a person would do anything to bring it to an end. Listening to my father's drunken snores beside me, it at least seemed plausible. I rolled to one side, careful not to tug on the line, and went to sleep.

CHAPTER TWENTY-TWO

"I don't have a plan for this contingency," Dad called from the other side of the fence. "Nothing at all."

I stared at the dog's teeth, bared in a snarl. "You don't have a plan for any contingency," I called back, careful not to make any sudden movements.

The original plan had been mine, the inspiration Derek's, and Dad's support was technical. We set out to find a dissatisfied customer from Lotus by cross-referencing referrals listed as coming from the consulting group with hospital and county health records and soon discovered something unexpected: as many as one in ten of the patients listed as coming from Lotus seemed not to exist. "I don't understand," Dad said, staring at his paper-covered study wall. "They're registering these patients but they're ghosts, just like the night watchman. But how does the money work? They're not billing an insurance company for the care. They're not billing a ghost family. They're just creating names on paper and turning handsome profits."

I didn't know. I was, at that point, dividing my focus between the investigation and my plans for the musical revue. Dad, meanwhile, tracked down the real-life patients who had been referred to the Mullens Center by Lotus and then narrowed those to families living reasonably nearby and from that smaller pool picked several whose cases, according to the county, had ended particularly poorly. This was the third of those; after the first two hung up on us we decided to try arriving unannounced, so after lunch we made our way to a two-family house in New Birmingham with a locked door and a broken buzzer. Dad suggested I go around back and see if I could spot any signs of life, which was how I found myself face-to-face with a Doberman.

"Dad," I said, trying to keep my voice steady, "go get your leftovers from the car."

"My leftovers?"

"The burrito," I said. "Get the goddamned burrito."

Dad had insisted on going by a Mexican place with hot sauces that reportedly managed to punch through his post-TBI blunting of taste. I heard his retreating footsteps, the car door open and then close, and his return. "Throw it," I said, "aim for the far corner of the yard, over by the shed."

A moment went by during which I imagined my father, standing behind me, safely on the other side of the locked gate in a chain-link fence I had just climbed over, weighing the relative merits of a delicious double bean, beef, and cheese grande versus the life of his only child, a son who had, after all, failed to earn a single college credit by the age of twenty-three. Then the foil-wrapped burrito sailed overhead. It landed with a thud in just the right spot. The dog's head swiveled, he sniffed, and then he bounded toward it.

"Run, Lukas!" Dad called.

It was terrible advice. I ran and the dog, no fool, saw one meal that would sit nicely until later and one that was rapidly escaping. He barked once and came after me.

I ran as hard as I could and the fence was not far, but the dog was faster. I grabbed the chain-link and placed one foot high on it, preparing to swing the rest of my body over, a position that offered my ass to the approaching Doberman. It took full advantage, sinking its teeth in on the left side.

It was not a gentle scream. The feeling of being bitten is primal and visceral, another animal trying to wound and consume you. I screamed not only in pain but in protest, sending my objection to the gray clouds hanging over New Birmingham that day. I screamed even though the dog did not care, was probably excited by it, and I screamed rather than doing something functional, like getting the rest of my body over that fucking fence.

Dad saved me. He leapt forward, grabbing me by the collar with one hand and reaching around with the other to seize the animal by its jaws. He was incredibly strong, having applied his overdone version of physical therapy for months, and he immediately pried the dog off and lifted me over the fence like I was a child. My knees gave out and I clung to him. The dog snarled and barked inches from my face but safely on the other side of the chain-link. A door banged open behind us. "Just what the hell is happening out here?" a voice said.

"I need first aid supplies," Dad said, "and I need to see this dog's vaccination records or I am taking it to New Birmingham Medical Center, decapitating it, and having a pathologist examine it for rabies."

There was a moment of silence as I struggled to my feet and turned. A woman was standing on the porch. She wore a baggy, shapeless dress and canvas slip-on shoes and she held a cigarette in one hand. She was probably in her early fifties and had brown hair that hung around her shoulders. She took a drag and looked from one of us to the other. "It's not my dog," she finally said.

"That," Dad responded, "is entirely irrelevant."

The woman walked to the edge of the porch. The dog looked at her and barked. "Shut up, Princess," she said. It obeyed.

"Your dog's name is Princess?" I asked.

"I told you, it's not my dog. I didn't name her, and I don't care if you decapitate her. Who the hell are you people and what were you doing in my backyard?"

"We're looking for Dakota Flynn," Dad said.

"That's me."

"We want to talk to you about Ford."

The woman's eyes narrowed and she took a hard pull on her cigarette, then dropped it to the porch and ground it beneath her shoe. "Why the fuck would you want to do that?"

"Tell her who you are," I whispered.

"My name is Dr. Richard Moore. I'm a psychiatrist. I'm investigating adverse outcomes at the Mullens Center over at NBMC. I understand that you had one."

"It was about as goddamned adverse as you can get," Dakota Flynn said, "but why would I want to talk about it?"

"Because we want to do something about the situation," Dad said.

"With all due respect, doctor, I'm not interested in helping to make that place better by telling you all the ways they failed my son."

"I don't care about making it better either," Dad said. "But I would like to protect the next family with a vulnerable child who has the misfortune to be sent to Mullens. And to Lotus Consultants."

"How did you know we were with them?"

"It's in the record. The hospital tracks referral sources."

"What did you say your name was?"

"Dr. Moore. Richard Moore. This is my son and assistant, Lukas."

"Hello," I said, one hand clutching my punctured and bleeding ass cheek.

"She bit you on your rear?" the woman asked me.

"She sure did."

"Well," she said, "you'd better come inside."

I hobbled up the steps to the front porch and went into the house. There was a closed door to my left and a flight of stairs to my right, and to my dismay Dakota went up them. I gripped the banister and followed, each step burning. "Hurry up, Lukas," Dad said.

"I'm going as fast as I can," I hissed. "A fucking dog tried to eat me."

"She wasn't going to eat you," Dad said from the stairs behind me. "She was just defending her territory. We do need to worry about rabies, however."

"Great."

"We'll have the dog tested if there's no proof of vaccination."

I imagined Dad walking into Dr. Mancini's morgue with a Doberman struggling in his arms, decapitating it with the largest knife on hand, and then passing the head to Mancini for analysis of the neural tissue or whatever it was they did to look for rabies. I thought that the pathologist would take it in stride, probably pop a Life Saver into his mouth and dig in. I found it strangely comforting and almost funny, and despite my pain I had to stifle a laugh.

The steps led to another door and through it an apartment. Dakota Flynn stood to one side and watched us come in. I scanned the living room. The walls were lined with bookshelves, the kind you assembled yourself and nailed a cheap, thin backing to, and the shelves were filled with books. Books and plants. Green leaves popped out everywhere and vines wound their way from shelves down to the floor. There was an old couch, a worn chair with a reading lamp positioned behind it, and in the corner a very old woman sat by the window, an oxygen canister beside her and a clear tube snaking up to her nose. She watched impassively as Dad and I entered and Dakota closed the door. "Bathroom is that way," she said.

I walked down the hall and into the bathroom. Dakota followed, opened a linen closet with a half-size door, rummaged, and came out with a first aid kit, which she handed to me. "I'm sorry about the dog," she said. "It's my downstairs neighbor's. George. I don't like him, or his dog, but I don't use the backyard anyway and Princess guards the house, so . . ." She shrugged and left me holding the red kit.

Dad entered and shut the door. "Drop your pants," he said.

"Absolutely not. Let's do this interview and then you can take me to urgent care."

"You want a strip mall doctor to take care of you? I went to the Yale University School of Medicine."

"You're a research psychiatrist with a suspended medical license."

"You need that wound cleaned. Drop your pants; I used to change your diaper."

"I am confident that you never once changed my diaper."

"I must have." He frowned. "I'm sure I did, didn't I? Maybe when your mother was sick?"

I drew my hand away from the back of my pants. It was sticky with blood. I did need help. "All right," I said. I unbuckled my pants and pulled them down, turning to the sink. Dad lifted the back of my shirt and studied the injury.

"It's not bad," he said. He opened the first aid kit on the closed toilet seat and rummaged around for a few moments. "Hold on," he finally said. "This is going to sting."

It did, but he cleaned the wound well and applied an adhesive bandage supported by a good deal of medical tape, and five minutes later we made our way back to the living room where Dakota Flynn was sitting near the old woman, smoking another cigarette, looking at her phone.

"Should you be doing that by the oxygen?" I asked.

Both women looked at me. Neither spoke. Dakota took a long draw and tapped her ash into a can of Diet Sprite. "You had questions for me?" she asked. "About Ford?"

"First I have questions for this neighbor, George," Dad said. "Stay here, Lukas."

"I don't think that's a good idea," I said. "Why don't we—"

But Dad was already through the front door and down the stairs. I stood, awkwardly leaning against the wall in the doorway leading from the living room back to the bathroom, and the two women and I looked at one another as down below we heard Dad pounding on a door and then the door open and a man ask him who he was and what he wanted and then Dad go inside and the voices become fainter and more muffled. I knew that I should go down to intervene, but frankly I did not want to navigate the stairs other than to leave this place for good and I also did not mind the idea of Dad losing his temper with the owner of that dog. I heard him say "records" and "rabies" and the sound of the other man's voice, then furniture shifting, then a long period of silence. Then Dad was coming back up the stairs and into the Flynns' apartment, closing the door behind him. He nodded once to me. "We're all set, Lukas. The dog's records are up to date."

"Well, that's a relief."

Dad sat on the couch, facing the women. I remained standing, not wishing to stain their furniture or to experiment with the effect that sitting would have on my injury.

“This is Ford’s grandmother,” Dakota said. “My mother.”

Dad nodded to the woman. “Pleased to meet you. I’m Richard Moore, and this is my son, Lukas.”

“I told her you were investigating Lotus Consultants and the Mullens Center. She wants me to talk to you.”

The older woman’s expression did not change but something flickered in her eyes. Dakota withdrew another cigarette. I flinched as the lighter flared. Dad said nothing. She took a drag, situated the soda can on the windowsill so that it aligned with her arm, draped over the back of her chair, and began.

Ford Flynn died when he was sixteen years old. He died by suicide, on Halloween night, jumping off a newly constructed fifteen-story building in downtown New Birmingham into the upper Hudson River where it snaked through town on the way south to its far larger and more cinematic incarnation in the big city. She noted that the building’s janitor had locked the door to the roof three hours before he jumped and that the police inferred that he had been hiding up there and had therefore spent at least three hours contemplating his act before completing it. She related all this with little expression and with the support of two more cigarettes, pausing to suck on them so hard that I thought she would aspirate the filters. Dad listened carefully, nodding his head a little but otherwise sitting very still. I watched him as much as I watched her, wondering what he was getting from this terrible story.

“Tell me about the care he received,” he said.

“Oh, he received all sorts of care. Therapists and psychiatrists. Nothing helped. I’m a social worker myself, not working anymore but I have a master’s from Rutgers, and I’m convinced that most mental health science is common sense watered down by snake oil and dressed up in whatever jargon is in fashion. No offense, Dr. Moore.”

"None taken," Dad said. "When and why did you connect with Lotus, and how did you afford them?"

"You think we're poor?"

"You're a retired social worker and this apartment is not in the nice part of town. Lotus is in the business of selling access to rich people."

"You speak your mind, don't you? Well good, that will make things go faster. We signed up with Lotus almost exactly two years ago and as for the money, you're right: even if I was still working for the state, my salary would have covered only a fraction of the cost. Ford's grandmother, his other grandmother, had money. Ford's father left us years ago but when she died she left a trust for Ford, exclusively for health and educational expenses. That's why he was able to go to private school and why we were able to sign with Lotus. As for why we worked with them, did you ever work in the emergency department as a psychiatrist?"

"Not since my residency."

"The first time I took Ford to the ER they sent us home. I knew all the buzz words, knew the clinical language to describe what was happening with him, but they didn't take it seriously. They took it more seriously after he cut himself, took it seriously enough to admit him to the child psych unit, which they did after holding him in the ER for nine days waiting for a bed. Nine days sleeping on a gurney, not showering, not receiving any clinical care other than a benzo to sleep, in the middle of an emergency department. If you weren't crazy when you started that journey, you'd be crazy at the end."

"What does that have to do with Lotus?" I asked.

She turned to me. "Everything. It's like your father said: they sell access. You get to cut the line. Lotus promised a different path. Those were the words they used: 'a different path.' They reviewed Ford's records, met with us, and painted me a picture. Admission to a six-week therapeutic wilderness program in North Carolina. Then, transition to a day school near here with support for kids like Ford, and after that a move to a regular high school but a small one, where he'd receive a lot of individual attention, in time for college applications. And if the bottom fell out along the way the Mullens Center would be there for us and we'd have no wait in the ER, no visit to the ER at all. We were guaranteed direct admission to Mullens, when needed. After what we'd been through, that sounded pretty damn good. I worked as a clinical social worker for years, Dr. Moore. I thought I knew mental health care inside and out. What I didn't understand was that there is a parallel system, if you can access it. Lotus showed me that option."

"One you exercised," Dad said.

"Yes. Ford's state deteriorated. We never made it to the first step in the plan, the wilderness program. Ford needed to be admitted again and it was just like they said it would be: we drove right up to Mullens and went inside."

"And then?"

She snorted. "And then? There was no 'and then,' Dr. Moore. And then the bullshit started. As I said, I know what a psych unit is supposed to look like and this one was all smoke and mirrors."

"Tell me about it."

"It was put together to look like a fancy hotel, about as far from a psychiatric unit as you could get, but it was all a facade. What I remember most is the smell. They had these misters that sprayed a floral scent and it got on everything, covering up the usual hospital smells. It's still in some of my clothing. I can't stand it. They piped in nature sounds, gurgling streams and the like, and the walls were wood paneled with lovely murals painted in the hallways."

"It sounds nice," I said.

"Oh, it was nice," Dakota Flynn said. "And it was empty."

"They didn't have other patients?" Dad asked.

"They had other patients, but they didn't have many. What I mean, though, is the staffing. Even for the limited caseload they were chronically understaffed, and the people they had were woefully undertrained. I became suspicious the first time I visited Ford; I met the counselor he was supposed to be working with and the young lady clearly had no mental health training. I mean, none. She had memorized parts of the *DSM*; phrases, diagnostic terms, but when I referenced multiaxial diagnosis to see if she knew what I was talking about, she looked at me like a deer caught in headlights and practically ran away. It was the same with everyone: the aides, the desk staff . . ."

"The psychiatrists?"

"A resident came through once a day. At one point they had Ford on Risperdal and he was having terrible GI symptoms. I wanted the prescription changed and it took them six hours to get a doc to do it. Six hours, at what was supposed to be a premier psychiatric unit!"

"Did you meet a psychiatrist named Jason Grant?" Dad asked.

Dakota Flynn paused, hand halfway lowered to the soda can. "Dr. Grant?"

"That's right. You knew him?"

"He was Ford's psychiatrist."

"What did you think of him?"

"He was the only genuine thing in that fucking place." She sat very still. I watched the ash grow on her cigarette until she finally lowered it the rest of the way and tapped it in the can. Then she raised it to her lips and took a long drag. "I was very sorry when I heard what happened to him."

"The records show that Ford went into Mullens three times," Dad said.

"Yes. He couldn't stabilize in the community. I'm not convinced that he stabilized at Mullens, but at least it was a locked setting. There were times when he needed 24/7 monitoring, he was so acutely suicidal. They gave him that. A nurse told me that one time Dr. Grant stayed after his shift to personally sit by Ford while he slept because no one else was available. Every time I complained about the staffing or about a counselor, I got a note or a call from Dr. Grant saying that he was making it right, that it would be better. I believed him, you know? I believed what I wanted to believe."

"All right," Dad said, "so the Mullens Center was an overpriced, understaffed unit with surface amenities but no real quality care, is that about the size of it?"

"That's some of it," Dakota said, "but not all. The rest of it is about the money."

"Oh," Dad said, sitting straighter, "please do tell me about that."

Dakota turned to her mother. "Do you need a break, Ma?" she asked. The older woman shook her head, almost imperceptibly. Her eyes were on my father. "Well," Dakota said, "I do. This is the most I've talked about Ford's story in some time." She dropped her cigarette into the soda can and rose. "I'll be back in a moment." She retreated to the other end of the apartment, leaving me and Dad with her mother.

I pushed off the wall and limped to one of the shelves. The books largely centered on mental health topics, depression and psychotherapy, and some were clearly old textbooks. I didn't know the names of any of the plants lining the shelves other than a cactus. Botany was the sort of thing I'd never taken to; it all just looked green and leafy to me. Dad was sitting with brow furrowed, rubbing his temples. I wondered whether he was getting a headache from the exertions of the day.

Dakota returned, a notebook tucked under one arm. “The money,” she said, reseating herself next to her mother, “took some work.” She opened the notebook on her lap. “I worked for the state,” she said, “and I have friends who were eager to help, after what happened to Ford. Some of the information they accessed was not exactly proper. I need to know that there won’t be any repercussions for them.”

“I’m not reporting anything to anyone,” Dad said.

“Good.”

“But back up a moment,” he continued. “Why were you looking into the financial side of things to begin with? Simply because of the understaffing?”

She shook her head. “No. There was that, this curious way they seemed to have poured money into the facilities but not the staff, but there was more. I was convinced that there were kickbacks. I still am.” She tapped the notebook in her lap.

“What sort of kickbacks?” I asked.

“Payments from Mullens to Lotus for sending patients.”

“They seem to have a relationship,” Dad said, “if Mullens is guaranteeing access for Lotus clients.”

“That’s right, they do. Lotus was up-front about that with us at the start. The man, Rafael, said that they have an exclusive service agreement where Mullens promises to get Lotus clients right in, whenever they need. The flip side of that, I figured, is that Lotus is only routing clients to Mullens, not to other, traditional, less expensive facilities.”

“That’s a far cry from kickbacks,” Dad said.

“I know it is. That’s where one of my friends at the state came in. There had been an audit, about a year before we signed up with Lotus, that uncovered a suspicious pattern of payments from the Mullens Center to Lotus Consultants. Sporadic payments booked as business expenses. Like they were going out to lunch every couple weeks but way, way bigger than a lunch."

"What came of the investigation?" Dad asked.

"It went away. Shut down, no findings. My friend . . . well, my friend says that happens sometimes in Albany, depending on who you know, and that was the part of the story he really did not want to talk about."

"All right," I said, feeling left behind, "so . . . you were paying Lotus for what they did, and you were paying the Mullens Center for what they did, but then there was this third thing, this payment from Mullens to Lotus?"

"That's what a kickback is, Lukas," Dad said.

"But what's the problem? I mean, Mullens was pretty empty, right? So, they were just paying for business. Marketing. Like a theater giving away free tickets to get bodies in the seats. I'm sure Mullens was paying out less than they were getting paid by families, so they still came out ahead."

"It's unethical," Dad said. "Highly unethical."

"It's also bad business," Dakota said. "Your assumption about the payments is true, but just barely. They were sending so much back to Lotus that their margins on Lotus clients were razor-thin." She flipped through the pages on her lap. "In some cases, I'm convinced they were losing money."

"There's something else," Dad said. "Apart from the cash flows we're talking about, there was one more. Lotus was a major donor to the Mullens Center. One of their biggest."

"I didn't know that," Dakota said. "Apart from what I've told you, what my friend was able to get for me, I wasn't able to unearth much more on Lotus. I was sort of obsessed for a while, you know? Convinced that they'd steered us in the wrong direction, that Ford would be alive if we'd done things differently. I went there, demanded to meet with them, tried to pull financial records. I have this damn notebook full of leads, all going nowhere. I probably look like a crazy lady." It made me think of Dad's study wall, covered in notes and papers.

"They're owned by a firm called Burned Stone Partners," Dad said.

"Yes. About which virtually nothing is available. It's an endless web of bullshit, closed offices and disconnected phone numbers, documents that refer to each other and never lead you anywhere. Eventually I had to give up. It wasn't helping. It wasn't helping me grieve for Ford, and nothing I found was going to help either. It was like an itch I had to make myself stop scratching."

Outside, in the backyard, Princess began to bark. "That damn dog," Dakota Flynn said. "Usually she's quiet, but she's having a hell of a day."

"May I?" Dad asked, gesturing to the notebook. She nodded and held it out. Dad rose, retrieved it, and returned to the couch, opening it and studying the pages. "You put a great deal of time into this," he murmured.

Dakota glanced at her mother and lit yet another cigarette. I barely flinched this time. "I knew something was wrong," she said. "I still do. I just can't look for it anymore. I can't let it consume me." Princess's barking grew louder. "Jesus," Dakota said. "Fucking dog." Dad studied the notebook some more.

"You said Princess is usually quiet?" I asked.

"Usually. Not today."

"When she barked earlier it was because I was in the backyard."

"That's right. The landlord needs to fix our doorbell, though most people aren't as persistent as you."

I limped across the room to a window between my father and the two women and looked out on a wedge of the backyard. I could hear

Princess but I couldn't see her. I watched and a moment later there was movement at the edge of the house, by a row of trash cans. "Someone may be out there," I said.

"Could be George, taking out the trash or something," Dakota replied.

"Do you mind if I take some notes?" Dad asked, absorbed in the pages in front of him and ignoring both me and the dog.

"Be my guest," Dakota told him.

He took his small notebook out of a jacket pocket and scribbled in it. I hobbled back to my spot leaning against the wall. "You said something a moment ago," Dad said. "About closed offices."

"That's right."

"So, you went to an office and found it closed?"

"I did. Twice. Once here in New Birmingham and once in Albany. I can't travel much, Mom needs me, but I drove there and I pounded on the doors, looked in the windows, spoke to the neighbors. There are other offices for them too."

"Do you have the addresses?"

"The page with the blue sticker."

Dad flipped to it. "I know one of these," he said. "I've seen it before." He wrote in his notepad and then looked up, meeting Dakota Flynn's eyes. "I have a headache."

"So do I," she replied.

"We appreciate your time," he said. "This has been very informative." He stood and set her notebook down on the couch, then crossed to the front door. I limped after him.

"I have a question for you," Dakota said. "I looked you up on my phone while you were taking care of your boy. Yale Medical and all those publications. Given that you've wandered into my living room and taken an interest in my son, I think I should get to ask you something."

Dad turned at the door. "Yes?"

"Do you think it would have made a difference? If we had done things differently? Gone to the regular psychiatric unit, got Ford to that program upstate? Might it have changed things?"

Dad was quiet for a long moment. "I don't know," he finally said. "I don't know if anything could have made it different. But I've listened to your story, I've listened to the way you tell it, and I know you did everything for that boy that you possibly could and whatever else he was at the end, when he was on that roof, he was most definitely loved."

Dakota's mother turned her head and looked at us, her eyes boring into my father, her nostrils flaring above the plastic tube. After a moment she nodded.

Dad went through the door without another word and I hurried after him. We returned to our car where I took a few moments figuring out how to situate myself in such a way that my ass would not scream in protest. "You're all right to drive?" Dad asked, sitting beside me and flipping through his notebook.

"I'll make it work," I muttered. I turned the car on, winced as I shifted my weight to look over my shoulder, and pulled out. "You want to get a new burrito?"

"That would be nice."

It wasn't until after we drove away that I realized Princess had gone completely silent.

CHAPTER TWENTY-THREE

Misty was helping Alice tie her shoes. They were sitting in an empty school cafeteria, Alice facing away from one of the tables, Misty kneeling in front of her. Again and again Misty tied a knot, again and again Alice tried to imitate her. I watched from the hallway. Misty's back was to me. Finally, I approached. "Maybe I could help?"

Misty turned and looked up. Her face was flushed and she looked exasperated. "Lukas. What are you doing here?"

"Meeting with Mr. Jollett." Budget cuts to the Faith public schools had hit the arts department with particular ferocity and our old high school drama teacher was leading art classes at the elementary school one day a week.

She blew a strand of hair off her face. I hadn't seen Misty since she stormed out of our house the day after her brother was found, not counting our intervention when she was tailed by Joanna Bartlett. I'd called her afterward and tried to explain as succinctly as possible; she listened for a bit, but once it was clear the Accountant wasn't involved and that the incident boiled down to an unhappy ex, she cut me off and got off the phone. Crouching in front of Alice and her untied shoes, Misty looked me up and down and then turned back to the task at hand without further comment.

"Do you want some help?" I asked again. "My meeting isn't for a few minutes and I've been tying shoes for about twenty years."

“Mom tried to show me,” Alice said, “but she’s tired a lot and sometimes she cries. And Emery’s no help; Emery’s always with his stupid rockets.”

“Here,” I said, “let me.” I knelt in front of Alice, the wound on my rear end protesting, and took her laces in my hands. “Watch this.” I contemplated for a moment and then Alice watched as I executed a slow-paced and simplified version of a bow. “Do you think you could do that?”

She bit her lip and nodded. She couldn’t do it the first time, or the second, but after my third demonstration she successfully completed the knot. Alice’s face lit up in a radiant smile as Misty and I stood.

“You were doing it the way you do it,” I said to Misty, “which is natural. But you just kept on showing her what you do and hoping she’d finally imitate it and that won’t work. You need to look at it from Alice’s point of view.”

Misty stretched her back. “I’m no good at this, Lukas.”

“Sure you are. You just need practice.”

“I’m not sure I have the patience.”

I shrugged. “You can probably practice that too.”

“Are you going to start walking to school with us again, Lukas?” Alice asked.

I glanced at Misty. “I don’t know, Alice, I’ve been pretty busy in the mornings. I’ll see you at rehearsal though.”

“But I liked our walks.”

“Me too. I have to get going. Great job, Alice.”

Alice gave me a high five and I headed for the cafeteria exit.

“Lukas?” Misty called.

I turned back.

“Are you and your father still . . . working?”

“Yeah,” I said. “We are.”

She nodded. "Okay."

"Do you want to get together sometime? Come over for Chinese food or go out for coffee? I could update you."

"I don't know. I don't know if it's good for me. Maybe I'll let you know?"

"Okay. Let me know anytime."

I left in search of Mr. Jollett and found him in the school art studio, spattered in paint. "Four years of drama school," he said. "Macbeth. Willie Loman. Then two more years for a master's degree in teaching." He used a damp paper towel to scrub at a purple handprint on his trousers.

"Is this still a good time?" I asked.

"It's not going to get better." He took me to the staff room and poured us very strong coffee and listened to me explain the situation. "Basically," I concluded, "I have fourteen special-needs kids and a few more weeks to get them to sing more or less in unison, to say nothing of the choreography."

He nodded and sipped his coffee, still picking at paint on his knee. "Have you developed a rehearsal schedule?"

"Yeah," I said, "but I don't think it's in the right order. I have kids sitting around, getting bored, and parents showing up late or pulling people out early. I mean, some of the kids have soccer beforehand and have missed a ton of time; maybe I should do their numbers later? But then that's not fair to some of the others . . ."

"Do you have a budget?"

"Sort of. The organization sponsoring us promised to help out with costumes and sets and stuff, but I'm not really sure how much they're ready to pay."

"Did you start out with some sort of lesson plan, in terms of orienting these kids to performance expectations?"

"Uh . . ."

He chuckled. "So, you genuinely have no idea what you're doing."

"Absolutely none."

He opened his briefcase and brought out a notebook. "I'm lending this to you," he said.

"What is it?"

"My director's book from *Hamlet*."

"The one I was in?"

"I haven't done another."

I opened it. The first page was covered with notes on props and materials for sets in Mr. Jollett's neat handwriting. "I could give you a textbook," he said, "or tell you to take a class. Ultimately, if this is something you want to do, you'll need lots of classes and textbooks. For now, though, read through my side of what we did."

I flipped a few pages, reaching the cast list and scanning down to the leading role. "You have notes on me."

"I do."

I studied it silently for a moment. "It says here that my elocution was weak, I moved awkwardly during swordplay, and that I was arrogant."

"Your elocution came a long way over the course of the production." He smiled. "Take heart, Lukas. You were a sophomore, the youngest leading man in a long time and the youngest since. It's natural for you to have had some rough edges that needed sanding. That's much of what education is about."

"Why did you cast me if I had rough edges? There were talented juniors and seniors."

"There were. They let me know it. Their parents did too. But I saw something in you. Not elocution and certainly not grace with a sword. You had a quality of honesty that you brought to the performance.

There was a truth in you. That's what made you a fine Hamlet. It's what the character is all about: thrashing through illusion to accept the truth of what's right in front of your face the whole time."

I looked farther into the notebook. "Thank you for this. I'll return it."

"Do. I have a complete set, stretching back to the first production I directed, thirty-eight years ago. And let me know if you want to borrow some of those textbooks or look into the classes."

I stood. "I don't know if I'll be any good at this. I don't want to let these kids down."

"That fact alone means you're far ahead of most other people who might try their hand at it. Do you enjoy the work?"

I nodded. "I do. I didn't expect it, but I do."

"What do you like most?"

I thought of Alice's face when the knot came together. "The moment when it connects," I said. "I've just had a few of those, but that's it: that moment."

Mr. Jollett nodded. "You have potential, Lukas. I've never been wrong about that."

On my walk home I got a call from Jules Pierre, whose texts had been tapering off. "Bro," he said without preamble, "this Mamet thing is huge. Huger than huge."

"Hi Jules," I said, "how's the weather in Manhattan?"

"What?" he asked. "The weather? Who the hell knows? I've been in my office for the last twenty-seven hours straight. Now listen to this." He rapidly listed six or seven names, all of which I recognized. He sounded like he was powered by too much caffeine or maybe something stronger.

"That's who's auditioning for this thing?" I asked.

"That's who they've cast, brother, but I might be able to get you a look for understudy if we move fast and if you stop playing at being a fucking nurse and get your ass back here where it belongs. Is your dad better yet?"

Dad had been confused again the night before. The cord woke me and I got him settled. That morning he'd again wanted to tie his own tie; when he wasn't able, he'd thrown a full cup of coffee against the wall in the kitchen. He immediately apologized and insisted on cleaning it up for himself, which he did while I knotted three ties for him to choose from. "Not really," I said.

Jules exhaled loudly. "Listen," he said, "we all have fathers. It's complicated, I get it. But your career is drying up while you're away. It's not something you can just hit pause on and then restart whenever you feel like it. You had momentum with *Streetcar* and that is totally going to be gone. Plus, you're getting older. You're only going to be leading man material for so long. Are you working out? Have you gained weight? You might need new headshots."

I held the phone away from my head while Jules opined about the necessity of using the correct facial sunblock/moisturizer. I closed my eyes and took two slow, deep breaths. "I have to go, Jules," I interrupted. "I appreciate the heads-up about the Mamet. I'll do the best I can. I'll use a moisturizer with SPF." I hung up before he could respond and put the phone back in my pocket, tucking Mr. Jollett's notebook firmly under my arm.

Dad was in my room when I returned to the house. He was at the desk, shuffling through some papers on NBMC letterhead. "I've been working with Mancini on the chemical burn issue," he said as I entered. "We've been running some experiments with tissue samples. I'm more convinced than ever that the body lay somewhere, exposed, before going into the water."

I shivered, both at the thought of what that meant and at the idea of the two doctors conducting experiments on tissue samples in the hospital basement.

Dad set the papers aside, picked up the notepad he'd been using when interviewing the Flynns, rose, and turned to the wall of papers. "By the way," he continued, "I finally made the connection." He stepped over and tapped a sheet midway up the wall. "This is it. The address."

"One of the ones from Dakota's notebook?"

"That's right. It's attached to Burned Stone."

I stepped closer. He had set up a sort of family tree for the Grant family, pages on Owen and Lucia with lists of their activities and memberships alongside photos printed out from fawning newspaper stories in the *Ulster County Courier*. Misty and Garrett had similar setups below them. The paper he was focused on was off to one side. "Frank Grant," it said at the top. There were photos printed out of *The Boston Globe* online, mostly from a series of stories five years before on construction irregularities. They showed a tall, broad man with clear resemblance to his brother, Owen, invariably wearing a rumpled flannel shirt, work boots, and gripping an impressively large cigar in his teeth or between two fingers. An address in South Boston was written on the sheet. I looked at it, then looked at the notepad in Dad's hand. It was the same building; suite #9 on the notepad, while on the sheet Uncle Frank was listed at #5. "They're neighbors? What does that mean?" I asked.

"It means we're taking a trip. We're going to Uncle Frank's. It was family trips to his house on Lake George that punctuated Jason's mood the summer he and Joanna were together: first, the Fourth of July and then Labor Day. Something happened each time. There's something else too." He returned to the desk and picked up Jason's research proposal, flipping to the page with "Lotus" in the margin. "The *L*," he said. "It matches Owen's handwriting."

"That's what you said."

"But Frank and Owen are brothers. They probably went to the same school. They probably learned the same letter formation from the same nuns in South Boston."

"Nuns and handwriting seem to be coming up with surprising frequency."

"We go where the data takes us, Lukas." Dad shook the proposal in my face. "This could have been Frank's note, not Owen's."

"We still don't know what it means, if anything."

"That's why we're going."

"Alternatively," I countered, "we could not go to Lake George. We could stay here. You could work on your rehab and maybe get a consulting gig. I could finish directing this revue. We could get on with our lives. If you really think Jason Grant's death was foul play then we can go to the Faith police and they can look into it."

"Jason didn't trust the police. He told Joanna not to go to them."

"Well, to be honest, Dad, that may have been a few days before he tied a weight to his wrist and walked into a lake, so we can't be totally confident about his state of mind. And even if something else did happen to him, and even if he was right not to trust the police, so what? So that means they don't investigate? He's still just as dead."

Dad shook his head. "It won't let me go, Lukas. I have to see it through. I need to have the truth."

I sighed. "All right," I said, "we'll go. But let's try to make it a day trip, okay? I have a tight rehearsal schedule. I have work to do."

Dad smiled. "That," he said, "is exactly what I like to hear."

CHAPTER TWENTY-FOUR

My phone rang on the New York State Thruway. I didn't recognize the number. "Lukas," a voice said, "it's Joanna. Joanna Bartlett. From the other day."

I was unlikely to forget. "Hi Joanna," I said, "is everything okay?"

"Yeah. I thought of something, though. You know how your father asked me about Jason's handedness? The whole tennis/soccer thing?"

"Yeah?"

"There was something."

"Put her on speaker," Dad said from the passenger seat. "I need to hear."

I thumbed the phone to speaker and set it in the cup holder. "You're on with me and Dad," I told Joanna. "Go ahead."

"I'm still not sure about his handedness," she said, "but neurologically speaking, lateral dominance isn't only about the hands. I remembered the telescope."

"What telescope?" Dad asked.

"It was August. There was a meteor, I forget which one. RX2-something. Jason was into that stuff and he brought a telescope over to my place and set it up on the roof. The thing was that the meteor was only going to be visible at four thirty in the morning, so he woke me in the middle of the night and we went up in our pajamas. It was perfectly clear, the city was quiet. I looked through the telescope but

I couldn't see it so Jason stood behind me and helped. I remember his arms around me, guiding the telescope, and he leaned over to look for himself. And when he did, it was over my right shoulder and he used his left eye."

"Are you sure?" Dad asked.

"I remember the moment perfectly," she said. "I think about it all the time. It was one of our last nights."

"Tremendous," Dad said, clapping his hands together. "Absolutely tremendous! Excellent insight, particularly for a Harvard student."

"Why is this important?" Joanna asked.

"We're just looking into a few things," I said before Dad could open his mouth. "We're still clearing up some details about what happened."

"Will you tell me?"

"Tell you what?"

"What you find out. When you get to the end of this investigation you're doing, will you come back and tell me?"

"Yes," I said. "We'll tell you whatever we know."

"All right." She was silent for a moment. "I should go . . ."

"Did you see the meteor?" I asked.

There was silence for another moment. "I saw it," she said. Then the line went dead.

Driving was difficult with the puncture wound in my ass. I sat on a little cushion Dad had procured for me but it was still rough. "Dad," I said after a few minutes, "have you thought through what we're going to say to Frank Grant when we see him?"

"See him? We're not going to see him. Frank is in Boston."

"How do you know?"

"Because we have an appointment with him at his office there for one thirty this afternoon."

"I don't understand . . ."

"I don't want to see Frank, Lukas. He's not going to tell us anything. I want to see his house and the surrounding grounds. I called his office in Boston, posing as a developer. He's expecting Earl Grey at one thirty."

"Earl Grey? Like the tea?"

"It's what popped into my head. You should be pleased; planning has been a bit of a challenge over the last year. I think this represents some progress."

"Yeah, good job. That's some decent frontal lobe functioning."

"Thank you."

"So, you think the house will be empty?"

"Frank's a bachelor, from what I understand. And Misty said her parents were in Faith?"

"Yes." I'd called and asked for her uncle's address, explaining that we were trying to corral some stray mailing information that came up when we went through Jason's personnel file from the medical center. "He was maybe having his checks forwarded there at some point?" I lied. "You know how Dad is. He has to dot every *i*."

Misty did not seem particularly interested. She gave me the address, I thanked her, and then casually asked whether she and her family were going to be in town over the coming days, making up a half-assed story about a neighborhood BBQ.

"I don't think we'll be up for it, Lukas, and I'm not sure my parents are eager to see your father again."

"Understood. Are you doing—"

"I have to go, Lukas." She hung up.

We exited the Thruway for a sparsely populated two-lane road. I thought about Misty as I drove. I thought about her asking my father for words that would make her loss bearable. Maybe he hadn't done the best job possible, but it still wasn't a fair request on her part. What are you supposed to say at moments like that? Dad wasn't a clinician. He was like a faithless priest who refused to give the sacraments; the bread remained bread, the wine remained wine, the words remained unspoken, and Misty continued to grieve. If my father was too unapologetic about the terrible reality she faced then it reflected some combination of his pre-injury personality and his post-injury deficits, but her pain still wasn't his responsibility.

"Turn, Lukas."

"Huh?"

"This is our turn."

I almost skidded off the county highway onto a smaller road. There was a canopy of trees overhead and no other houses around. Ten more minutes of driving brought us to a long driveway leading to an isolated waterside property on the north bank of Lake George. I turned the car off and got out, eager to take pressure off my ass. Dad came around to stand beside me, a backpack slung over one shoulder.

"This can't be real," I said.

It was three stories tall and it was all stone and glass. The door was one and a half stories, a semicircle of iron-bound oak that would have been more at home in a castle. It was flanked by enormous windows. There was even a turret on the water side. "Is that . . . a gargoyle?" I asked.

"I believe it's technically a grotesque," Dad said. "It doesn't look like there's any route for it to spout water."

I wasn't interested in the architectural terminology, but grotesque seemed like an applicable term. The process of building this hideous modern castle had clearly taken its toll on the land around and it had yet to grow back. What might have once been a lawn had been reduced to dirt and mud by construction machines, and some of their tracks were still evident. Trees had been cut down, or in some cases perhaps inadvertently knocked down. There were jagged stumps and trunks strewn haphazardly in the underbrush. It looked like the house had been gouged out of the earth, leaving a trail of destruction as it resisted being born. "Why spend all this money on the house and not bother with any landscaping?"

"It's not about beauty, Lukas. It's about power." Dad walked toward the building and I followed. The driveway was empty and there was no sign of life inside.

"What are we looking for?" I asked.

"I want to inspect the grounds."

We circled around, studying the windows. There were three units for central air on the side. We reached the back and I looked at the water. That, at least, was beautiful, and I walked toward it. The ruined lawn sloped down to the side of Lake George. There was a small dock. "I'm going down there," I called to Dad, who was standing with his hands in his pockets studying the lake side of the house, the main features of which seemed to be massive picture windows for appreciating the water.

The dock was as neglected as the other exterior features of the property. It bobbed in the water. Some of the wood was rotten and I stepped carefully over what seemed to be the least reliable planks as I made my way to the end, ten or fifteen feet out, and looked down. It was very still. I could imagine fishing at such a spot, if I ever fished. There was even a bit of line tangled on an exposed nail along the edge.

As I stood at the end of the dock a wind picked up and I shivered. There was a loneliness there, something I couldn't put my finger on. For all the grandeur of the house behind me I found the spot to be very sad. I looked down, scanning the surface of the water, and I spotted something: under the nail with the fishing line was another exposed nail and there was a bit of fabric on it. I crouched, reaching out and pulling it free. It tore a little. I held it up and studied it, rubbing it between my fingers. It was stained and sun bleached but it looked like a scrap of khaki cloth.

"Lukas! Come here."

I stood and turned toward shore. Dad's voice was coming from the far side of the house, the one I hadn't reached before peeling off. I stuffed the fabric in my pocket and hurried back.

Dad was waiting by a small shed on the periphery of the property, set near what once would have been the tree line but now was just a row of stumps. It was made of wood planks and listed about ten degrees to the right. He was standing in front of the door looking down at a heavy lock that looked to be far newer and sturdier than what it was attached to. "What is it?" I called as I approached.

He looked up and pressed a finger to his lips. He was listening. I stopped beside him and listened too. A rustling. "Something's inside," he murmured.

I stepped back and looked at the shed again. It seemed so rickety that I thought I could probably kick a hole in a wall. Anyone locked inside and unable to get out must be weak, or small, or tied up. "Maybe we should . . ." I began, wondering where the nearest police station was. Dad didn't wait. He walked over to the edge of the lawn, picked up a rock, returned to the door, and in one swift motion brought it down.

The lock itself held but the latch it was attached to tore away. Dad pulled the door open, the other arm cocked with the stone as though he was going to throw it at whatever was inside. Something ran out of the shed, passing within inches of my feet, and a cry caught in my throat. It was just a chipmunk. I looked up; the inside of the shed was very dim but it seemed to be empty. I followed Dad in.

There was an earthy smell, sweet and organic, and I immediately wanted to step back into the fresh air. I looked around. There were bags of gravel along one side; the path up to the front of the house was lined with it. A few old gardening tools, a shovel and hoe and a rake, presumably from the days when this property had a live lawn or even a garden. Not much else. “Lukas,” Dad said, “do you have a light?”

“Your phone does this, too,” I said, turning on my phone’s flashlight.

“I can never get it to go on, and then I can never turn it off. Shine it over there.”

I lifted my phone, illuminating the far corner of the shed. There was a pile of cans and at first I thought it was paint. I stepped closer, the smell grew stronger, and I almost dropped the phone. “Dad . . .”

“They’re chipmunks, Lukas. Just dead chipmunks.”

Their desiccated bodies were clustered around the cans, the bottom layer of which were rusted, a hole chewed in one of them. Dad walked over and picked up an intact can from the top of the pile, returning and looking at it closely under my light. “This is what I was looking for,” he said, satisfaction in his voice.

“Chipmunk corpses?”

“Builder’s lime. This place is covered in stonework.” He took my phone, bending over and shining it on the dirt at our feet. “It’s dry now but this shed is in no way watertight. When it rains there must be puddles of this stuff in here.” He stood and turned in a full circle, shining the light on the walls of the shed, the ceiling, and then on the dirt floor once again.

I remembered the results of Mancini’s autopsy and Dad’s mention of tissue studies. “Dad,” I began, “will that stuff burn skin?”

"It will, particularly when mixed with water."

"Do you think—"

"Mancini said Jason's lungs were full of freshwater. We never considered that it might have been from a different lake. There's only one way to know for sure, though; we have to get this to the lab."

"But this is . . . it must be the place . . ." I bent over, resting my hands on my knees. I thought that I might be sick; the shed seemed to swing around me and the smells of chemicals and dirt and something sweet were overwhelming.

"Steady, Lukas," Dad said, resting a hand on my shoulder. "One breath at a time."

I nodded, stood, breathed, and gratefully stepped back into the daylight and the fresh air, glancing back and trying not to shudder as Dad closed the door. I put my hand in my pocket and felt the strip of fabric from the dock. I took it out and handed it to him. "I found this," I said, "down by the water. It was caught on a nail."

Dad took it, squinting and rubbing it between thumb and forefinger.

"What do you think it is?" I asked.

"Lukas, who do you think the last person to see Jason Grant alive was?"

I thought for a moment. "I don't know. He was in Cambridge, with Joanna, and then he left. They found his things by the lake—what was it, three days later? Those were work days, so maybe people at the medical center?"

"But we don't know, do we? You're assuming."

I looked past Dad, at the closed door to the shed. "He was here. He never made it back."

"That is also an assumption. A hypothesis, I should say. We haven't actually spoken to anyone who saw him after he came back from

Cambridge. We need to get to the lab." He took the backpack from his shoulder and stuffed the can inside. "We have what we came for. Let's go."

I looked around, at the absurd monstrosity of the house, at the ruined land, and then at the lake. The water lay still, the surface just barely rippled by a soft breeze. The dock was empty but I could imagine a boy fishing there, a young Jason Grant on a family visit upstate. A chill ran through me. We turned and walked away from the lake and the shed in silence. "Are you hungry?" I asked. "We could—"

"Lukas, wait—" Dad reached out to grab my arm as I turned the corner around the side of the house. He was too late.

The blow caught me just under my left eye. My head snapped to one side and I stumbled backward, arms flailing, the ground rushing up to meet me. "That's far enough," a voice said, and I heard the mechanical click of a gun cocking.

CHAPTER TWENTY-FIVE

The man was old and clearly out of shape. His chest was heaving and his vein-riddled cheeks were flushed red. He was holding a shotgun in shaking hands.

"I assume that isn't a prop?" I asked my father.

"No," he said, crouching beside me, "that one is real." Dad stood back up, hands spread, palms out. "Easy there, friend. We're not looking for trouble. We're friends of the Grants."

The old man gulped for air. "Party is tomorrow," he managed.

"Ah, tomorrow," Dad said, striking his forehead with the palm of his hand. "Of course it's tomorrow! Lukas, I told you I thought it was tomorrow but you insisted on driving up today."

"Silly me," I said from the ground, gingerly poking my tender cheekbone.

The man lowered his gun. "I'm Watkins," he said. "I manage the house for Mr. Grant. I'm stocking the liquor cabinet, getting things ready."

"We understand," Dad said. "We're trespassing. We're lucky you used your fist and not the firearm."

Dad was technically right, though he wasn't the one who had been hit in the face. The man nodded to me. "Is he okay?"

Dad looked down. "Oh, he'll be fine. I'm not really a clinician but I'm confident he's sustained no more than a mild concussion."

"You're a doctor?"

"A psychiatrist, yes."

I wanted to signal Dad that he shouldn't reveal our true identities but I was having a very hard time focusing.

"Psychiatrists? So, you're some of the gentlemen from Lotus?"

"Indeed," Dad said. "We're consultants from Lotus. We work with Rafael."

"Yeah, we're putting you folks up on the third floor, but the thing is the ceiling had a leak. It'll all be set by tomorrow but right now everything's covered in plastic . . ."

"Oh, it's no problem at all," Dad said, "it's our fault for mixing up the dates. We'll head off to a hotel."

The man nodded regretfully. "I'm real sorry about this," he said. "I hope Mr. Grant . . ."

"There's no need to mention this to Mr. Grant," Dad said.

Watkins heaved a sigh. "I sure do appreciate that." He looked down at me again. "He's definitely okay?"

"Absolutely," Dad said, reaching down and heaving me to my feet. The world swam and I felt like I might throw up. "Sorry to trouble you. Come along, Lukas." He wrapped his arm around my waist and half dragged me past Watkins. We crossed the front lawn—using the term loosely, as there was barely any grass—and reached the car. "I think I should drive," Dad said.

"You haven't driven in over a year."

"You can barely stand up." He opened the passenger door and dropped me into the seat. I bit my lip to keep from crying out and grabbed the cushion from the driver's side, tucking it beneath my still-sore ass. Dad placed the backpack with the builder's lime between my feet and circled around the front, getting in and fiddling with the mirrors. While he worked I rested my head on the dashboard and then sat back and looked around. Watkins had parked a large SUV a short way up the driveway where he had come around the bend and presumably first seen our car. "All right," Dad said, starting the engine, "just like riding a bike." We lurched forward and backward as he executed a clumsy K-turn.

"Look out for the SUV," I said. Watkins had left it in the middle of the driveway and there was limited space. As we approached, however, it backed up and to one side, allowing us a wide berth.

"Looks like he has a partner," Dad observed. As we passed I peered in the passenger side window and saw who it was. The Accountant was sitting at the wheel.

Although I was very tired, I didn't think that I would be able to rest. I held the can of lime in one hand and rubbed my face with the other. My thoughts were racing but Dad sat silently, focusing on the thruway. "Can I ask you something?" I finally said. "You tried to stop me from turning the corner back here. How the hell did you hear Watkins sneaking up on us?"

"You didn't hear him?"

"No."

He shrugged. "You were probably lost in your own thoughts," he said. "Contemplating the past, considering the future. The present gets filtered out. Sounds reach your ears but go no further. You see or hear but you don't truly observe. It's actually quite exhausting, but in this case it proved useful."

A cell phone notification sounded.

"Lukas, could you check that for me? I want to keep my eyes on the road."

I agreed with the sentiment. Dad was driving a solid fifty miles an hour in the center lane, cars passing us on both sides, and his knuckles were white on the wheel. I retrieved his phone from the cup holder and tapped on the incoming text. "It's from a 617 number. It says: sorry, package is undeliverable, address is incorrect."

"Ah," Dad said, "thank you. Please give him a thumbs up, or whatever it is you're supposed to do."

"You were sending someone a package?"

"Yes, via private courier."

"What was it?"

"An empty box, sent express to Burned Stone Partners at the address in South Boston obtained by Dakota Flynn."

"The one in Frank Grant's building?"

"Correct. Suite nine."

"But the guy—the courier—he's saying the address is wrong."

"Indeed. My guess is that he's standing at the end of a hallway in a nondescript building in South Boston holding an empty box and looking at suite eight."

"So, where's Burned Stone? Where's number nine? It's not even there?"

"No," Dad said, "I didn't think that it would be. This has all been quite clarifying."

I did not feel clarified, though that was likely the product of the blow to the head Watkins had given me. "What's clear to you, Dad?"

"Several things. It's been obvious to me, ever since we met with Dakota Flynn, that the relationship between New Birmingham Medical Center and this corporation, Burned Stone partners, is fraudulent. Burned Stone owns at least two companies, Hiring Consultants and Lotus, that are doing business with the medical center. We know, from Derek and Mancini, that Hiring Consultants is doing a lousy job, not even filling positions that exist on paper. And we know, from Dakota Flynn, that Lotus is steering a lot of money to the Mullens Center and Mullens is sending a lot of it back. Finally, we now know that Burned Stone is attached to a nonexistent address in Frank Grant's building and Frank Grant is connected to this figure you call the Accountant who was following Misty and apparently dissuading the private investigator she tried to hire from doing any actual investigating. I'd say that's a fairly clear picture."

"Of what?"

"Of money laundering, Lukas. Of Burned Stone, whatever it really is, using the New Birmingham Medical Center, where Frank's brother Owen just happens to be chairman of the board, to clean dirty money. There are probably multiple streams: shitty construction, which explains the fountain in the lobby; dummy hiring, which is why the front desk is understaffed and there's not enough security at night; and donations to the Mullens Center and kickbacks to Lotus for fake patients. Who knows how far it goes, or where the dirty money comes from? I'm sure Frank has all sorts of operations running up in Boston."

I stared at the highway ahead of us. I had the barest understanding of what money laundering was, just a vague sense that it was often associated with organized crime and that the people involved didn't like outsiders interfering. "None of this is what we were looking for," I said. "We were trying to find out what happened to Jason Grant. What does all of this have to do with him?"

"That," Dad said, "is the ongoing mystery. Quiet down now, Lukas, I need to focus and you need to rest. We have a bit of time before we're back in Faith."

At the pace we were going, he was right. I rested my aching head against the passenger side window and closed my eyes.

CHAPTER TWENTY-SIX

The man must have been at least eighty years old. He lay face up, eyes closed, shoulder length white hair falling back. There was an impressive cut descending from the notch just below his throat through the center of his chest and belly.

"Life Saver?" Dr. Mancini asked.

I took two. My breath felt sour inside my mouth and I popped the wintergreen and bit down.

"You look like hell," he said.

"That from a doctor who works on dead people."

He laughed. "You're still better off than my patient here."

The body didn't bother me as much as I would have thought. Maybe it was because I was sleep-deprived; Dad and I had arrived home hours before and I'd tried to rest but I couldn't. Everything hurt, and on top of that every time I closed my eyes some stray noise would make me jump back to consciousness, convinced that the Accountant was there. Dad, on the other hand, fell right to sleep on the couch with his clothes on. "What did he die of?" I asked.

Mancini shrugged. "That is the question. The answer is likely to be boring but his people deserve it anyway. And what brings you here this evening, Lukas? To be honest, it looks like you need one of my colleagues upstairs for your face, and if I'm not mistaken you're heavily favoring your right leg."

I limped over to a metal table along one wall and set down the bag I was carrying. "Dad and I want to give you this." I reached in and took out the can of builder's lime we'd taken from Frank's shed. "Can you tell us whether it matches the burns on Jason Grant's body?"

Dr. Mancini studied the can. "Very interesting. I can tell you whether it is consistent with them. Could I testify that this is the only product that could have caused those marks? Certainly not. But I can give you a reasonable probability of fit."

"We also have this." I withdrew the scrap of fabric from the bag and set it on the table.

Mancini bent low and scrutinized it. "Again, interesting."

"Could it have come from Jason?"

"I didn't keep samples of his clothes so it's not possible to match the fibers. I have photos, but I don't need them. It's similar to the pants he was wearing."

"But you couldn't testify that it's the same."

"I myself am wearing khaki trousers. So are thousands of other men. I should have kept a sample."

I stepped back from the table and sighed.

"Do I want to know where you obtained these?" Mancini asked.

"Probably not."

"And your father is all right?"

"He is. He's resting."

Mancini studied the bruise on my face for a moment before turning back to his table. "You seem to have yourself caught up in a nasty business. You should think about getting out before things get worse."

"I made that case just yesterday but at this point I think we need to see it through."

He chuckled. "As I diagnosed: a romantic."

I limped back around his table and looked down at the old man. "I don't feel like a romantic."

"How do you feel?"

"Just tired. And in pain."

"That seems about right for the condition."

"I don't know what's romantic about this situation."

"Your reasons, however you would articulate them. I suspect you would point to the need for closure, for those who can still find it. Perhaps for justice, though I doubt that's at the heart of it. Rather, for truth. I find that to be romantic."

"Like you want to tell his people what happened to him," I said, glancing down at the body between us. "You said you were a romantic too."

"I am." Mancini picked up a scalpel. "The problem with being a romantic," he said, "is that it can only turn out one of two ways: either you find something to attach your passion to, or you turn bitter."

"Did you find something?" I asked.

He gestured to the cadaver between us with the gleaming blade in his hand. "This. And, much later, Derek. And now, Lukas, I need to open Mr. McCafferty. He won't mind if you're here, but I don't know if you're ready to see the inside of a human torso?"

I considered for a moment. The idea of staying in this chilly basement with Dr. Mancini, munching on Life Savers, didn't strike me as all that bad. I had an evening obligation, however, and I didn't want to be late. "You'll look at the chemical sample?"

"Yes. Just as soon as I'm done with this."

I made my way to the door.

"Lukas."

"Yes?"

"Keep a close eye on your father."

I half turned, nodded, then let myself out into the empty hall. I just had time to grab something from the cafeteria before rehearsal.

"There's No Business Like Show Business" is a song that always rewards exuberance, and my cast was not short on that quality.

I stood in the third row, arms folded, and felt utterly delighted. Brian, the boy I had spoken with at the Down Syndrome Foundation dinner about the secret of bravery, was center stage, arms spread, belting it out like Ethel Merman herself. It had taken a long while to get him there. For the first couple rehearsals he wouldn't leave my side, hovering next to me in the high school auditorium. Sometime around his fourth visit I was able to walk him onstage so that he could experience the songs while looking out, but he still didn't sing along and I had to stay next to him. A few nights after that Alice, who evidently had no stage fright at all, walked him into the ensemble and I was able to go back to my spot in the auditorium, and now here he was, the biggest ham, the loudest voice, drinking it all in.

"Let's go on with the show!" they sang, freezing in their final pose, and I clapped and cheered along with a small group of parents who had remained in the far corner to watch. "Fabulous," I called, "the best you've ever done it! I have just a few notes, but let's take a short break for water."

The kids broke up and walked toward the edge of the stage to another scattering of applause. Someone behind me clapped and I turned. Misty was walking down the center aisle. I peered beyond her into the shadows at the back of the house. "I thought that door was locked," I said.

"They're wonderful, Lukas. You've done an amazing job." She stopped in front of me and raised her eyebrows. "What happened to your face?"

There had to be a nicer way for people to ask that question. I told the kids that I'd had a minor bike accident and reminded them to always wear a helmet. "Uh . . . that's part of what I wanted to talk to you about." I had texted her a few hours earlier, still feeling woozy, and now I had no idea how to begin. "Let's go outside."

We exited through a side door into an empty parking lot. A dumpster was to our left and we took a few steps away from the smell of trash. Misty's hair was pulled back. She was wearing a light green sweater and a denim skirt and her usual canvas sneakers. She was so beautiful it momentarily distracted me from the twin aches in my face and my backside.

"Dad and I have been working," I began, stuffing my hands into my pockets and kicking an empty can aside. "We've been . . . um, making a lot of progress."

She crossed her arms and waited.

"We went to Lake George. To your uncle's house."

"Frank's? Why?" She reached out and took my chin between two fingers, tilting my face so she could more clearly see the bruise left by Watkins. "What exactly happened, Lukas?"

"I told you we found Jason's girlfriend. We've been following leads, looking further into the Mullens Center, some irregularities at the hospital. Just going where our questions take us."

"And your questions took you to my Uncle Frank?"

"Yeah. Well, to his house. There's this company, Lotus Consultants. They do a lot of business with the Mullens Center but there's something fishy about it. And they're owned by a bigger company, Burned Rock, which owns a third company, Hiring Consultants, and they also do business with New Birmingham Med and that's messed up too. Like, they're sending security guards who don't even exist and stuff."

"Lukas, what are you talking about?"

"I'm not explaining this well. My father has a better grasp of it, which is disturbing and probably means that I have a concussion. The point is that we've uncovered something, some sort of money laundering involving the hospital and particularly the Mullens Center, and we think that Jason was mixed up in things and knew about it too, and that he went to see Frank. And Misty, we think that maybe he never came back."

She stared at me. The kids' laughter from inside the auditorium sounded far away. "What are you saying?"

"We found some stuff. Builder's lime, in a shed. There's all this masonry . . . well, that's not important. We don't know for sure yet but we think maybe Jason's body was there before it was in Lake Prout."

"At Frank's house?"

"Right."

"You're saying Jason . . . died at Frank's?"

"That is what I'm saying."

"That Frank . . ." she trailed off.

I shrugged, hands still stuffed in my pockets. "Frank, your father. Garrett too, though I'm not sure exactly how. He had hard feelings toward Jason. Still does, I think."

"That is insane. That's . . . you understand you're talking about my family?"

I nodded. "I'm sorry. I'm sure this is—"

"I know my father is no angel, Lukas. I've never been the least bit interested in his business but I'm not stupid. I have ears. He talks to Frank all the time. They got caught paying off a building inspector once and another time there was a big fine over not having the right permits. Sometimes they have to push people around, guys from the unions and . . . I don't even know who. Dad's old-fashioned, he always tried to keep it from me and Mom. They're tough men, they grew up tough. Their father was gone and they were poor. And Garrett; I know Garrett's a fuckup. He's trying to get clean. I don't think it's working. That doesn't make any of them killers. That doesn't mean they . . . I mean, what the fuck are you saying here?"

I don't know what I had been expecting. I'd been bitten on the ass by a very aggressive dog and punched in the head and faced two guns, one of which was actually real but both of which were terrifying, and I had more or less done it all for her. I wanted her to be impressed. I plowed on: "There's something else, too. You know who we saw at your uncle's? The Accountant—"

"Shut up, Lukas. I don't want to know."

"Shut up? You asked us to do this. You're the one who wanted answers, who wanted to know the truth, remember? You wanted to solve your family—"

"And now I want you to stop," she said. "Stop looking. You and your father. I appreciate it, I do. I asked you to do it and you did and you're brilliant, both of you. But I don't want this. None of this matters. Jason is dead, his ashes are in an urn and we're going to scatter them on his birthday and that will be it, the end, and nothing else will matter." Her voice caught in her throat and she started to cry. "Nothing will change anything."

"The truth matters, Misty."

"Not to me it doesn't. Not anymore."

"I don't believe that."

"You don't? You know me so well? We hook up at the quarry and now you can read my thoughts?"

I took a deep breath. "I don't think we can stop," I said. "Things are in motion and we can't just walk away. I'm sorry, I am. I'm sorry if what we're finding is hard for you but I think that . . . I think that you need to know."

"You have no idea what's hard for me, Lukas," Misty said, "and don't you fucking tell me what I need."

I looked at her in the shadows of the parking lot. I wanted to put my arms around her. I wanted to find words that would make things better. "I'm sorry," I repeated. "I'm sorry, but this is the truth: We think Jason was murdered. We think he got dumped in Lake Prout so it would look like suicide. We think your father and Uncle Frank and Garrett were involved, and we think your uncle and father are doing some shady stuff with the medical center, and we think that Jason, because he was the doctor in the family, somehow got mixed up with the drug side of things—"

"Bullshit. My brother was a kind, good, wonderful person." Tears were rolling down her cheeks and her voice shook but she went on: "He was good, he loved me, and he was going to take me to see Ibsen and now he's gone and I'm never going to see him again."

"Maybe there was more to him," I said. "Maybe he wasn't only good. Maybe he was—"

The slap startled me, and then it stung. Misty caught me across my unbruised cheekbone. She didn't hit hard but the sound reverberated and I stopped cold. "Don't talk about him anymore," she said. "You didn't know him. You'll never know him."

I stood staring at her, one hand on the side of my face. Then she turned and walked back inside the auditorium.

"Maybe he was human," I said, finishing my sentence to an empty parking lot.

I took a moment to gather myself, a shifting breeze washing me in the smell of the full dumpster, and then I followed her inside, but she was already gone.

An hour and fifteen minutes later the kids were exhausted and so was I. We had drilled the songs, revisited the choreography, and rehearsed the curtain call. At the end of the night I said goodbye to Alice, Brian, and the rest. I chatted with parents, most excited but a few nervous. Finally, I was alone. I collected sheet music and stacked it on the piano and then I climbed the steps to the stage.

My thoughts turned to Manhattan and *Streetcar* and Stanley Kowalski. They seemed further away than ever. Myrton Styles was still getting rapturous reviews and there was buzz about a film adaptation. I remembered that I owed Jules Pierre a call; he had said "asap" in his latest text but with the events of recent days it had been lost in the shuffle. I reached for my phone and something moved in the shadows. It was just a moment, at the back of the house. I couldn't see clearly because the stage lights were in my eyes. I held a hand up in a vain attempt to block them and called: "Hello?"

I wondered whether one of the kids had come back for something they forgot, but surely they would have said something? I would have seen them entering by the stage. Then I thought of Misty, coming in from the back of the theater. The rear door that was supposed to be locked. I glanced to my left. The side door was just beyond the edge of the stage. I could step forward, vault down, and be outside in an instant. My car was parked nearby. I could return for my backpack in the morning.

There was no answer from the back of the house and no further movement.

My muscles tensed, preparing to move, and then I froze. Anger replaced fear, or at least joined it. If someone was here they were trespassing in my theater. They were intruding on my rehearsal. "Who's there?" I called. I stepped down to the edge of the stage and peered into the darkness. It was a large auditorium for a high school, and with the stage lights on and the house lights off there were many rows and an entire mezzanine sunken in shadow. There was nothing but silence.

"Mr. Moore?"

I jumped, spun, and almost screamed.

"I didn't mean to startle you, sir."

Lester Smith, the high school custodian, stood just offstage. He was holding a mop and pushing a bucket. Lester remembered me from my days as a student but he still called me Mr. Moore now that I was back in a semiofficial capacity. "Lester . . . hi."

"Are these your sets backstage?"

I walked over and peered into the wings. "Yes, some of the parents painted those. We're going to set them up next weekend. Are they okay there?"

"Sure are. I just didn't want them to get moved if you needed them."

"Thank you." I turned and walked back onstage, looking out, still tense.

"You all set, sir?" Lester asked.

"Yes, I was just putting things away. Can you get the house lights?"

Lester turned and made his way offstage. There was a click, a thump, and a moment later the lights came up in the auditorium. I looked out. It was empty.

"Anything else you need?" he asked.

"Have you seen anyone tonight? Anyone hanging around the school?"

He frowned. "I've been up on the second floor for the last hour. No one's up there."

"You going to be around for a while?"

"Need to mop the stage."

"All right, I'll get out of your way."

Lester set to work and I went back out into the house, retrieving my backpack from the third row. Then I walked down the center aisle and pulled on the door. It was open. I stepped into the school lobby.

It was quiet and still; the old, scuffed white linoleum floor, the trophy case with generations of achievements by the Tricounty Bobcats, and next to that a mural of one such bobcat, caught in mid-leap. It was meant to look fierce but I'd always thought that the artist captured a look of quizzical annoyance instead. It's probably hard to depict animal facial expressions. To my right, the front doors of the school were made entirely of glass and faced out to the main parking lot.

I looked around. Not much seemed to have changed in the five years since I left Tricounty High. Maybe there were one or two new trophies in the case; the swim team had been dominant. I peered through the doors. It was well lit outside and there were no cars but there were also plenty of shadows beyond the lights, out toward the field house and the tennis courts. Standing there I had the distinct feeling that something in the dark was staring back at me. I pivoted and went back into the auditorium. Lester was onstage, whistling something off-key, mopping.

I slowly walked down the aisle, then turned and went into the second from back row until I reached the approximate spot where I'd seen movement. It was empty, but the fifth seat in from the aisle, unlike all the others, was flipped down. I stood beside it and breathed in deeply. There was a scent, faint but unmistakable. Deep, rich. The smell of a cigar.

CHAPTER TWENTY-SEVEN

I dreamed of mothers and lost children. Lucia Grant and her drowned son. Dakota Flynn and Ford, on that rooftop for three hours. My own mother, separated from me by four hundred miles, an international border, and a lifetime of unspoken words. Even Mrs. Quinlan across the street. Emery was still there, launching his stupid rockets, but at some point he would either grow up and go to MIT or else blow himself sky high.

I woke around lunch, showered, and spent some time with Dad in my room going over the new information. He needed to see it all laid out so that he could make sense of it. It was like his mental worktable was damaged and he couldn't keep all the information internally available, but when he saw it stretched out on the wall it came into focus. He showed me his notes on Burned Stone, Hiring Consultants, and Lotus, his theories about cash flow in what I could only assume, in my extremely inexpert understanding, constituted money laundering. Fees and donations going into Mullens and the broader New Birmingham Medical Center, construction contracts and salaries and referral payments going out. It all seemed so abstract. It didn't seem like anything worth killing for.

"Look," Dad said, "here." He pointed to a new dry-erase board propped in the corner. A three-ring Venn diagram was drawn on it.

One circle was labeled *Medical Center*; a second *Burned Stone, etc.*; and the third *Boston $*. At the point where they all intersected in the center he had written *Grant brothers*. "The money coming out of Boston is dirty," he said. "It doesn't matter how; there are a hundred ways. Drugs, prostitution, extortion, whatever. And Faith is a giant washing machine. It gets funneled here into supposedly legitimate operations, including the medical center, and then ultimately invested in the growing Ulster County real estate market. It's simple, really. It's just that Owen must have a hundred different strands."

"I still don't understand how Jason winds up dead. I don't understand what his body was doing in Frank's shed at Lake George, and I don't understand how it wound up in Lake Prout."

"We have to assume," Dad said, "that Frank and Owen had something to do with Jason's death. My guess is that he was involved in some way; maybe he was just writing prescriptions for his brother at first and then he got pulled in deeper. He was caught in the web, and presumably he was being compensated, but then his involvement with the Mullens Center led him to better understand his father's businesses and he wasn't happy. Maybe he wanted a bigger cut."

"It doesn't fit with what Joanna said," I protested. "She said he thought the profit margins were obscene."

"You have to think about what he didn't tell her, Lukas. He realized how much money was sloshing around and he thought more of it should be going into his pocket if he was the one running the program, he was the one with access to the meds. She's an artist, an idealist, and he was sleeping with her. You heard how she talked about him. She thought he walked on water; would he be likely to tell the whole story?" Dad tapped a corner of the original dry-erase board where he had drawn a timeline, just below Al Pacino's mutilated photo. "Fourth of July, and then Labor Day. Joanna said he came back from the Fourth with a weight on his shoulders and that it was lifted at the end of the summer. Maybe they finally caved to his demands."

"And then what?"

"Maybe he eventually wanted more."

"I don't know," I said. "That's a pretty cynical read. Maybe it's the opposite. Maybe he wanted out, sort of like Joanna said although she doesn't know the whole story. Maybe he really did just want to be a good doctor and help kids." I took one of the dry-erase markers and extended the timeline beyond Labor Day to Halloween. "The Ford Flynn suicide, at the end of October. That was when Jason began his research into kids who weren't getting help, right? And he started preparing the funding proposal. I made myself read the damn thing, you know. Twice. He wanted to run the center through public health grants and he was all about serving poor and working-class communities in Ulster County. Maybe on Labor Day he told his dad and his uncle to fuck off."

Dad nodded and pinched the bridge of his nose between two fingers. I could almost see the wheels turning, struggling to shift from one track to another. "All right," he said, "Jason comes back to Faith after medical school to do his residency and gets more than he bargained for. Frank doesn't seem to have any children of his own. Jason is the eldest of Owen's; Misty is off becoming an actress and Garrett is . . . well, Garrett. Jason was the heir."

"And he didn't want it."

"Perhaps not." Dad rubbed his jaw. "The note on the proposal. 'Lotus.' One of them, Frank or Owen, wanted Jason to get funding through their shell company alongside, or maybe instead of, traditional sources like the National Institute for Mental Health. He wasn't happy about that, I remember that from our last conversation. He might have said no."

"And that made them kill him?"

Dad paced back and forth in front of the board, his excitement growing. "Why did they want him to take that money in the first place, Lukas? So they'd have a hook in him. Remember what Garrett said to Joanna in Cambridge? He wouldn't get his hands dirty. It's classic: You don't want someone to talk so you make them complicit in your wrongdoing. They'd let Jason in on their secrets; if he wasn't going to join them then they'd at least want some insurance against his exposing them. If Lotus was funneling their dirty money to Jason's new venture, then he'd be dirty enough that he could never talk. But he refuses, and things come to a head. Maybe he went to Lake George to confront them, thinking they wouldn't really hurt him, though he was scared enough to call Misty and visit Joanna first. And ultimately maybe he underestimated what they were willing to do."

"That's dark, Dad. That is very fucking dark. But even if it's all correct, and they killed their own son and nephew, how did his body make its way from one lake to another?"

Dad smiled. "I think I have an answer to that question, Lukas: ceramics."

"Ceramics?"

"Our dinner at the Grant house. You made a mistake. Remember I said you were a terrible liar? You were rattled and started talking about all the talents Jason had, listing activities you saw in photos on the wall, parasailing and such. And you mentioned ceramics."

"So?"

"That wasn't depicted in the photos. Nothing artistic was. I don't think his parents knew about the talents—and I use the term very loosely—that Joanna was cultivating. When his father heard you say that he must have put it together with the visit I'd paid them shortly before the memorial and realized we were interested in Jason and were doing some digging."

"Your powers of observation were on display that night too. The cat's eye."

"I wonder if they ever got it checked out? Likely benign, but still . . ."

"Focus, Dad. All right, so Owen realizes what we're doing . . ."

"And Jason's body immediately and conveniently washes up right where it was supposed to be, on the shore of Lake Prout. No need for further investigation. As my old professor Dr. Myers used to say, 'the effect reflects the intent.' The effect was supposed to be for us to stop looking into the disappearance."

"Except that you noticed the ligature marks."

"And Mancini saw the evidence of chemical exposure."

I nodded. Somehow, it all fit better than I had ever expected. A weird sort of order had emerged from the chaotic dry-erase, from the wall of taped documents. "And now they know for sure we're onto them. The Accountant saw us at Lake George. He'll have told Frank and Owen. Someone, I'm sure it was Frank, was watching me last night. We need to take this to the police."

"Jason didn't trust the police. He told Joanna not to contact them if she was in Faith or New Birmingham."

"The FBI, then. Don't they handle organized crime anyway?" I had a vague sense this was the case from movies. It seemed like the FBI was always bothering Joe Pesci.

"Precisely my thought; we'll take it all to the FBI office in Manhattan, make a presentation. You're an actor, you'll be very effective.

But not quite yet. We're close, Lukas, but all this is still speculative. I need one more visit to Mancini and the lab to review the sample we took from Frank's shed. One more day, two at most to get the results. They're watching us. They want to know what we know, but once we go to the FBI they won't dare make a move."

"I still don't like it. It's not safe. Maybe we should . . . I don't know, get a gun or something."

"Don't be ridiculous. I took the Hippocratic oath."

"I thought you weren't a clinician."

"I'm still a doctor."

"Maybe a prop gun, like Joanna?"

"Do as you like. I wouldn't start waving it at the people we're dealing with, though. They're likely to have real ones." Dad looked at his watch. "I'm heading to the lab."

"I'll drop you off and then I have to go to the theatrical supplies shop. I need to pick some things up for the revue."

Dad was silent in the car on the drive to New Birmingham. He didn't seem agitated the way he had after Joanna Bartlett challenged his hypotheses. He was tense, coiled. I didn't interrupt him, and when I pulled up in front of the medical center he started a bit as though waking. He undid his seatbelt and looked out the window.

"I drove myself here every day for twenty-four years."

"I know you miss it."

"I thought I did. Now, I'm not so sure. I think what I miss is unraveling a mystery. Maybe it doesn't matter so much what mystery it is, though, whether it's one of neurotransmitters or of a disappeared psychiatrist. Maybe what matters is the feeling of purpose."

"What are you going to do when this is all over? When we turn our evidence over to the feds?"

"That," Dad said, "is what I've been thinking about." He patted my knee. "Time will tell, Lukas. We are always starting over. I'll see you in a bit." He got out of the car and walked through the massive rotating doors into the marble lobby with the malfunctioning fountain.

I drove to the other side of town to see about the kids' costumes. Traffic was terrible and then the boxes couldn't be found. An hour went by, then another before they were located in a corner of the shop's basement. My cell phone rang a moment later. It was Dad. "Lukas," he said, "where are you?"

"Still at the shop. Where are you?"

"Outside the medical center. I had my meeting with Mancini."

"And?"

"The specimens match."

I let out a breath. "I knew it."

"No, you didn't. It was a hypothesis. That was why it had to be tested. Your feelings about it—"

"I know: were true but irrelevant."

"In any case, he says there's a high degree of specificity. There's something else too. Derek looked at the HR records. Jason wasn't at work Monday through Wednesday of the week he disappeared."

"Because he never came back from seeing Joanna, and wherever he went next."

"Presumably Lake George."

"I'm going to be a little bit longer, Dad. There's been a screwup with the costumes."

"It's all right, Lukas, I need to learn to live without you at some point. There are such things as taxis; I'll take one home."

I paused. "All right," I said, "I'll see you soon."

I felt unsettled. I called my mother but her phone went straight to voicemail and I didn't leave a message. I wished I could call Misty. I even thought about calling Jules, just to have someone to talk to, but he'd just berate me about all the auditions I'd missed out on. Almost an hour later I finally had the costumes, makeup, and props. The logistics I needed to deal with just for this little revue were dizzying. If I ever did something like this again I was going to need a stage manager. Still, I was making it work. I'd read through Mr. Jollett's *Hamlet* notes a dozen times and he had been right: it was an entirely different thing to experience that show, which I remembered so well as an actor, from the director's side. I was slowly developing my own methods of planning and organizing, figuring out the inner bones of a production, all the things that have to happen but that the audience will never see or applaud.

The guy at the register gave me a 10 percent discount for the trouble and I loaded it all into the back of the car and drove out of New Birmingham, thinking things over. The pieces fit, the theory worked. We would lay it all out for the FBI and then they would get their warrants, do their searches, and find the proof they needed to bring a case. And then what? Frank, Owen, and the Accountant would be arrested, presumably. Garrett too. There would be a trial. What would happen to Misty and her mother? Would they lose everything? Their house, all their money? Was that why Misty didn't want us to continue? She'd made a big deal of not taking her parent's money, of taking out student loans for Yale and wanting to be self-sufficient. What if it wasn't true, though? What if she was more attached to the family fortune than she let on? I felt guilty for thinking about it but I reminded myself that my feelings were TBI.

As I reached the city line I called Dad to see if he wanted me to pick up some dinner. The call went to voicemail, my father's overly formal voice inviting the caller to leave a message. "Hey," I said, "it's me. I should have stopped at the burger place but I'm already past it. I can get pizza or Thai or Chinese, though. Give me a call back."

Five minutes later he hadn't called. I tried again. Again, voicemail. I didn't leave another message. I gripped the wheel tighter, sped up a little. He was probably in the bathroom, I thought, or he had been in the bathroom and he left his phone. He had the ringer off. He probably made a big mess with the coffee and was cursing and hammering his fist on the counter and trying to get it all cleaned up on his own.

I pulled into the driveway and slammed on the brakes, torn between nagging worry and irritation at the mess I knew I would find. The front door was unlocked and I let myself in. "Dad?" I called, sniffing the air for the scent of burnt coffee. Nothing. No smell, no response. "Dad?" I walked through the living room, looked into the bathroom, the kitchen. The coffee maker sat on the counter, pristine. Upstairs. Back down. By the time I'd completed my second circuit through the house, my stomach in knots, the conclusion was inescapable: I knew we had locked the door when we left. My father had been here, and now he was gone.

CHAPTER TWENTY-EIGHT

I stood in the middle of the living room. The house was very still. I tried to force myself to think. Not just to think, to look. To observe. To actually see.

We'd waited too long. We should have gone to the FBI the night before, or that morning. Even if we didn't have the lab report, we should have done it. Now it was too late.

There was something different; I could feel it. Something in the room had been moved, rearranged. Dad would have known right away but Dad was gone. I scanned the couch, the remote control tossed carelessly to one side, Dad's reading glasses on the end table next to a glass of water from the night before. I walked into the kitchen. The precarious spice rack, so prone to tumble when Dad was angry, sat neat and full in the corner. The morning's breakfast dishes were still in the sink.

On to the dining room. Dad's chair and mine were slightly ajar where we'd left them this morning and mom's old chair was perfectly aligned and undisturbed.

There had to be something.

I could hear my heart hammering. Sweat poured down my sides. The living room; there was something different about the living room. I tried to breathe deeply and turned in a slow circle, focusing my thoughts, not letting my feelings crowd my vision, trying to see as if I had a 7 percent reduction in frontal lobe volume and there was no filter on my senses.

Then I had it: our rope. I walked over to the shelf nearest the couch. That morning I had set the spool down on the second shelf. It was always on the second shelf. Now it was on the third. I picked it up. The end of the line stuck out from the bottom, not tucked in the way I always left it, and the end was carelessly frayed rather than the clean, careful cut I made every morning. In that moment I knew: someone had used it to bind my father.

I looked around again. If he'd been threatened or overwhelmed in some way and then restrained . . . then what? Where would they take him, and how? It was a quiet residential street, but you couldn't count on it being empty in the evening. People would be coming home from work. Kids would be playing. Emery might be launching a goddamn rocket. You couldn't just take someone out of their house with their hands tied behind their back.

And then I thought of the one place I hadn't looked and I raced into the kitchen, through it to the side door and wrenched it open, stepping into the garage.

We hadn't used the garage for anything other than storage in years. It smelled of old paint and leaves and gasoline. I flipped the light on and saw that things had been shoved to the side, the lawn mower tossed on top of a pile of leaf bags and old trash barrels in the back. I stared at the empty space in the center of the concrete floor and imagined a car backing in and staying just long enough to receive my father.

I slammed the door and raced through the house and out onto the front walk. Emery was sitting on his front steps petting his dog with one hand and examining a small plastic rocket with the other.

"Emery," I called, "have you seen my father?"

He shook his head. "Not since this morning."

"Has anyone else been around my house?"

"Like who?"

"Anyone, Emery!"

"Nope. I might not have seen them though, I've been prepping for another launch."

"Great," I said, looking up and down the empty street, "that's just great."

"Yup. Almost got run over by a car, just like your dad did."

I turned away, wondering what to do next, who to call, and then I stopped. "Who almost hit you with a car, Emery?"

"Mr. Grant. He's turned into a really bad driver. He sort of weaves back and forth and sometimes he rubs up against the curb. One time, last week, at night, it took him three tries to get his car into his driveway."

"When did this happen? Him almost hitting you?"

"Maybe half an hour ago. Maybe forty-five minutes. I was crossing the street because I'd been out in the woods scouting locations—"

"I know, for the launch. Emery, was he coming out of my garage? Did he turn right and go down the hill? Was he alone, or . . ."

"No, no, no, Lukas. He wasn't coming out of your garage and he wasn't going down the hill. He was alone, going up the hill. He was going home."

I turned and ran. The timeline didn't make sense. Dad couldn't have been home for more than forty-five minutes if he was just leaving the hospital when he called. Even if he got a cab right away, even if there was no traffic leaving New Birmingham—an outside possibility at this time of day—Owen couldn't have met him, subdued and bound him, taken him somewhere, and made it back on time to almost hit

Emery. Maybe Emery had been wrong about the time? Maybe Owen had someone else do his dirty work, maybe the Accountant? My mind raced through possibilities.

I didn't slow down as I reached the Grants' driveway, passed Owen's BMW, and leapt up their front stairs. The front door was unlocked and I threw it open and burst inside. "Owen Grant!" I cried.

The house was silent but I sensed somebody listening.

"Where are you?" I demanded, taking another step in.

"Lukas?" Misty stood at the top of the stairs staring down at me.

"Where is he?"

"My father?"

"Yes, your father, your goddamn father." I walked farther into the house, turning the corner into the living room where Owen Grant was struggling up from his armchair. A half-full glass of whisky sat on the table beside him. I crossed the room in two strides and shoved him back down. "Where is he, you son of a bitch?"

Now it was Owen's turn to stare, his mouth halfway open.

"Where is my father?" I yelled.

"Lukas," he began, "I don't—"

I'd never hit anyone in my life but I'd taken classes on stage combat. This was the same, just without pulling it back at the end. I slapped Owen hard across the face.

"Lukas!" Misty screamed from the doorway.

"Where is my father?"

The room was very still.

Owen Grant looked up at me, then he gestured to the armchair across from him. "Lukas," he said, "sit. Let's talk about this."

I stepped back but did not sit down. "Listen to me," I said, "I do not have time for bullshit. I know about you and your brother. I know about your operation. I know what you're doing with the consulting firms and the construction company and the medical center, the payments and the fake employees, all of that fuckery. I mean, I don't necessarily understand it all, but my father does and the FBI will too."

Owen stared at me for another moment and then burst out laughing. "Well," he said, "it's about damn time somebody figured it out. Holy Christ, we have phantom security guards and desk attendants running the place and nobody says boo. I was going to start staffing the OR with invisible surgeons to see if anyone would speak up."

He stood and shuffled to the sideboard. A red mark stood out on his cheekbone and he rubbed it absently with one hand while rummaging through a collection of bottles with the other. "You don't look like you would hit hard, Lukas, but you do." He settled on something and brought it back to the chair. He sat, poured himself a full glass, then held the bottle out to me. I shook my head and he set it on the floor by his feet. Misty cautiously approached, standing behind the couch.

"Where is your brother?" I asked.

"So far as I know Frank is in Boston, running our 'operation,' as you call it. There, or at his lake house."

"We've been to his lake house. We know he's hosting some sort of gathering but I don't think he's actually there. I think he's here, in Faith, with the Accountant."

Owen peered curiously over the top of his glass. "My brother has an accountant?"

"That's just what we call him, the blond guy in the suit . . ."

"Oh, Harold. Yes, Harold does look like an accountant, now that you mention it. And you've visited the lake house?"

"Lukas," Misty said tentatively, "if your father's gone missing we should call the police. You said that he wanders—"

"At night, he wanders at night. And that's not what's happened here; he's been taken. By your father and your uncle and probably your brother and some fucking guy named Harold." I looked at Owen, who was steadily draining his glass. "Tell me where they are."

"Your father is a research psychiatrist," he said. "I looked into his record. Nobody likes him, but everybody respects him. The department chair said he's a genius, the most tenacious scientist she's ever had the opportunity to meet in person, and even so there are no circumstances under which she would ever let him out of the hospital basement and near a real patient."

"He doesn't want to come out of the basement," I said. "He wants to do his research and he doesn't give a shit what some department chair says."

"Admirable. Why is a man like that looking into consulting contracts and construction arrangements?" Owen stared at me and his eyes did not look as cloudy as they had a moment before.

I hesitated and glanced at Misty. "Dad . . . notices things," I said. "Especially since the accident. He can't keep anything out. He picks up on everything. It's like a curse."

Owen raised his eyebrows and took another drink. "Like the cat's eye," he said. "Those retinal lesions turned out to be benign, by the way."

"Oh. Good."

"Lukas, I do not know where your father is, but if he's missing I very much doubt that my brother or Garrett have anything to do with it. Frank leaves things in New Birmingham to me. If Richard has been acquainting himself with our business, then the most Frank would do is give me a call."

"And what would you do?"

"I wouldn't disappear him in the middle of the day, if that's what you mean."

"You don't seem that concerned," I said.

"About your father? Misty's right. He probably wandered off looking for a snack and he'll come wandering back soon."

"I mean about what we know. Money laundering, that's what it's called, isn't it? Fraud. Whatever the hell your family is doing in Boston to make the money in the first place. You're not worried about all that coming out?"

Owen considered for a moment. Then he swung his arm in a wide arc, flinging the amber liquid in his glass across the pristine white couch. Misty, who was standing behind it, gasped and looked down at the crescent of whisky. "I find," Owen said, "that I don't care about things as much anymore." He pronounced the word "things" with a severity and contempt that signaled a life spent pursuing them. "So far as I'm concerned, they can take it all. All of it. The house, the furniture, the cars. I don't give a shit." He looked mournfully into his now-empty glass. "I will miss the scotch, I suppose."

"They do more than take your scotch away for murder," I said.

Owen looked up at me. "Murder? What are you talking about?"

"Jason. We know what happened to Jason."

Owen was silent for another moment. "I understand what happened to my son," he said. "Water may have filled his lungs when he walked into that lake, but he died of a broken heart because he lost faith in me. He came to understand that his father lacked—in his words—'integrity.' I am responsible for his death. That doesn't make it murder."

"He didn't die in Lake Prout. He was dead before his body went in. When was the last time you spoke to him?" I turned to Misty. "When was the last time you spoke to your brother?"

Neither responded.

"He went to Cambridge," I said, "the weekend before he died. And then he went to the lake house and he never came back, and now Frank is here and he has my father and I need to know where he is."

For a long moment nobody moved. The color had drained from Owen Grant's face and he stared at a point just beyond my shoulder, so transfixed that I imagined he could see his dead son accusing him. His focus was so eerie that I started to turn and look and that was when he came out of his chair, hurtling toward me. I barely had time to raise my arms before his hands closed around my neck and we crashed to the floor. He was shouting and Misty was screaming and I was dimly aware of Alice's lamp falling and shattering beside me.

I pried at his fingers with one hand, trying to find space for air. My other arm was twisted below me and my shoulder was screaming in pain. I wrenched it around, dragging my hand through the shards of Alice's lamp and coming up with a sharp piece of ceramic. I slashed at his face.

Owen cried out as I opened a cut along the left side of his jawline. He released me and rolled off, clutching the wound. I gasped and rolled the other way. Misty was forcing herself between us but I couldn't quite grasp what she was saying. Stars were bursting in front of my eyes and my field of vision was narrowing. All I wanted was to draw air into my lungs. Jesus, I couldn't imagine drowning. I couldn't imagine doing that to myself. However Jason Grant had died, I hoped it hadn't been like that.

Then everything went black.

~

"Lukas, get up." Misty was crouching beside me. I pushed myself to a kneeling position and looked over my shoulder. Owen was gone. "Are you all right?" she asked. "Can you breathe?"

I tried to speak. My voice was hoarse and felt like it was being squeezed through a narrow tube. "Where is he?"

"He's gone."

"Where?"

"I don't know."

I rose and wobbled to the window. The BMW was gone, but a new car was in its place. A familiar SUV. I turned, still shaky on my feet. "Misty," I croaked, "go lock the front—"

"Hello, Lukas." Garrett stood in the doorway to the living room. The Accountant was beside him.

CHAPTER TWENTY-NINE

"Where are we going?" Misty asked.

No one answered. She sat in the back of the SUV with the Accountant beside her and directly behind me, a gun resting in his lap. I was in the passenger seat; Garrett drove.

Minutes passed. My throat ached and my hands were shaking. I wished I could speak with Misty alone, communicate with her in some way. I felt, somehow, that I understood Garrett better than she did. Her eyes had been wide with shock as her brother and the Accountant led us out of the house and into their car. I wanted to try to explain things to her, at least as much as I understood, even if it would not make our situation materially better.

"Jason was an artist," Misty finally said into the silence.

Garrett's eyes shifted to the rearview mirror. "Bullshit. Jason didn't have a creative bone in his body."

"He was. He just didn't tell any of us." Misty was trying to sound bold, but her voice shook.

"Your family probably doesn't know you're still dabbling in Matchbox cars," I observed. "People have their secrets."

"Hmm." Garrett stared at the road.

"I thought you might be interested," Misty said, "given that you were an art history major before you dropped out of Cornell. Or was it business, in the end? Sociology? You changed so often none of us could keep track."

"Hmm," Garrett said again, softly, not deigning to defend his academic record. "What about it, Lukas? Have you seen my late brother's oeuvre?"

"Yes."

"And what did you think?"

"I think it was better than I could have done."

"Thematically, though? I'm curious as to his topic."

I thought about the lopsided mugs and bowls in Joanna Bartlett's kitchen. About the sketchbook, never quite capturing the texture of her hair or the proportions of her face but nonetheless conveying something of the artist's feeling. The word "integrity" looping in and out of a birch forest. "I think he was trying to make something special. I think . . . I think maybe he was trying to be something more than his family wanted him to be."

Garrett snorted. "It would be hard to be more than our father wanted for him. Dad saw him winning a Nobel in medicine or some bullshit like that."

"Not something grand, Garrett. Something real. Something authentic, even if it was small and anonymous and imperfect."

"And you find that laudable?"

"I do."

"Be honest, Lukas: When you're trooping around to those auditions, getting shot down for part after part after part, are you really doing it in the name of art, or are you after something different?"

"Such as what?"

"Oh, say that article *Playbill* did about your understudy. The one that should have been about you. That sort of thing."

"You're full of shit, Garrett," Misty said from the back seat. "Lukas has more authenticity in his little finger than you have in your whole goddamn body."

"Does he, now? Truth and beauty, that's all he cares about? That's why he's been running all over New Birmingham with his ridiculous father, playing detective? It has nothing to do with wanting to get into my little sister's pants one more time?"

"Jesus, Garrett, I'm not your little sister. We're twins."

He chuckled.

"My father and I are getting this detective thing down," I said. "One of the few things we haven't quite figured out, though, is exactly why you killed your brother. I have a feeling it was more than simple jealousy, though I'm sure that was part of it."

Garrett shook his head slowly, stretching the twisted muscles in his neck, eyes glued to the road. "I didn't kill Jason, Lukas," he growled. "I tried to save him. He could have saved himself, if he had just played along. If he had just taken the money that was sitting on the fucking table. If he could lower himself to get his hands even just the slightest bit dirty." He hammered the wheel with one fist, punctuating each of the last three words.

"You're a little obsessed with dirt on people's hands, aren't you?" I asked. "My sense is that you'd already gotten him plenty dirty. Was he writing prescriptions for you? Connecting you with doctors and pharmacists who would? Friendly nurses who had access?"

Garrett was silent for a moment and then he laughed, a single angry bark. "Jesus, no. We have our own suppliers, Lukas. Can you imagine Jason dealing drugs? When we were kids he wouldn't take a bill from Dad's wallet without leaving an IOU." He laughed again but it caught in his throat.

"You met him in the woods between our houses, days before he disappeared."

"Yes, I did."

"Why?"

"To warn him. To tell him what he needed to do, to be safe. The same reason I followed him to Cambridge. He wasn't talking to me by that time but I thought if I could get to him first, if I could just make him listen to me, get him to throw Frank a fucking bone . . ." Garrett shook his head again. His knuckles were white on the steering wheel. We were outside of town now, the tires whirring on county highway. The sun was meeting the horizon.

I guessed where we were going. My stomach clenched and I gripped the door handle. I had no doubt that any effort to jump from the vehicle or to wrestle control from Garrett would result in the Accountant shooting me from behind, and even if I did manage to get away it would leave Misty alone with her psychopathic twin and his associate.

The indifferent miles wore on and there was nothing left to say. I wanted to remind Garrett of our childhood together, of the friendship we'd once had, but I knew it was pointless. That person was gone.

I wondered where my father was. I wondered if I would see him again. "Garrett—" I began.

"We're done talking," Harold said. It was the first I'd heard him speak. His voice was low and pleasant, much like you'd expect an accountant's to be. He conveyed calm competence. I looked out the window as Garrett turned into the parking area beside another car, this one with Massachusetts plates. We had arrived at our destination.

CHAPTER THIRTY

"There's something lonely about a lake," Frank Grant said. He stood, hands clasped behind his back, looking out at the water and the reflection of the setting sun. He turned to me. "Don't you think so, Lukas?"

"Actually, I do," I replied. "I've always been partial to rivers."

He nodded. "Rivers can be very peaceful."

I was sitting on a rock beside my father. His hands were tied behind his back and his ankles were bound with what I recognized as the yellow cord we used to tie ourselves together at night. There was a bruise on his cheekbone and dry blood on his upper lip. Harold stood behind us, gun in hand. Frank was maybe ten feet away. He was bigger than he'd appeared in the newspaper pictures on my bedroom wall. Lucia Grant stood beside him, Misty and Garrett behind her.

"There have been some very interesting developments," Dad murmured.

"I've been explaining to your father," Frank said, "that it is important for me to understand exactly what the two of you have been up to." He spoke in a calm, conversational tone, as though picking up a thought he had casually set down a few moments before and turning it over in his mind. "I believe we were coming close to an understanding, though now the situation has changed."

"Nothing has changed," Dad said. "You leave Lukas alone and I tell you everything. It's simple."

"Less simple now," Frank said, "because he's been here and he's seen us. Before, it would have been conceivable that you had some sort of fit and wandered off, fell in a hole and were never found. Started having brain damage spasms or some shit like that."

"That is not how traumatic brain injury works," Dad said.

"Shut up, Dad," I said quietly.

"There's no reason for him to butcher the science."

Frank sighed and gripped a cigar in his teeth, turning away from Lake Prout to shield it from the wind as he struck a match.

I glanced at Garrett, wondering whether I might find a flicker of sympathy in my old friend's face. After parking the car he had taken a moment to dump a handful of pills in his mouth. He was sitting on a flat rock, holding his head in his hands. "People know where we are," I said. "They'll tell the police if we go missing."

"No, they don't," Frank replied between intense drags as the cigar caught light. "And we own the police."

I involuntarily moved closer to my father, our shoulders touching, and for a moment I thought that he was shaking. He had every right to be, but it was a relief to realize that I was the one who was quivering and that he was totally still.

"If it was just the two of you, I'd drop you both in the middle of the lake," Frank continued. "I'd be enjoying a bourbon at my lake house by midnight."

"I doubt it," Dad said.

"You don't think so?"

"Oh, I think you would kill us and that you could do it by midnight. And I assume you enjoy bourbon. I don't think you would drop us in the middle of the lake though. It's about seventy-five feet deep out there."

Frank snorted, turning back to us and releasing a stream of smoke through his nose. "Perfect."

"Maybe. But people are creatures of habit. I think you'd weigh us down and drop us where you dropped Jason's body, which was very likely not in seventy-five feet of water given how quickly you had your assistant retrieve it."

Frank studied him. His jaw clenched and unclenched around the cigar. "Variety is the spice of life," he finally said. "I'd enjoy taking you out to the dead center of the lake and making you watch while I put your kid in, still breathing."

I felt my body shake but was curiously devoid of emotion.

"However, as I said . . ." Frank half turned away and glanced toward the others. "It's not just you two. Things are complicated."

Lucia stepped forward, standing alongside her brother-in-law. She brought Misty with her, one hand resting lightly on her daughter's arm. "Not so complicated," she said. "Misty has never been interested in the family business."

"Very simple, in fact," Dad agreed. "You've already killed a nephew, why not a niece? And you"—he directed this at Lucia—"were apparently complicit in one child's murder. I'm sure the second will be even easier. You'll still have the third, though he's clearly the runt of the litter."

"Dad," I whispered, "I'm begging you: please stop talking."

"Misty is not going to be murdered," Lucia said in the brisk and unruffled tone of someone declaring that she would decline dessert that evening. "Misty is going back to New York City to pursue her acting career. She is going to outgrow this childish determination to make her own way and will allow her parents to finance a Park Avenue condominium that recently became available. She is going to have lunch with several producers I know and she is not ever going to be curious about the boy down the street who she had the very temporary misfortune of dating in high school."

Misty started as though just waking up and turned to her mother. "Mom?" She looked at Harold, then at Dad, then at me, and finally back to her mother. "I don't understand."

"Jason was always the smart one," Frank muttered.

"Misty." Lucia took her daughter by both arms. "There is nothing to understand. This is not about understanding. You do not want or need to understand. Understanding is a burden. If you grew up the way I did, the way your uncle and your father did, then you would know that, but you and your brothers had a pampered upbringing and this is the result: You think when you should act. You try to understand instead of moving to adapt. I am telling you what you are going to do, and you are going to do it."

"But I want to know," Misty said. "I want to know the truth."

"No," Lucia said, "you don't."

"I need—"

The crack of the slap reverberated over the water. Misty's head flew to the side and she stumbled back, but Lucia still held her with her other hand and she did not fall. We were all silent for a long moment.

"Misty," Garrett finally said, rising to his feet and slurring his words, "you really need to shut up and do exactly what our mother tells you to."

Frank spoke: "I'm not sure, Luc. This is just like the situation with Jason. Once they know, they know. It doesn't matter if they say they're going to keep our secrets. It doesn't matter if they have some other chickenshit career going. Sooner or later they're going to grow a conscience and we're going to be fucked."

"This is not like Jason," Lucia said. "Jason was . . . unique. I can manage Misty. There is nothing to be unsure about. I'll handle her, you take care of the two of them."

Frank rubbed the back of his neck, glanced at Harold, then looked at us as though contemplating the scope of a job.

"Lukas," Dad said quietly, "I have something to tell you."

"Okay," I said. I felt increasingly far away, as though I were looking down from above. My stomach was hollow and my mouth was dry.

"I am very proud of you."

"TBI," I said. "Maybe true, but irrelevant."

"No," he said, "it is true and it's very relevant."

Frank Grant stepped toward us. Garrett, standing unsteadily a short way behind his uncle, met my eyes for a moment and then turned away. Dad twisted toward Harold. "I have a question for you," he said. "Can you guess my son's middle name?"

"What are you talking about?" Frank asked.

Dad looked at him. "Lukas here. What's his middle name?"

"How the hell should I know?"

Dad turned back to the man we knew as the Accountant. "Mind reading," he said. "There's more of a science to it than people think. Some interesting studies, actually, mostly out of Belgium. Janssen and his group are doing some very innovative work with a double-blind format and I find it persuasive. Give it a try."

"You had your bell rung far too hard," Frank said. "You want to talk about mind reading? Just—"

He never finished the sentence. Dad, with his lack of a filter, had heard something the rest of us missed, behind him and to the right, and he had distracted Frank and Harold just long enough. Owen Grant appeared from the darkness and brought a rock down, hard, on the back of Harold's head. There was a sickening crunch and the Accountant crumpled to the ground.

"Get your hands off of my daughter." Owen advanced onto the stone beach. Dried blood from the cut I had given him crusted the side of his face and stained the front of his shirt. His eyes were fastened on his wife. Frank, Garrett, and Lucia all stepped back.

"To be honest," Dad said, "Janssen is a total quack; really just an unbelievable moron."

"I don't care," I said. "Give me your hands."

He peered at me. "Lukas, what happened to your neck? Did someone try to choke you?"

"Please, Dad, turn around."

Dad twisted so his bound hands were toward me. The line had been wrapped around his wrists multiple times. It was cutting into his skin. I tugged, trying to find a way to loosen the knot.

Owen moved away from Harold's prone body and approached his brother. "You killed him," he said. "I need to know why. He went to see you and he never came back. You killed my son, and you dropped him in this lake, and you let me believe that he killed himself because he was ashamed of me."

"Not mutually exclusive," Dad observed to Owen's back as I tugged helplessly at his bonds. "He was indeed ashamed of you. It was crushing for him when he understood the true scope and nature of the family business, as well as your expectation that he would inherit it. I imagine it ruined his Fourth of July weekend."

Owen turned to stare at Dad, who continued: "By the end of the summer, of course, he found his moral compass. He found the strength to tell you that he wanted no part of it. And he was cutting his own path, wasn't he? He had a vision for the Mullens Center, and it was not as a laundromat for money coming out of South Boston. And you were just fine with that, weren't you, Owen?"

Owen blinked and nodded, his mouth slightly open. Frank took a tentative step, his boots crunching in the gravel on the beach. Owen spun toward his brother, raising the rock, and Frank stepped back again.

Dad continued. "You were all right with it. You would have been fine with a son who was nothing other than a devoted child psychiatrist. A daughter who was a talented actress. And a third child who was just as dirty as you and your brother but half as smart and hooked on narcotics. Two out of three isn't bad. What you didn't understand, Owen, was that Frank wasn't all right with it."

"Don't listen to him, Owen," Frank said. "He's a fucking head case. I'm your brother—"

"Go on," Owen said to Dad.

"Frank didn't trust Jason. He recognized something you also saw in your son: Honesty. Dedication. Integrity. For him, though, that was a threat. He sent that man, the one likely now dying of a subdural hematoma as a result of the blow you gave him, to keep an eye on Jason. He kept his employer abreast of Jason's activities, and Frank came to the conclusion that he would feel safe only if Jason was sufficiently complicit in the family business that he'd go down with you if affairs ever came to light. That's why he got hold of the funding proposal Jason was developing for Mullens; it's why he wanted Jason to take family money via Lotus. He wanted Jason to be dirty. But Jason wanted no part in it and he went to the lake house to confront his uncle, to have it out once and for all." He shook his head and looked past Owen to Frank. "Ridiculous architecture, by the way. You have truly atrocious taste."

I groped on the ground behind us, looking for a sharp rock I could use to attack the cord.

Owen turned to Frank. "Is what he's saying true?"

Frank gazed back at his brother for a moment, then took his cigar from his mouth and tapped ash onto the shore. "Those are the facts, Owen. Those are the facts. Facts are not the same thing as the truth . . ."

"Well," Dad said, "the truth is that you drowned Jason in Lake George, likely at the end of your dock. Then you put him in the shed and brought his belongings to this spot so that it would look like suicide. Finally, when the search was called off, you delivered the body, lungs conveniently full of fresh water, to Lake Prout. You tied a weight to his left arm—that was a mistake, by the way—and you dropped him in shallow water not far offshore. Frankly, I would have just burned his corpse or buried it in the woods, but I suppose you wanted it to be in the right place. Sort of an insurance policy, in a way. And indeed you used it. You"—Dad directed this last at Lucia—"realized we were making progress in investigating Jason's disappearance and you called Frank and arranged for the body to be brought back up and found in the hope that it would close the issue." He shrugged and turned from Frank to Owen with the satisfied but disinterested look of a doctor completing a challenging diagnosis. "Credit where it is due, Lukas is the one who connected many of these dots. And Dr. Mancini was also instrumental."

I picked up a rock with a sharp edge and sawed at the cord, thinking about doing to Dad what Owen had just done to Harold in an effort to get him to stop talking.

Owen was shaking his head with the disoriented look of a man who had woken in the midst of a terrible dream. He turned to his brother, his wife, and his surviving children. "Lucia?"

For all the times I had seen her, I'd never really looked at Lucia Grant. She seemed to fade into any room she entered, agreeably blending into her surroundings. She was an unimposing woman, short and small boned, tiny alongside her husband and brother-in-law. "Jason was weak, Owen," she said. "He had none of your strength, none of mine, none of Frank's. Even Garrett's, when he's in the right frame of mind. He couldn't live with it. He was going to expose us."

The bond around Dad's wrists finally gave way under the sawing pressure of the rock. "Now my ankles," Dad said softly. "You do it, I can't feel my hands." I slid off the rock to crouch by his feet. Owen and Frank, both focused on Lucia, were half turned away.

"It's true, Owen," Frank said. "Jason came to see me with a binder full of papers on Burned Stone. All the evidence he needed to expose us, everything we built. He said he would do it too, if I didn't fuck off and leave him and his center alone. He said he'd turn it all over to a newspaper."

Owen shook his head. "No."

"Yes." Frank tucked the cigar back between his teeth and cupped one hand in the other, loudly cracking his knuckles. He looked down at Harold, who showed no sign of moving. "The little son of a bitch had no idea, Owen. That was the problem: he had our blood in his veins but no blood on his hands." He looked back up at his brother. "You raised him in that big house, sent him to those fancy schools while I was back home fighting like a pit bull to keep what was ours. And here you are, in your new life, pillar of the goddamn community, chairman of the board. And that's fine, brother. That's fine. That was always the plan, and the plan worked. But one thing that was never going to happen was for your boy, with his Ivy League degree and his clean fingernails, to tear down what I built up. Never. I was not going to let it happen, and sooner or later it would have if I had stood by and done nothing."

Owen's mouth opened but no words came out.

"That all," said my father, "is extremely interesting." The group turned to us just as the line around his ankles broke. I dropped the stone and took his arm, pulling him to his feet. We could run, back the way Owen had come. We'd circle back to the road. We had a chance.

Instead, Dad took a step toward the brothers, rotating and rubbing his hands. "I do have a question, though," he said, and I realized that even if it proved fatal he was utterly unable to let the puzzle go. "Jason went to Lake George to threaten you," Dad said to Frank. "He knew exactly who you were by that time. He knew you were very dangerous. He was blackmailing you; he wanted you to let him walk away from Lotus, no strings attached, or else he would expose you. He met you at an isolated house in the woods where he was in fact murdered. It seems foolish for him to have gone, and though I did not know Dr. Grant well, I do not think he was a fool."

"No," Frank said, "he was no fool. He told me that he'd left the originals of the papers back in Faith and that if anything happened to him they were going to be mailed to the *Ulster County Courier*."

Dad considered. "I assume he didn't tell you who he left them with?"

"He did," Frank said. "He needed some persuading, but he did." He glanced at Lucia.

"He said he left them with his mother," Dad said.

Frank nodded.

"He didn't think you had any part of it," Dad said to Lucia. "He thought it was just Owen and Frank. And when he was 'persuaded,' he said the papers were with you because he didn't think Frank would hurt you. He thought Owen would protect you."

It was quiet on the beach for a moment. Each one of us was alone with what Dad had just said, but only I had stood on the dock by that cabin, only I had looked out at the empty water where Jason Grant had died. Frank had been right, I thought: a lake is a very lonely place.

"You persuaded him," Owen said softly.

Frank turned to his brother. "Owen—"

It was too late. Owen Grant sprang across the distance between them. He struck his brother in the midsection, head down like a battering ram, and the two of them crashed to the ground. Owen raised the hand holding the rock but Frank caught it and pushed his brother to one side. They grappled, rolling over each other on the rocky shore, tumbling closer to the water. Garrett started toward his father and uncle, paused, then stepped back and tripped, landing flat on his back.

"Come on," I said, taking Dad's arm. I pulled him away. He stumbled a bit but kept his footing. We reached Misty and I took her hand. She looked dazed and I found myself trying to climb the trail half carrying her and towing my father, whose extremities still seemed to be numb.

We had gone no more than a dozen steps when Misty twisted away, turning to look back at the shore. Garrett stood paralyzed. Frank and Owen had reached the waterline. Owen had lost the rock and was atop his brother, straddling his chest with hands planted on his face, pushing him underwater. Frank was struggling, flailing and forcing his face above the surface for short gasps before being driven down again. Owen's bloody jaw was set and clenched and his eyes were on his task. Then Lucia was behind him. She stood on the edge of the water and raised one arm, and I could see the light glint off the gun in her hand as she pointed it at the back of her husband's head.

"No!" Misty screamed.

Owen turned his head to look at her, momentarily loosening his grip on Frank, who in that moment of opportunity struck him in the neck. Owen slumped to one side as Lucia pulled the trigger. The shot rang out, reverberating over the lake, and Frank, who had been pushing himself out of the water, fell back.

Misty ran toward her parents and I ran after her. I didn't know what her mother would do; it seemed entirely possible, given the ice in her voice when she had addressed Owen moments before, that she would simply shoot each of us and be done with it.

Misty reached her father. Frank's blow had connected with his windpipe and he didn't seem able to breathe. She shoved Garrett out of the way and knelt beside Owen in the shallows, wrapping her arms around him and trying to lift and pull him away from her mother. "Help me, Lukas," she called. A few feet away Frank was still moving in the red-stained water, crawling toward shore. I splashed into the lake behind Misty and started to bend over to help. Then my eyes met Lucia's and I straightened. Her gun was lowered but still held before her. Her face was entirely calm.

"Did he really give you copies?" I asked.

She raised her eyebrows. "Excuse me?"

"Jason. He didn't know you were involved in Burned Stone, in Lotus, in everything. When he went to see Frank, did he actually leave copies of the papers with you?"

She considered me for a moment. "No," she finally said. "He was bluffing, and he chose the wrong bluff." She raised the gun and in that moment Dad stepped between us.

"It's time for you to go," he said.

"What makes you—" she began.

"You have to," Dad said. "Now." He nodded toward the far shore where the lake curved to the east. Blue lights flickered in the trees. "Someone heard the shot, probably at the campground. They're opening up for the season. It's your bad luck that a trooper must have been fairly close; they tend to park at the speed trap on Highway 41. You may own local law enforcement, but I expect the New York State Police are out of your price range. They'll be here in approximately four minutes, given the quality of the road."

Garrett stepped to her side. "Mom, come on." Lucia didn't move. She looked at me and Dad, and then at Misty.

"If you were willing to shoot your daughter," Dad said, "you wouldn't have tried to persuade her to go back to Manhattan."

"You have no idea what I'm capable of," Lucia said.

"I didn't say capable. I said willing."

Behind us, Owen's breath came in ragged gasps. Frank lay on the rocks just above the waterline.

"Are you testing my will, Dr. Moore?" Lucia asked. The hand holding the gun didn't waver.

"I have no opinion about your will."

"I would have thought character assessment was your expertise."

"My expertise is adenosine metabolism, primarily in *Rattus norvegicus domestica*, or what you would call the ordinary lab rat. There are some clinical applications. Predicting psychopathic behavior is not one of them."

I closed my eyes. The upside of being shot, I thought, was that Dad would finally stop talking. Execution was one situation he couldn't make any worse.

Then Misty was beside us. "Is it true?" she asked her mother. "What Dr. Moore said? What Uncle Frank said? He drowned Jason, right there by the dock? Is that what happened? Did you know this whole time?"

"It's irrelevant," Lucia said. "He's gone."

"I need to know. I need to know the truth."

"It doesn't matter," her mother replied. "In the end, it doesn't make a difference."

"Truth is truth," Dad said. "It does matter, especially in the end."

The road did not run alongside the lake the entire way and the flashing lights were no longer visible in the distance. A siren reached us on the wind, however. "They're moving quickly," Dad observed. "I'm revising my estimate to two and a half minutes." I was not sure that time pressure was what the situation called for. There was a moment of silence, the seconds ticking down in my head.

"It is what happened," Lucia finally said, her eyes on Misty. "And I knew. I knew because I was there, watching from the window." She looked at my father. "There should never be any question about my will, Dr. Moore." She raised the gun, aiming it directly at his chest, and as she did so I wrapped my arms around my father from behind and heaved him out of the way, hurling him into the shallow water, leaving nothing between myself and Lucia Grant. My momentum carried me to the right as the shot rang out and I felt as much as heard the bullet pass close by my left ear.

"Lukas!" Dad cried, coming up sputtering, trying to regain his footing, slipping and falling on the slippery rocks at the bottom of the lake.

I found my balance and Lucia held the gun for a moment, aimed squarely between my eyes. Then she smiled and stepped back, lowering it. "Unlike Frank," she said, "I don't take any pleasure in killing. People die when they have to. You, Lukas, now do not have to. Do you know why?"

"Why?"

"Because there are four bullets remaining in this gun. There are five of you, assuming Harold is indeed dead, and it's just as well to leave five of you alive as it is to leave one."

"That," I said, "is very . . . interesting." I couldn't think of anything else to say.

Then she was gone, moving toward the road with Garrett wobbling beside her, and in a moment they were out of sight.

Dad was beside me, soaking wet. He grabbed my shoulders and looked me up and down before concluding that I was unperforated. "Lukas," he said, "that is by far the single dumbest thing you have ever done, and that includes your decision to become a professional actor." Then he briefly embraced me and turned his attention to the men lying on the ground. Misty knelt beside her father and Dad looked down at Frank who, to my inexpert eye, seemed to have been shot in the shoulder. "I'm just a psychiatrist," he said, "and I'm not a clinician, but I believe that he will live."

Frank, capturing the moment, cursed and then moaned incoherently.

Owen lay just a few feet from his brother. I could see his chest rising and falling, and looking closer I could see that his eyes were open. Still, he didn't try to move and he didn't respond when Misty laid her hand on his chest. He was looking elsewhere, out into the falling darkness over Lake Prout.

Dad turned his back on the scene, facing the water, and I stepped beside him. Behind us the sirens grew louder. In another moment we would hear the trooper's footsteps coming down the path, but for a moment nobody spoke.

"Why didn't he really leave copies with someone?" Dad mused. "Lucia was right, it was a dangerous bluff and it wound up killing him.

Perhaps it was too much of a risk? The person might have looked at them while he was gone."

For once I knew that my father was wrong. More than that, I knew the answer, though in that moment I chose not to share it and to let silence fall over the lake once again.

CHAPTER THIRTY-ONE

I sat alone on Joanna Bartlett's couch, holding my tea. It was in a lopsided mug, created by Jason Grant in an effort at ceramics his parents didn't know he had made. An effort I revealed in a careless slip, setting in motion the events that led to their downfall.

Joanna sat across from me sipping her own tea. A thick pack of papers rested on the table between us alongside a stamped envelope addressed to the *Ulster County Courier.*

"He brought them to you on that last visit to Cambridge," I said. "That was why he had to come in person, before he went to Lake George. He anticipated being in danger and so he gave you the papers and instructions to send them if he disappeared. Why didn't you do it?"

"I almost did," she said. "I took them to a blue box and nearly dropped them in, but I couldn't."

"They'd have no way of tracing them back to you."

"That wasn't the issue. I wasn't afraid."

"What, then?"

She considered. "I told you about that night, on the roof?"

"With the telescope?"

"Yes."

"You told me," I said. It had been the occasion when she observed Jason using his left eye to peer at the meteor.

"It was a beautiful night. Have you ever seen meteors, Lukas?"

"I thought I did, once, but it turned out to be an airplane. Very disappointing."

She shook her head. "You know a meteor when you see one. I remember that night so well not because of the meteor, though, but because of how exhausted we both were. I couldn't believe that he wanted to go up there and see it."

"Why were you so tired?"

"There was a teenager. Sixteen years old. Clinical depression, suicidal. He'd already made several attempts. He was on twenty-four-hour suicide watch but we were understaffed. We always were."

"That was part of the racket."

She shrugged. "The unit nurse made me help out and I had the late-night shift. I was supposed to sit, just outside his room, and keep watch. They thought that if he woke up and no one was watching he would take advantage of the opportunity and find a way to kill himself."

"I can't imagine wanting to die so badly."

"Neither can I, but he did and he was as serious as cancer. So I sat, and I watched, but the minutes went by and it was two in the morning and I couldn't do it. My eyes closed and I dozed off."

"What happened?"

"Jason was there when I woke. Sitting beside me. He'd already worked a full shift. I deserved a reprimand but he just pulled up another chair and sat and kept watch on that sick, sleeping boy until he and I woke in the morning. And of course then it was time for another shift; by the time the meteor came he'd been awake for almost forty-eight hours."

I knew who the boy had been.

"It didn't matter in the end," Joanna continued. "I heard that boy died by suicide anyway, on Halloween night."

"We came across his case during our investigation," I said. "I think it mattered. It wasn't forgotten."

"I'm glad for that."

"You knew what would happen," I said. "You read the documents. You didn't want the center to close."

"That's right. It took me a while to put the pieces together but I understood what it would mean. The Mullens Center, maybe the entire hospital would collapse. It was his legacy. It was what he believed in. He tried to set it on a different path, and to some extent he was successful. There are programs there that wouldn't exist if not for him. Clinics for children without mental health coverage, school outreach programs. It was where he sat up all night so that a boy could sleep safely. I couldn't do it."

I drank my tea and looked at the papers on the table. They didn't matter anymore; the FBI and the IRS were tearing the medical center apart along with the Grant family finances, Burned Stone and Lotus and Hiring Consultants, all of it. Frank and Owen Grant were in custody; Owen with the federal authorities for fraud and Frank with the county for murder. Harold survived his head trauma and would be charged as Frank's accomplice. Lucia and Garrett had been apprehended at an airport in South Carolina just a few days after disappearing from Faith.

"Is your investigation over?" Joanna asked.

I nodded. "It is."

"I'm sorry I didn't help you. I'm sorry I kept this from you. I never really knew whether you were working for his family or not."

"I understand. It's all right. We put the pieces together for ourselves."

"You seem to be talented private investigators."

I smiled. Strangely, she wasn't wrong.

"Did you find out anything more about him?" Joanna asked.

"About Jason?"

"Yes. I knew him, of course. I knew him very well. I loved him. It's just . . ." She paused and looked down into her mug. "When someone dies, the process of knowing them just stops. It's like they're set in amber. I wish I could discover just one more thing."

I didn't know what to say. I felt that I had learned a good deal about Jason Grant. I knew where and how he died, and where his body had lain before being dropped into Lake Prout with a weight mistakenly tied to the wrist on his dominant hand. I guessed that I had seen the last sight his eyes had taken in when I stood at the end of the dock on Lake George. I knew the final lie he told, the bluff he'd tried to pull off, thinking his uncle might spare him if Frank believed that Lucia had the papers on the table in front of me. And I knew why he didn't tell the truth, no matter what kind of "persuasion" Frank and Harold were employing. "We found out that he loved you," I said. "He truly loved you, and he loved you very much."

Joanna nodded. "Thank you," she said after a moment.

A black cat emerged from behind the sofa and leapt into her lap. Joanna smiled and stroked its fur. "Your father was right," she said, "about the mice. I went ahead and got a cat."

"Sometimes he gives good advice."

"Apparently so."

"What are you going to do?" I asked.

"I'm going back to school."

"Harvard Med?"

"That's right. I'm going to graduate and I'm going to be a child psychiatrist."

"You'll be good at it."

"I hope so."

"You will. I live with a good psychiatrist, and I know one when I see one." I set the misshapen mug down on the table beside the papers and stood. "Goodbye, Joanna."

"Goodbye, Lukas. Give your father my regards."

"I will." I walked to the door.

"Lukas."

"Yes?"

"When you finally see a meteor, you won't think that it's an airplane. You won't mistake it for anything other than what it is."

It took a few years, but when it happened she turned out to be absolutely right.

I brought a cushion out to the front stoop and sat on it. My ass still hurt where the dog bit me, though the bruises on my face and neck were healing. I sipped a cold beer. Misty sat beside me with a glass of iced tea. Her packed car was parked by the curb at the end of my driveway.

"Tell me about the part," I said.

"It's off-Broadway. Unknown playwright, unknown director, just out of school. Zero budget." She told me about the play and the part that her agent wanted her to audition for. I drank my beer and listened, not as a fellow actor who wanted my own shot at the stage and not as a sometime boyfriend who wondered if we were on or off. I listened as a friend who wanted the best for her, as someone who knew what she had been through and wanted nothing more than for her to have better days ahead.

"It sounds great," I said when she was done and my bottle was empty. "It sounds perfect for you."

"You think so?"

"I really do."

"If I get the part will you come see it?"

"I'll be there on opening night."

She smiled and sipped her tea. "What about you, Lukas? What are you going to do?"

"I'm thinking of going back to school."

"Really? Where?"

"Ulster County Community, to start, and then I'll probably transfer to SUNY and commute."

"You'll stay here? With your father?"

"He still needs me."

"And you'll study theater?"

"I'll minor in theater. I'm going to major in education. Mr. Jollett is getting close to retirement; someone will need to replace him at Tricounty."

Misty stared at me.

"What?" I asked. "You don't think I'd be a good teacher?"

"No," she said, "I think it's perfect. The revue was amazing. All the kids love you. You know how to talk to them, how to get them to do things they didn't think they could. You knew what to say to Brian, remember? That night at the dinner, you told him the secret to being brave, and then you stuck around and helped him actually do it. I think you'll be a wonderful teacher."

"Thank you."

"When did you decide?"

"I've been thinking about it for little while now, but I made the decision back on the beach. I thought I was going to die. I was sure of it. And do you know what I thought about? The revue. Not getting to see the revue. Not being there for the kids."

Misty nodded and squeezed my hand. We hadn't talked much about the beach or about her family, but a few days before she'd spent a long time in my room with Dad and the dry-erase and the papers and photos, and when she came out something was different about her. Something was resolved. After she left I asked Dad what they talked about. He shrugged and patted my arm, looking very tired. "The truth will set you free, Lukas," he said, "but it usually hurts like hell."

We sat for another moment and then she set her empty glass down on the bottom step. "I have to go." We both stood. "Thank you, Lukas. You did what I asked you to do."

"Did I?"

She nodded. "You helped me find my brother."

"I'm sorry for how it turned out."

She looked up the hill, in the direction of her old house. "All you can do is decide to look. You have no control over what you find."

"That sounds about right."

"Are you sure you don't want me to give you the name of the guy who works at the hotel? That security footage is still available."

I shook my head. "No. Thank you, but no. It . . . it won't matter."

"Your father said that the truth always matters."

"Maybe it does, but maybe I'm not as devoted to it as you and he are."

"I think you're perfectly devoted. I think you'll find your own way to it, in your own time, and when you do you'll be ready." Misty stepped forward and embraced me for a long moment and then turned and walked to her car. "Oh!" she called, turning back. "I forgot one thing." She opened her trunk and took out a brown paper bag, hurrying back down the path to me. “Will you give this to Emery? I already said goodbye to him and Alice, but it finally came in the mail this morning.”

I looked inside the bag. It was an altimeter for a model rocket. “I’ll give it to him,” I said. “It’ll probably burn up within the week, but I’ll give it to him.”

Misty smiled. “Goodbye,” she said.

“Goodbye.”

She returned to her car and got in and I watched her drive away. She never came back to Faith but I told her the truth about opening night. I was there for her debut and I have been in the audience for all twenty-three opening nights Misty Grant has had in the years since. I am always there, and she always sees me when she comes to the foot of the stage for her bow, and she always smiles.

After she was gone and I had stood on my empty front walk for a few minutes, letting my thoughts settle, I gathered myself and crossed the street. I rang the bell at the Quinlan house and waited, but no one answered. I thought about leaving the bag in the mailbox but I wanted to see Emery’s face when he got his present. I walked across the front yard and around the side. I had never been in their backyard but it was where he launched some of the rockets and I thought that he might be tinkering.

The smell caught me first, and I knew what I was going to see a moment before turning the corner and entering the garden: rows of lavender flowers, lining the back of the house, clustering around a bench in the center of the yard, arrayed around a set of oak trees. Lilacs, like those found beside my injured father at Forty-Third and Vine. Mrs. Quinlan was on her knees, tending one of the plants. Her back was to me but she turned as I entered and then she stood. “Lukas,” she said.

“Hello, Mrs. Quinlan.”

She followed my gaze to the flowers. We were both silent for a moment, and I knew. Someone who was distraught at the accident scene but never appeared afterward, never called or made any effort to see if he was all right. It didn't make any sense unless it was someone who saw him across the street every day. Some mysteries are solved by observation and persistence, and some are solved when you finally walk into the right backyard.

I stepped forward and held out the paper bag. "This is for Emery. From Misty."

She took it. "Thank you."

I nodded and started to walk away, then turned back. "You could come see him," I said. "He'd probably like that. You could all come, you and the kids, we could order Chinese. Or you could come and see him alone."

Mrs. Quinlan held the bag with the altimeter and looked at her flowers. "He asked me not to."

"Why?"

"I think it was because of you."

"Because I came home?"

She nodded. "He didn't want you to know. He didn't want you to be ashamed of him."

"I'm not ashamed. It turns out that I'm quite proud of him, actually."

"It's not just that," she said. "I've been afraid."

I understood, maybe better than anyone else could. "He's still him," I said. "He's different. In some ways he's better and in some ways he's damaged, and he always will be. But he's still him."

She looked up at me and nodded. "All right. I'll come soon."

"Good." I turned and walked back to the front yard, glancing down at the shrubs where I'd found Dad searching in his delirium, an easy place for a secret lover to tuck or retrieve a note or a gift back when there was the need for such maneuvers. It could have made me feel angry or hurt, and maybe it did, but more than anything else it made my father seem human and I was grateful for it.

I crossed the street to my own house, up the walk and the front steps and into the living room, past the spool of yellow rope sitting on the second shelf, and dropped onto the couch. On the screen Hugh Grant was pushing his hair out of his face and smiling at a girl.

"I've made a decision," I said.

"What's that?" Dad asked.

"I'm going back to school."

"Ah, good. NYU?"

"No."

"City College?"

"No."

"Not Columbia? It's an Ivy. Your high school GPA wasn't stellar, as I recall. I might know some people, I suppose. I could—"

"I'm staying here, Dad. I'm going to commute. We're staying here, together."

Hugh seemed concerned on the TV screen. His brow was furrowed and he was biting his lower lip.

"If that's what you want," Dad said. His voice sounded different. Constricted. I didn't turn to look at him.

"It's what I want. I'm going to be a teacher."

I felt his eyes on me. "Will it be hard to step off the stage?" he asked.

I shook my head. "Someone else can have the spotlight. Teaching will make a difference, and in two thousand years Myrton Styles will be just as dead as Marcus Aurelius."

Dad nodded. "Well, you have excellent timing. I'm going to have tuition benefits."

"What do you mean?"

"The hospital called."

"And?"

"They made me an offer."

"And?"

"And I'm going to take it. Don't worry, you won't have to drive me every day. I negotiated for a car service."

"I wasn't worried. Congratulations."

"Thank you. There aren't many jobs you can do with a seven percent reduction in frontal lobe volume. It turns out that hospital administrator is one of them; the brain damage might even be an advantage."

The management at New Birmingham Medical Center had been cleaned out in the wake of the Grant scandal. Dad wasn't getting his medical license back but they needed smart, experienced doctors to help rebuild. Derek had been promoted to head of accounting and he'd recommended Dad for an open administrative role.

"When do you start?" I asked.

"Monday."

"That's not much time. We have a lot to do. We need to make sure—"

"Yes, yes. I'll be ready. I know I can count on you."

I sat back and looked at the screen. "Do you ever wish you had gone to Nebraska?" I asked.

"Not even for a moment. Now be quiet and watch the movie; it's getting to the good part."

Hugh was running. We'd seen it before, maybe a hundred times, and Dad was right: it was getting to the good part.

I sat beside my father and let myself enjoy it.

ACKNOWLEDGMENTS

I am grateful to Reiko Davis and Adam Schear at DeFiore and Company for their guidance in developing and supporting this book, and to Luisa Smith and her team at Mysterious Press and Penzler Publishers for their editorial and design expertise.

William Kent Krueger and Hank Phillippi Ryan provided much-needed encouragement along the way, for which I am deeply appreciative. Thanks as well to fellow writers Erica Ferencik and Edwin Hill for their support.

So much appreciation to Jenna Blum and her never-ending writer's workshop, including: Trisha Blanchett, Hillary Casavant, Mark Cecil, Tom Champoux, Jenn De Leon, Chuck Garabedian, Julie Gerstenblatt, Edwin Hill, Alex Hoopes, Sonya Larson, Kimberly Hensle Lowrance, Jenna Paone, Jane Roper, Whitney Scharer, Adam Stumacher, Grace Talusan, and Kate Woodworth.

Much love to my parents, Jonathan and Rebecca Moldover; to my sisters and brother, Anna, Abigail, and David; and to my children, Jacob, Nora, Nathan, and Charlotte.

My wife, Leah, is my first and last reader, and everything I write is for her.